A Place of Justice

Elisabeth Ludlow

First edition 2024

Front Cover Design by Elisabeth Ludlow

For David

Table of Contents

ABOUT THE AUTHOR

CHAPTER ONE

The Student Kitchen
May 1978

Luke had had enough. The essay was due in tomorrow morning at nine o'clock, and he'd slaved over it, on and off, for the last week. He wasn't satisfied with the current draft, but his brain hurt, and he was bored. What more was there to write about the *Pensées* of Pascal? He got up to make another coffee. Various items were waiting to be washed up in the bowl and for a moment, he was tempted to tidy up. The sink needed cleaning, too; there were vegetable peelings in the plughole from last night's supper, and the washing-up bowl was dirty. But his heart wasn't in that project either.

The coffee was good – strong, Kenyan, and a satisfying energiser. He looked out of the window and breathed in the summer air. Strange and good, that in Edinburgh, it should actually be warm on an evening in mid-May. There was a rather dramatic glimpse of the back of the castle from this student kitchen, and its grandeur always inspired Luke. In the future he would always remember that he'd lived with a view of

Edinburgh Castle during his second and fourth years. The façade would have been preferable, but although the side viewable from their flat was plain and lacked the panache of the front, this former royal residence, fortress, prison, and now major tourist attraction was a significant historic feature of the city.

"Are you still working on that essay?" Archie burst into the room, long hair flying, cheeks flushed from his bike ride. His distinctive Edinburgh accent always struck Luke as a marriage of posh English with a strong shot of Scottish. It was undeniably what might be called an "educated" Scottish voice. He'd entered the room talking; Archie was always on the move, always active, frequently doing three or more things at once. In his second year, with four years of medical studies still to go, he was thriving on student life. The two had crossed paths simply because they'd both ended up in this flat, yet they'd got on well this year and had become good friends. These days they rarely saw Tina, their other flatmate; since January she'd spent most of her time at her boyfriend's flat in Stockbridge. Occasionally she would return for an item of clothing or to study in peace, but in reality, the flat was occupied by two and not three tenants.

"Yeah, I'm up to here with Pascal." Luke hesitated. "*Tout le malheur des hommes vient de ne savoir pas demeurer en repos, dans une chambre,*" he continued, knowing that he'd be asked for a translation. "You've just done what Pascal didn't approve of. Crashed into my silence. He thought the source of man's unhappiness was that basically he couldn't be in a room by himself, contemplating. But I'm glad you came in. Don't go! I'd had it with solitude."

Archie smiled. "What you need is a break from work. Have you had anything to eat?"

It was seven o'clock, and Luke hadn't eaten since midday. He hoped Archie was hinting at making dinner. His flatmate was a chef *manqué*, and any meal he prepared was hugely appetising. "Are you offering to cook?" he ventured, collapsing into a more comfortable chair and putting his feet onto the one opposite.

"Lasagne and salad with fresh French bread!" replied Archie, brandishing a baguette just purchased from the *boulangerie* near the Western General Hospital where he'd been working. In effect, it was the only French bakery in Edinburgh, recently opened and currently very popular with students.

He pottered around the room gathering utensils and ingredients, red wine in hand, having poured Luke a glass of the same. The pans and wooden spoons, the tin-opener and colander, the chopping board and salad servers were all a mish-mash provided by their landlord, but then they'd clubbed together, Tina as well, to buy a bright yellow pottery dinner-set to cheer themselves up, helping to imagine they were in Provence rather than grey Edinburgh. As Luke dozed, Pascal a distant memory, and food a pleasant imminent event, Archie conjured up his usual culinary magic.

"We'll imagine we're at the *Café Royal,*" he proclaimed, locating red napkins, bright cutlery, and two smart wine glasses. A candle was lit in the centre of the painted wooden table, and they sat down to their Italian repast.

"How's the application process going for next year?" asked Archie as they tucked into the meal.

"Another dreaded subject," laughed Luke in a mix of humour and despondency.

"Sorry, on to lighter things?"

"No, it's good to talk about it. I've got a place to do the Law Diploma in London, but zero replies from law firms for funding or articles. I'd hoped studying French and Italian might help, but I guess there are countless other language graduates expecting those skills will appeal. I'll keep sending out my applications, and keep hoping. They updated the training regulations last year, so I need to stay current with any changes."

"Glad I have four years to go. I hope you find the funding soon, mate."

They ate in silence for a few minutes. The window was still open. Sounds of people walking along the street below wafted up to the kitchen. An occasional car drove past, and a dog barked incessantly.

"Have you tried any of those recipes?" asked Luke, switching subjects to lighten the mood. He was looking at *The Joy of Cooking*, left behind by a former flatmate from New York. Hailed as a classic in North America, the book had yet to make an impression in the UK, but a lone copy occupied their flat. The book sat on one of three rather lopsided high white shelves containing medical textbooks, a French dictionary, a couple of Frederick Forsyth books, a tattered copy of Erich Segal's *Love Story* donated by Nancy, a former resident, and various other recipe books. Below the shelves was the ubiquitous noticeboard beloved of all student flats, overflowing with paper, much of it loosely attached with a drawing pin and about to float away, highlighting events, amusing quotations, restaurant and theatre publicity, and the occasional invitation. Luke and Archie would have liked more invitations on their board, but the ones that came in were proudly and prominently displayed.

"I was thinking of trying their Chocolate Mayonnaise Cake," chuckled Archie. "It's supposed to be one of the top ten recipes, so it can't be as bad as it sounds."

Luke grimaced at the peculiar mix of sweet and savoury. The sound of the front door being unlocked broke abruptly into their conversation. Tina? Surely not; she hardly ever came back. The kitchen door opened to reveal Ricky, her boyfriend, who didn't look very happy.

"Hi! Just come round for some of Tina's clothes," was his explanation for appearing in the flat. "She's got a really bad headache."

"Terrible," commented Archie. "Tell her to take three tablets if it's bad. The packets say two, but it's OK to take three. She hasn't been well for weeks. How's her work going?"

Ricky sat down on a tall stool which tottered slightly as he sat. He lit a cigarette and looked thoughtful, managing to appear stylish at the same time. He had graduated two years ago, and worked in advertising. "She's up and down. One day she's fine, and the next she's in bed all day, moaning about her head and her stomach. She's been to the doctor, and they're not worried. I think it's stress."

"Have a coffee?" offered Archie, managing to locate a clean mug. He poured the remaining coffee that Luke had made, still vaguely warm. Ricky took the "I Love Paris" mug and continued unburdening himself to Tina's two flatmates. "We're getting married," he announced, quite casually, as though breaking the news that he and Tina were going to see a new film.

"Congratulations!" said Luke, always ready to say the right thing.

"But a bit of a surprise," added Archie.

"She's pregnant," Ricky added, puffing on his cigarette. "Parents wouldn't like a baby appearing without a ring. So we're getting hitched. Tina's headaches and stomach aches are work and personal stress, and then there's sickness as well because of the baby."

"Double congrats!" exclaimed Archie in his jolliest voice, aiming to raise the mood as they absorbed the two bits of big news. He pointed at a card on the noticeboard.

"Annie and Simon have had a baby!
Tommy joined us at 4.20 am on 12th May.
Nappy days!"

The postcard was illustrated with a Shirley Hughes-style drawing of a jolly baby. Luke winced at the poor attempt at humour. "How are you feeling about all this dramatic news?" he asked, even though the answer was glaringly obvious.

Ricky got up and looked at the castle. He leant over the messy sink. He was silhouetted against the draining board, an old upright hoover stuck in the corner beside him. "It's just life," he said, attempting a casual shoulder shrug.

Luke and Archie were surprised. They didn't really know Ricky that well, and yet here he was sharing his innermost feelings with them. They felt a bit embarrassed.

"Can I get Tina's clothes for you?" said Luke. "No, it's fine. I know which ones she wants," replied Ricky. He put his coffee down and left the room hurriedly.

Two minutes later, he left. "See you!" he called from the corridor.

"Give Tina our love!" shouted Archie just before their guest slammed the door shut.

"I've got to get out for a while," said Luke.

"I must do some physiology," countered Archie. "And should we send Tina a happy message?"

"Not sure," replied Luke. "Happy isn't how I'd describe Ricky. Let's leave it a few days and see if we hear any more news or updates from them."

So Luke meandered off to his favourite pub, the iconic Deacon Brodies Tavern, bumping into a friend on the way, and enjoying a leisurely couple of hours before his return to Pascal. Archie diligently immersed himself in physiology.

The kitchen was submerged in a mellow light on Luke's return. Archie's studies were over for the day. 'Never Comes the Day' from The Moody Blues was playing on the stereo that was the joy of their kitchen. With no living room in the flat, their full tally of music was housed there, as well as Archie's stereo player. A sheaf of LPs was stacked up under the noticeboard. Moody Blues was a favourite.

The lone angle-poise lamp had been switched on, and pale light from the street enabled them still to see the castle. Archie was lounging on a vast turquoise beanbag on the floor next to the table, drinking coffee, and nearly asleep. "Back to Pascal?" he queried.

"Yes, I'll work in my room," replied Luke.

"No need," said Archie, "I'm going to bed; I'm cream-crackered. Physiology was worse than Pascal. Great sleeping tablet."

The phone rang, and Luke answered. "Hold on, I'll get him." Archie got up dozily and took the receiver. "Hi Mum! What? No! No! No! When?" Luke tactfully left the room. Two minutes later Archie called him back. The call was over. Archie blurted out the news. "Duncan has had an accident on his bike. He was in a collision with a car in Leith. He's in intensive care. I'm going to the hospital now." Duncan was Archie's younger brother. His face was ashen and the usual effervescent personality was subdued and perturbed.

"I'm sorry," said Luke. "Let me know how he is." He put his hand on Archie's arm, the only way he could think of to show his sympathy.

"Yeah, I'll be in touch," said Archie, rushing out of the door with an uncharacteristically sombre face.

The kitchen had morphed into a dark, solitary place again. Conversations and dramatic news – marriage, pregnancy, a serious accident – had filled it. Life events had seasoned it. Lasagne, coffee, and wine had punctuated the evening. The sink was clean. Dishes had been washed and silence had engulfed the room.

Coffee wasn't strong enough now. Luke poured a stiff gin and tonic and settled down with Pascal once more. He had eleven hours to finish his masterpiece.

Le silence éternel de ces espaces infinis m'effraie. Yes, the silences and also the enormity of marriage, pregnancy, and a serious accident were terrifying too. *Infinite life changes frighten me,* thought Luke, bastardising Pascal. But revisiting the quotation accurately, the endless silence of a universe with no known boundaries was significantly worse. What was Pascal? Was he a scientist, philosopher, religious fanatic, or brilliant writer? Whatever he was, Luke must write. And so he wrote, sipped his drink, wrote again, thought a bit, drank some more, wrote some more, and eventually, at half past midnight, finished the essay.

***

Morning came at six-thirty. Although the essay was written, it disturbed his dreams. Pascal featured large in them. He was standing over Luke, discoursing about his wager. "If you say you believe in God, you'll be secure when you get to the other side. And even if he doesn't exist, it's the best option for now – just to be safe. Believe me."

Luke realised that the ringing of the phone was what had woken him. Guessing it was Archie, he stumbled into the kitchen to answer it.

"Hi, Luke here!"

"It's me, Archie. Afraid he's still in a coma. They can't say how this will pan out. So I'm staying with Mum and Dad for the moment. I'll come back when I can for clothes and maybe some books. I'll keep you posted."

"Take care," was all Luke could say. And then, as an afterthought, "Say 'Hello' to your parents."

"Will do. Cheers, mate." Archie had rung off. His parents lived in Morningside, an upmarket city area, doubtless the origin of Archie's posh accent.

Nearly two hours to kill before he would wander off to Buccleuch Place to hand in his essay. The doors wouldn't be open before eight-thirty. Luke put the coffee on, had a shower, and enjoyed the sun dazzling him from their east-facing window. Later that morning, he would have to knuckle down to the last few weeks' revision for his finals. He'd go to the George Square Library, and find his favourite spot, overlooking the square and gardens. He'd be disciplined and would draw up a final revision timetable for the next couple of weeks.

A book on the leaning shelves caught his attention. *The Great*

Railway Bazaar. Claire had bought it for him, four months after they'd met. It had just been published and served as inspiration for anyone who wanted to enjoy a continental adventure, or a journey further afield to Asia, especially a bohemian adventure, chronicling all they saw. Claire, now in Frankfurt, working as *Lektorin* and language assistant at Goethe University. Claire, who now he never heard from. Claire, who was officially an "ex-girlfriend." No longer his girlfriend.

And yet he could see her clearly, in this room, making a cup of tea, dressing a salad, assembling the ingredients for a quiche, reading Dickens or Brontë. She wasn't classically beautiful. But when they first met, he couldn't take his eyes off her. He had spied her in the university library, walking to and fro, checking out a book, nipping out for a coffee. She was slim, with carefree hair; she wore cheesecloth smocks, Afghan coats, and Fair Isle jumpers. They enveloped her figure, but he could see that it was a good figure below the layers of bohemian clothing. And she had a sweet smile, one that engulfed him when they talked. She was knowledgeable about her academic area, having read all of Dickens, Trollope, Austen, and Thackeray. And when she told him the plots of some of these books, her face shone with enthusiasm.

They'd met in early January – her third year, his second. They teased each other about the age difference – just three months – but her August birthday put her a year above his November one. The six months in Edinburgh together were idyllic; she'd become an integral part of the Lothian Road flat. The Inter-Rail holiday in the summer was truly memorable. Then he had to go abroad, nine months in France, with occasional visits to Italy. The plan was to meet every month. It was hard; neither of them had much money. So the plan petered out somewhat. Meetings became every other month rather than monthly. It wasn't as much fun as before. Claire occasionally mentioned Ben, a young lecturer. And then more frequently. And suddenly it was all over between Luke and Claire. She told him when she visited him in May. Her plan for the following year was to work in Germany, and Ben was going with her to a new academic job. Luke guessed that the situation was the other way round, that it was more a case of Ben moving to a job in Germany, and Claire had found work there so that she could be with him. So he accepted it and tried to forget Claire. Not easy.

The book on the shelf, the "I Love Paris" mug, the patchwork cushion on the comfy chair that Claire had bought on the Inter-Rail holiday in an Italian market, all of these things reminded him of her. The ditsy maroon Laura Ashley cushion, bought from the shop in Lothian Road, spoke to him of Claire. The view of the castle brought back memories of their time together. They'd spent late evenings gazing out of that window, embracing each other, planning the future. It was romantic, and it was unrealistic. She was lovely, but she wasn't for him.

There was a knock at the front door. At seven o'clock in the morning? Who could it be? A young man, slightly out of breath from climbing the stairs and with a concerned expression, was standing there. Who could be anxious at this unearthly hour, so ridiculously early in the day?

"Is this where Christina lives?" he asked in a deliberate voice, in an accent that Luke couldn't exactly place.

"Well, yes," replied Luke, feeling not entirely truthful.

"Christina Braun?"

"Yes."

"I need to see her," the stranger said emphatically. He was young, smartly dressed, and carried a small travel case.

"I'm sorry; she's not here at the moment."

"May I come in? I need to talk to someone about Christina."

Luke hesitated. Did he really want to invite a stranger into the flat?

"I just want to tell you about Christina and her history," he continued. "Please, may I come in? I'm an old friend of hers." As a quasi-visiting card, the stranger produced an old photo of Tina; to Luke's surprise, the worried stranger was in the picture sitting next to her, in a group of five people around a table in a café.

"OK, come in for a minute," replied Luke slightly intrigued, and growing more sympathetic.

They went into the kitchen, and the stranger took off his jacket and looked around. "I'll take it," said Luke, hanging the jacket over a chair. "Would you like a coffee?" *"Bitte!"* replied the visitor.

"So you're German?"

"I'm Friedrich Schultz." He walked around the kitchen. He was jittery. He looked out of the window. "Splendid view you have! Edinburgh Castle."

"Yes. We're fortunate." Luke handed over the coffee. This time, appropriately, in an Edinburgh Castle mug.

There was a pause. Luke waited for his unusual visitor to explain what he wanted.

"When will Christina be back home?"

This was a tricky one. Who was this person? If he was here on official business, best not to indicate that Tina didn't live here most of the time. "This evening, I guess. What was it that you wanted to tell me?"

"That's *Kölner Dom*," commented Friedrich, gazing at the small picture on the wall next to the window. It looked like a cheap tourist purchase, hurriedly posted in the kitchen on someone's return from their travels.

"Yes, we visited a couple of years ago," replied Luke. We, not I. Claire was still a presence in this room. She'd been with him when they visited the cathedral. They'd stopped at Cologne station during the Inter-Rail summer. *Hier handelt die Welt.* Luke remembered the slogan on the platform. The world comes here to do business.

"Christina is in a difficult situation. I need to see her urgently." He drank the coffee greedily. Luke guessed that he'd come straight from a long journey from Germany, most likely hotfoot from Waverley Station, following many hours on the train.

"Well, come back tonight. Come at eight o'clock. Christina should be here then."

"*Gut. Ich komme zurück.* At eight o'clock."

Friedrich downed the remains of his coffee, shook Luke's hand, and left, not having divulged the promised information about Tina's history; it had simply been a ploy for admittance. Luke was left with the dilemma of how to produce Tina within the next twelve hours, having first handed in his essay. He didn't have an address for her in Stockbridge, just a number for a phone which was rarely answered. How would Pascal have handled this situation, one flatmate with a brother in intensive care and another being hounded by a strange German visitor? Which inspiring *Pensées* would he have offered? *Je ne sais pas quoi faire; je vais m'asseoir un moment dans cette salle, je vais réfléchir, et je vais attendre.* Possibly. You don't know what to do, so you sit here in this room, and think.

Luke looked at the picture of Köln. Why hadn't he torn it down? It was another unfortunate reminder of Claire. He took down a larger poster, one of Che Guevara, and giving thanks for Blu Tack, covered up the famous German cathedral, replacing it with the world-renowned depiction of the Cuban revolutionary. Revolution triumphing over God-worship. Yes, that was good. Without much hope, Luke dialled Tina and Ricky's number. No answer. He'd try later. He had a last look at the essay, made a final change to a couple of sentences, and set off for Buccleuch Place.

The kitchen was empty and silent, apart from an occasional bark from somewhere nearby. Then the rain started. It was a drizzle, then a solid downpour, rapidly becoming a real Edinburgh soaking. Five minutes after Luke had left, Archie returned. He hung up his raincoat in the hall and ambled into the kitchen, aiming straight for the coffee machine and gratefully filling up a white pottery mug. Walking over to the stereo, he put on a Beethoven piano concerto, and then collapsed into the sole chair suitable for relaxation. The combination of the chair, soothing music, and warm coffee enveloped him, and he dozed off.

An hour later, Archie was roused from a pleasant slumber by the front door opening. Luke appeared in the door frame of the kitchen.

"Hi," he said, "How are things?" with a sympathetic expression on his face that didn't really help Archie. The words asked how he was; the face said, "You're in a bad situation, mate."

"He's still in a coma. They say they'll know more after the next scan. It's a tough time. I'll go back to my parents tonight. They're pretty distraught." Luke deepened his "sorry" expression but didn't really know what to say.

"Have you studied anything like this?" he asked hesitantly, thinking a medical student might have more insight than most. "No, it's too specialised for me. He might regain consciousness; it just depends on the scale of the injury. It's a waiting game at the moment."

"And I've got my exams in three weeks," he said almost as an afterthought.

"Coffee? Beer? Wine?" offered Luke.

"Another coffee, yes, thanks."

Luke kept up a stream of uncharacteristic patter while preparing and then pouring a fresh coffee. A sand-coloured pottery mug this time, from a craft fair. He hadn't noticed that Archie already had a mug in play. "A stranger called to see Tina this morning. He was German and seemed pretty stressed and keen to find her. Friedrich. I've rung Ricky's number, but there's no reply yet. I'll keep trying. I didn't tell Friedrich that she's currently staying somewhere else. There might be some sort of legal issue, and I didn't like to complicate matters."

"Odd," commented Archie. "We don't know much about her. She must have done something before she started studying anthropology. She's at least twenty-four."

Luke dialled Ricky's number once again. It was ten-thirty. If Tina was in, she must be awake by now. The phone was answered. "Hi!" It was Tina's voice. "Tina! It's Luke. How are you? Feeling better?"

"Yeah, I'm feeling fine today. Think I'll toddle down to the department and find my tutor."

Luke didn't feel it was the right time to offer double congratulations on the impending marriage and birth.

"Tina, someone called to see you early this morning. He said it's important he sees you. Friedrich Schultz. He's coming back here at eight o'clock. I didn't tell him you were living somewhere else."

There was a long pause at the other end of the line. "Tina? Are you still there?"

Tina laughed nervously. "Yes, I'm here! Friedrich! Great! I'll come back to the flat just before eight to see him. Kind of him to call in."

"Excellent. See you later then!"

Archie stood up. "I'd better go," he said, draining his mug and grabbing his raincoat.

"Here, take this packet of chocolate biscuits. I bought it on the way back this morning. Give it to your parents in the hospital." Luke produced the packet, a rabbit out of a hat, chocolate delights out of his backpack, thinking as he did so that the gift wasn't much compared with serious injury, but it was his personal token gesture. Better than absolutely nothing.

"Thanks, mate. See you soon!" Archie was off. *A day's revision,* thought Luke. *I'll make the most of it.*

***

It was a quarter to eight. Luke had just finished an indulgent but easy supper of Kentucky Fried Chicken and chips from the shop on the corner and a delightful Marks and Spencer slice of New York cheesecake, and was washing up. *Come on, Tina. I don't really want to have another face-to-face with the dour Herr Schultz,* he was thinking.

But Tina hadn't let him down. Minutes later she breezed into the flat and into the kitchen. She was a striking woman. Long, thick, dark hair bounced on her shoulders, her slim form was encased in a dark anorak and jeans, and her charming smile was as warm as usual.

"Hi, Luke!" She gave him a quick hug. "Hope the revision's going well! I'm plodding along with my coursework. Glad anthropology doesn't have as many exams as modern languages. Just two at the end of June." Her English was nigh on perfect, "plodding", flagging her acquaintance with colloquialisms. Still, she hadn't lost her German accent, giving her conversation an added charm. Luke doubted that she'd tried terribly hard to lose the accent.

He didn't know many pregnant women, nor did he have any idea how many weeks into her pregnancy Tina was. He was glad of the anorak, which meant he didn't have to guess how far gone she was from a casual look at her tummy.

"I'm doing OK. Just handed in my final essay, and hiding in the library every day from now on."

"Thanks for telling me about Friedrich. Old friend. Surprise! I'll take him out for a drink."

The doorbell rang. Tina went to answer it. "Hi Friedrich! Good to see you!" Luke heard sound effects indicating a hug and a kiss. They both came into the kitchen. "Good evening," said Friedrich.

"Come on, Friedrich, let's go out and have a drink in my favourite Edinburgh pub." Tina was bubbly and brisk. Friedrich looked marginally less worried than this morning and now at least pleased to see his friend. "Good idea," he replied.

From the kitchen window, Luke watched them down below, strolling along the road. Tina was talking nineteen to the dozen, and Friedrich was listening intently and nodding occasionally. She was sauntering along; his steps were more measured. Who was he? Where did he figure in her past? Was there a problem? Luke didn't much like the situation.

He gathered up his books and set out again for the George Square Library. The early evening sunshine was perfect, and the air was crisply warm, typically Edinburgh. He would be sad to leave in just over a month. Tina was moving in permanently with Ricky. Two new tenants would move in – Mike, another medic, and Emily, studying architecture, and he would be just a memory, one year out of many in the history of 89 Lothian Road, third floor, top right.

He would retain this remembrance for many years, this final chapter in his undergraduate life. Not counting his year abroad, the flat had been his home for two years, and it had been a welcoming home, not far from Princes Street, the Usher Hall two minutes' walk away, and the University fifteen minutes in the other direction. He'd loved its high ceilings, tall windows, birds-eye views over Lothian Road and Castle Terrace, and cosy friendship. And the castle had been a constant. They'd had many meals in the kitchen, Archie, himself, Tina and Ricky from time to time, Claire, various other friends; they'd held student dinner parties, all crammed into the kitchen and stretching into the early hours. Great meals. Lazy lasagne, salads, roast chicken, fish and chips, Kentucky fried chicken, sweet and sour chicken, and then more sophisticated attempts at *coq au vin* or *boeuf bourguignon* for the parties. Also just Claire and him, many times. But it was over now. Forget her! Think of the exams. He quickened his pace, and turned towards Lonsdale Terrace, from where a pleasant walk along the northern edge of the Meadows beckoned, taking him, looking neither to left or right and with a determined step, in the direction of the Library.

CHAPTER TWO

Grown-ups Now; Open-Plan Living
March 2013

It had light on three sides, and three thresholds. One was an open archway, from the hall. And two floor-to-ceiling doors opened onto the terrace, one on either side. The big window was central, a wide picture window for gazing out at the garden. The glazing was multi-pane, perhaps attempting to create a New England visual. The colour scheme was monochrome, offsetting fading. So the squashy sofas were cream. And so were the cushions, with light relief in shades of taupe and rust, in a mix of patterns. Halfway along the room were two tall cream bookcases, his and hers. Luke and Emily. His was full of law tomes, crime novels, travel books, and some cricketing literature. Hers had some architecture books, classic novels, and biographies. In each there was a small section on humour. Adjacent to the lounging area were a pale wood circular dining table and chairs, facing out onto one side of the patio and garden. And further back was a shiny dual E-shaped kitchen, cosying up to the walls on either side of the archway – marble work surface, solid oak doors, and stainless steel dotted around, containing every possible device for their family life. It felt intimate in that space; it was almost a separate room, the two long marble work-surfaces seamlessly dividing it off on either side.

The whole space was huge, a symbol of leisured financial security in deepest Highgate. And naturally there was a snug elsewhere in the house; this wasn't the only living space. The two garden doors opened onto spacious terraces, each furnished in a Daylesford lookalike style, and with a studied air of randomness. Below was an attractive garden, mainly laid to a gently sloping lawn, but with one spectacular herbaceous border. And beyond the garden, the roof of a neighbouring house was just visible, lower down the slope. To the left a tennis court could be glimpsed.

Emily was sprawled on one of the sofas, book in hand, but half dozing in the afternoon sun. She delighted in Sunday afternoons. Light lunch over; evening meal a long way off. No work until tomorrow at eight-thirty. She was working on a new project in her practice, and it had been on her mind yesterday, which slightly annoyed her, as she liked to keep to a five-day working week with zero weekend commitments. So today was a strict non-work day. Me-time and family-time were vital, and all-important for that well-being so prominently highlighted by all and sundry. Not a day went by without some helpful tips for positive glowing health, maybe on Google, or in the paper, or in an e-mail from a well-meaning friend.

Luke came in from his study upstairs. As usual, he didn't keep to a five-day week. He had a big case on, and would be in court all week, so had just done a couple of hours' preparation following their early lunch. It was an interesting case, and given its context, involving a family who had moved to London from Rome, he was glad of his undergraduate

Italian. He looked at Emily with her eyes drooping, and smiled. "Having a nice sleep, dear?" Emily grunted, and curled up more, resting her head on a large cushion.

She looked so like Claire. The first time he'd met her, on a return visit to Edinburgh, Luke had seen the resemblance; it was uncanny. They had the same build, similar hair, and Emily had that same warm smile. There the similarities ended, but it had been enough to spark Luke's interest. And she liked him, too. He was attractive, warm, intelligent, and he seemed to be interested in her. To her surprise, and to her delight, he was also happy to include Lily in their relationship, and freely called her his daughter rather than stepdaughter. Lily, to whom Emily had given birth five months after moving into the Lothian Road flat. Not at the flat itself. She'd gone home to her parents, and had the baby in their nearby hospital. Archie couldn't believe it. Was pregnancy at epidemic level amongst his acquaintances? First Tina, and now Emily, who'd rather sneakily concealed the fact until her room was secured. She'd committed to paying rent for the six months' absence, in return for Archie and Mike's agreement that she could return with Lily, at least for another year of studies, to trial a combination of architectural study and single motherhood. The father, a fellow student hailing from Aberdeen, had simply abandoned her. He wanted her to have an abortion, but she was adamant that the baby would live.

Emily's phone pinged. A WhatsApp – such an exciting new facility for fast messaging – or a text message, or an e-mail, or a Facebook post? She really wanted to sleep, but as usual inquisitiveness won over the desire for slumber, so she lifted the Android from her lap. "It's Felicity, WhatsApping," she told Luke, who, reading the Sundays, wasn't terribly interested. "Alice is out all day, and she wonders if she can come round."

"I'll go upstairs," was Luke's response. "You and she can have a chat in here."

Like Luke, a property lawyer, but at a difference practice, Felicity was ten years younger than them, divorced, with a teenage daughter. She and Emily had met at a legal social, had discussed just about everything apart from law, hit it off, and met from time to time.

Sending a quick welcoming reply, Emily gave herself a shake and got up to prepare a pot of tea.

After a morning of inertia, it would be good for her to see someone, and Felicity was always an upbeat presence. Born in Northern Ireland, she'd studied in Durham, done her legal training in London, and lived ten minutes from Luke and Emily.

"Hi!" In breezed Felicity twenty minutes later. "You know, I simply love this room. It does something incredibly positive to me, every time I visit you."

Emily smiled in pleasure. "Thanks. We enjoyed putting it together, every little touch. And along with the main bedroom, the aspect of this living space clinched our decision to buy. So glad you like it."

"No Luke?"

"He'll be down to say 'Hello'. How's your Sunday?"

Felicity perched on a high chrome stool next to the worktop. "Good! I took Alice to Maisie's at ten-thirty for their girlie brunch, and went home to finish reading my book. And then I had an idea."

Emily smiled. Felicity often had ideas, falling into two clear categories. The vast majority were shelved after deeper reflection. But some did develop into success stories. One impressive case in point was her plan to convert a corner of her large post-divorce house into an occasional local café. Her ex-husband was wealthy, and she had a good salary; there was a surfeit of space. Her genteel house was next to the river in central London, and thanks to diligent design work from Emily and a colleague, which included effective soundproofing and dividing the garden into three sections, two rooms on the ground floor had been transformed into a kitchen and a stylish eating area, the latter looking out onto the garden, with the river beyond. It had been cleverly divided from Felicity's large private exterior space by two beautiful high and fairly wide walls with a space between them, her very own "walled garden". The end-result was three distinct areas of the garden. And there was a parking area, accommodating up to eight vehicles.

It will never work, Emily had thought when presented with the idea by her friend. But strangely it did work. "The neighbours won't like it," Emily had objected. But the neighbours actually did approve, thoroughly, visited the café often, brought their friends, and appreciated its high standards and its peace. "And I still have my private, quiet space when the café's open. Well done, Emily!" Felicity had commented. Emily had prepared the space, and Felicity had registered with the local authority. Only open at the weekend for lunch and afternoon tea, the café was run by a capable mother and daughter team from Romania, and amazingly did make a small profit. Its appeal lay in the setting, its siting in a private home, and the limited-edition nature of available tables. The café was often fully booked. Felicity herself visited and avoided it in equal measure, depending on her timetable. She had always dreamed of running a café, but simply didn't have the time, so this venture fulfilled a long-held personal desire, yet implemented by others. She didn't charge rent; there was however a strict agreement to share details of each month's expenditure and income, and during very profitable months, Felicity took ten percent. 'Waterview Café' was one of her good ideas, and she was rather proud of it.

The current idea had been inspired by Felicity's visits to her elderly mother, now in a nursing home. She was distressed to see so many old people spending endless hours on their own, and was now full of zeal to mine the capital from their life stories. "How about if a few people – maybe not us, or maybe not us all the time – but history students, or 'A' level students, or other researchers – went in each week and asked some of the residents about their lives? Then, with their permission, some of this could be published. Possibly just for the home, or for the neighbourhood. It would stimulate the residents, and would be valuable oral history. Two birds with one stone!"

Luke had crept downstairs, partly to check out whether the chat was one he'd like to join in with, and had heard what Felicity was saying. "I think that's a superb idea," he enthused, listening to her lilting Ulster accent as she enthused about the latest project.

"Didn't realise you were there," said Emily.

"That is such a great idea," he repeated. "To make use of people's time, to inform others on social history, and to give those elderly people a fascinating purpose. You could start in one home and if it worked, it could be replicated in other homes."

"Hello Luke! Thanks for the thumbs-up!" Felicity was pleased at his positive response. And Emily was smiling and nodding in agreement. "Why don't you start with your mother's home, and get Alice to be one of your first volunteers in her holidays?"

"I'll broach it with the matron next week. Here's hoping she doesn't raise any objections. Though I can't see any problems, apart from the work of securing volunteers and getting residents on board. Someone would have to organise that, probably me. And I'll offer to draw up a contract for each resident to sign. Maybe their relatives would like to be involved too, and be reassured that this isn't anything to worry about, and doesn't breach data protection."

"Well done on another brilliant idea," said Emily. "Let us know how it goes, and if we can help."

"That is, from time to time," she added, not particularly wishing to make a new time-commitment.

"Let's take our tea outside. It's amazingly warm today, and we're wearing enough not to get cold." She didn't offer a biscuit, partly because there were very few in the house, but also because biscuits had become the enemy. Enemies to weight loss, healthy living, discipline. If there was a tasty packet in the house, Emily would eat them. Not all at once, but each time she had a drink, another chocolate digestive would beckon. So, no more treats when friends came round, either, she'd decided. Just something liquid, and preferably not alcoholic, certainly not before early evening.

Luke stayed inside. He owed Archie a message. They kept in touch regularly, and met when possible. Edinburgh and London weren't that far apart. "Good to hear from you," he started tapping into his phone. "Hope work going OK. Does that hospital give you any time off? Come and stay. We'd both love to see you." No kisses or exclamation marks, because this was a man-to-man message. Women sent kisses and dramatic punctuation to each other. Not Luke, and not most of his colleagues and friends.

Their friendship had lasted over the decades. Luke had done his best to be a support following Duncan's accident. In the end Archie had had to repeat a year; he'd spent too long at home that summer, helping the rehabilitation process, and his exam results were poor. Both his parents had full-time jobs, so for a whole year the three of them juggled huge commitments with looking after Duncan. They had professional help, but in a family where love abounded, they wanted to be as involved as possible in Duncan's care. Luke visited from time to time, trying to be a cheerful presence, taking Archie out for a drink or a meal, or to concerts at the Usher Hall. Thankfully his brother had largely recovered within the twelve months, though some cognitive challenges remained for a couple of years afterwards. Nevertheless Duncan had secured a good job in PR, and was now married with two small children. He'd chosen never to get on a bike again, and he forbade his wife and children from cycling.

Archie had married young, during his studies. Polly was a French teacher; they married during her probationary year, and his fifth student year, and initially all seemed well. She was dark, fiercely intelligent, musical, and – Luke couldn't find a better word to describe her – she sparkled. But there was a mismatch which didn't surface until a few years after their marriage. They were both fast-moving people, doing several things simultaneously, and aligning their lives proved problematic. Schedules clashed, and so did their individual friends. After five years they divorced, and a burden visibly lifted from Archie's face, and from his whole body. It was a release; Polly and he were simply a no-hope couple. They lost touch completely after the split.

Then Archie started talking a lot about Penny. Luke eventually discovered that she was a colleague, a haematologist at the Royal Infirmary. It developed into a solid relationship for a few years, but then it simply dissolved. In a rare moment of sharing, Archie confided in Luke that Penny had told him quite categorically that she couldn't marry him. It was a blow. He said it felt almost like a divorce. Penny liked to say that their split was a good split. She actually used the word "amicable", which Archie couldn't stand. "That's what people always say about divorces, all the time," he complained. "You read it in novels, in the tabloids, people say it out loud, in pubs, at the bus stop. 'They divorced amicably.' How can the end to a marriage be amicable? Do both people feel that the end was amicable? Aren't there any moments of anger, regret, longing for what was before? Amicable!! So on-trend, and often so inaccurate."

"Though really 'of the moment' of course, which is so important," he added with heavy sarcasm, at the same time seeming to forget about his own early divorce. Paradoxically, although his marriage had ended without drama, the finality of the unmarried relationship with Penny had hit him hard.

Currently Archie claimed to be happily single, but he kept a regular weather eye out for Penny's successor. Luke had a feeling that this would happen, but it was taking a fair few years.

Snippets of news had come through from Archie over the decades. Tina hadn't married Ricky. "Did you know that she was already married?" Archie revealed during a phone chat with Luke, shortly after he'd left Edinburgh.

"Well actually, no!" said Luke, amazed to discover Tina's back story.

"Friedrich is her husband. That's why he came to find her in May. They were having a trial separation, but in his view it was definitely only trial. Ricky had absolutely no idea; that news definitively scotched his about-to-be-illegal wedding plans with Tina. I actually don't know how she could have contemplated that possibility; I think she was stringing Ricky along a bit. Friedrich seemed to have some kind of weird hold over her. They both left for Germany shortly after his visit."

On a return trip which Luke paid to Edinburgh in the summer of the following year – a few days which fortuitously, enabled him to meet Emily for the first time – Archie had more news to pass on. "Tina's had the baby. A boy, Fergus. And I have the joy of being his godfather."

"A role I'm sure you'll carry out to perfection," commented Luke.

Several years later, Archie's update filled Luke in a bit more. "Surprisingly, I do carry out the godfather role rather well. I see Fergus almost as often as his father does. Ricky's with someone else in Edinburgh now, but he keeps in touch with his son, has him to visit, etc."

Fergus was now grown-up, and living in the UK. Five years after his birth, Tina and Friedrich had had a daughter, Marianne, now nearly thirty, who having done an impressive series of degrees, was just finishing university in Hamburg. Luke and Emily were now in touch with Tina themselves, seeing her from time to time on her London visits.

Luke was tapping the text to Archie into his phone – a sound which annoyed Emily intensely, even though she was equally guilty. "Tap, tap, tap," she would say, and he'd know that she was irritated. While he was tapping, Jessie came in.

"Where did you spring from?" he asked, not in an unfriendly way. Jessie lived in Shepherd's Bush, forty-five minutes away on the underground. He hadn't heard her come in.

"Hi Dad!" She kissed him. "I let myself in half an hour ago. I had to find something in my room". A medical degree and its after-training under her belt, Jessie was now in her first year as registrar and with several more exams still to complete, eventually heading for a consultant's post in gastroenterology. Luke was incredibly proud of all his children; he counted Lily as his. Lily's art gallery was a rising star in Hampstead; Xander, living in Reading with his wife Carla, was a maths teacher. And Jessie, a kind of "natural medic", had found her vocation – and also what seemed like her life partner, Jeremy.

She was now brandishing an old photo album with a look of triumph. "Got it! Looking for some incredibly old family pictures for Facebook. Wanted to show that I also have a Dad who wears ridiculous shorts on holiday".

She narrowly escaped Luke's attempt to commandeer the album. "Only if I'm able to access your very secret Facebook page," he insisted. "Otherwise that album stays here."

They both knew that Jessie wouldn't put anything absolutely secret or personally confidential on that page. "I'll invite you to be my 'Friend'," she promised.

"What are you working this week? Are you on call?"

"Twice," she grimaced. "Too many others on holiday."

"How's Jeremy? Working as hard as usual?"

"He's playing squash this afternoon. Hope he wins, or else we'll have a particularly silent evening when he calls round...."

Emily came inside, looking for more tea. "Hi, darling," she greeted Jessie. "When did you get here? Go and say 'Hello' to Felicity! She has a brilliant new idea, and I reckon she might try to enthuse you..."

"I'm afraid I'll need to work for a couple of hours tonight," Luke dropped into the conversation. "But to make up, I'll do dinner."

Emily looked at her husband. So dedicated, so gifted, so well-meaning, so handsome, yet often so unavailable. "OK, deal," she replied, knowing how much he loved his work and how he wanted to complete every task with an almost maniacal thoroughness. It fired him up, it completed him, it filled him with life.

"Oh, and I meant to say I'm going to a book launch on Tuesday evening," said Luke.

"Who by, and what's the subject?"

"It sounds highly academic, but the publicity appealed. Something about the initial decades of a century, using comparisons between the twentieth and twenty-first centuries. I think the author lives abroad, and is back doing a tour for his latest publication."

"OK, sounds good!" his wife replied.

The afternoon light had shifted; now it rather artistically highlighted a group of clean mugs waiting to be put into a cupboard. Multi-coloured and flowery, subtle grey, pastel striped, glazed cream, and a small textured jug, with an adjacent pristine and shapely wine glass – definitely not the kind of common and garden glass that would be picked up in a supermarket. The six items formed a pleasant still-life. The spring light was pure, with a sharp focus, and the objects stood out clearly against their shady surroundings, as if planted by a hidden artist.

Emily carried more drinks onto the patio, and Luke put the mugs away. He had a flashback to the mugs in his old student flat – I Love Paris, Edinburgh Castle and so on. Now he had graduated to the era of tasteful mugs, married mugs, mainly chosen by his stylish wife. He didn't object. In fact he rather liked the symbolism of his settled, happy life. Better than the student era with all its uncertainties, and fears for the future.

"I'm off," cried Jessie, planting a quick kiss on his cheek. "I need to do some violin practice before tomorrow's rehearsal." She added, "Felicity's idea is great, but not sure I'll have time to help. See you soon!" Luke wasn't sure when "soon" would be, but it sounded hopeful. "Yes, have a great week, and see you soon!" he echoed as she disappeared in the direction of the front door.

"Now what's in the freezer? What's in the fridge?" he asked the empty room. "Where are those great recipe cards with minimal ingredients, and just a couple of instructions? And maybe only ten minutes' preparation max. My kind of meal preparation."

From a state-of-the-art CD player, one of Mendelssohn's 'Songs without Words' filled the kitchen with peace and beauty, while Luke embarked on some creative Sunday afternoon cooking.

CHAPTER THREE

Her Study
March 2013

The room wasn't spacious, but it was just perfect for a study. It wasn't an office. Maybe it wasn't a study either. It was a hybrid of the two. Emily did a combination of research, professional reading, and actual work there. So a study, reflecting and taking in, and an office, getting things done. Yes, hybrid was the right word; it had a good solid ring to it. Emily did much of her planning in this space, though designs requiring more desk area were usually done in the central office of the architectural practice.

The study-office, the hybrid space, was due for a refresh. Up until now it had been a bit of a mish-mash of items, combining an old desk, a smartish swivel office chair, an assortment of bookshelves, and a comfortable chair either for Emily when relaxing with a hot drink, or for a visitor. She had her much-loved aid to reading, an ailing angle-poise lamp, and there were family photos dotted around the room. But what she was aiming at was more sophisticated, the inside equivalent of a man-shed. Her updated place would exude style and ambience, and would put a smile on the face of whoever chose to visit this private hideaway. Her partner-in-crime, the interior designer, was due to visit today. What fun they would have plotting the overhaul.

"Emily, do you have a minute?" Luke was calling up the stairs, just before going to work.

"Yes, just coming!" She ran downstairs. Always running. Emily moved quickly, and the stairs provided a bit of exercise. Not much, but a little.

"Archie's going to be down in London for a conference this week, and he has a few days free afterwards. Could we put him up? Sorry it's short notice, love, and we have Xander coming tonight as well. You know what Archie's like. He's just texted me."

"Of course. He can have Jessie's old room. It's virtually our guest room now. It will be great to see him. Have a good day!" Emily gave him a peck on the cheek and ran back upstairs.

Her plan for the day involved replying to a host of e-mails, preparing a second draft of the design for a house extension, and going into the office for a client meeting in the afternoon. The plan was swiftly derailed when her mobile rang. *I am not going to answer that,* she thought. But she couldn't resist looking at the number, and once she'd seen it was Lily, she couldn't ignore it.

"Hello darling. How are you?"

"I'm fine thanks," was the short reply. No news. No questions. A brief silence.

"What have you been doing?" asked Emily.

"Oh, this and that," was the informative reply. And then, "I went for a long walk yesterday."

Resisting the temptation to ask, "Who with?" even though this question was at the front of her mind, Emily kept up the conversation, "How nice. The weather was brilliant yesterday." And continued, "I guess you're at work at the moment. Would you like to come over for a meal this week?"

"Yes, that would be good,", replied her daughter. "I could do Thursday or Friday?"

"Come on Friday evening," said Emily. "We'll have an old university friend here from Edinburgh, so it should be quite sociable."

"OK, Great. See you then! About six o'clock?"

"Yes six, and we'll eat at seven. See you then, darling!"

Back to her work now. But something was niggling at Emily. She wasn't sure what was going on in her beautiful elder daughter's life. The gallery kept Lily occupied, and it was doing surprisingly well, thanks in part to Veronica, her mentor and its previous owner, and thanks too to an injection of cash from her parents. She seemed busy socially and had long settled into a smart two-bedroom apartment in Archway, not far from the Hampstead gallery. Lily was thirty-four, and attractive in a very individual way. Fairly considered in her conversation, she wasn't often given to easy laughter; yet in the right situation she would enthuse, and immerse herself in conviviality. She was loving, family was important to her, and Lily's heart reached out readily to those close to her. Moreover, her warm smile was definitely seductive when appropriate, and she was great company. There had been the occasional boyfriend though, as far as her parents knew, no-one serious to date. Emily loved her daughter greatly. She wanted her to be very happy, whatever happiness represented for Lily.

But she couldn't ever forgive herself that Lily wasn't in touch with her biological father. It had been a swift relationship in the late 1970s, following a student party in Edinburgh. Jimmy was from Aberdeen, tall, gregarious, studying English, and liked the look of Emily in her clingy dress, white PVC boots, and glossy hair. They had an intense three-week relationship, largely spent in Jimmy's room in Stockbridge, then a further five weeks' on-off liaison. When Emily realised she was pregnant, and after Jimmy could see that she was determined to have the baby, he fled. Literally. When she next went to see him, his flat-mate said Jimmy had moved, and hadn't left a forwarding address. She tried the English faculty, but they refused to put her in touch. She went to a couple of English faculty lectures, but he wasn't there.

Emily wondered if he had actually abandoned his degree course, and had left Edinburgh. She looked for him all the time whenever she went walking in the city, scrutinising every lookalike male figure in the street. One evening she went to the flat where they'd met, but no-one knew where he was. Angus, a kindly soul, invited her in for a drink, and was genuinely sorry that he couldn't help. He hadn't known Jimmy well; as was the way with student parties, Jimmy had been the friend of a friend of a friend of someone who used to live in the flat. And his surname was absolutely no help – Smith. They used to laugh about it together, Emily and Jimmy. "I am so ordinary," he would say, and Emily would caress his hair and tell him that to her, he was totally special.

So she was left with a vague memory of a tall Aberdonian redhead with an ultra-ordinary name, who had first charmed her and had afterwards abandoned her. Lily hadn't inherited his hair. Hers was very dark, and not even her face reminded Emily of Jimmy. She looked incredibly like her mother, a dark version of fair Emily.

They never spoke of her father.

Emily turned back to her Monday tasks. First up were the plans for a house extension in Crouch End. The three-bed terrace house had great potential, sadly matched in equal parts by the unrealistic demands of her clients. A couple in their late thirties and with too much vision had bought it in a dilapidated state, and Emily's challenge was to tone down their dreams while keeping them happy and while, importantly, retaining them as clients. She sighed; she'd been here before. An architect's nightmare was an idealist couple who had watched too many episodes of 'Grand Designs' when typically years of hard work and aching muscles were condensed into an hour of cosy viewing.

So Maddy and Tom's hopes of adding a vast kitchen-dining area, impressive study, bedroom, and en-suite just weren't going to work. Planning had been granted for an extension into their long garden, and Emily could see a beautiful kitchen opening onto the garden, and a study-cum-bedroom with a small shower tucked into a corner. And that was it. She embarked upon Draft Two.

The view from her study was eclectic. Emily could see their wide sloping garden with the low roof of next door beyond, a mixture of shrubs, the herbaceous border, and a lawn that was very green from the recent surfeit of rain. Some of the view spoke planning and work to her, though the fortnightly gardener would take care of much of the toil; other areas were more pleasurable and suggested leisurely afternoons. A church tower could be seen in the far distance, and on its right but thankfully fairly far away, a discouraging block of flats which had sprung up recently, designed by someone with very different tastes to Emily. On balance it was a good view, and in idle moments it lifted her spirits. But she did try not to gaze out of the window. Too much to do!

***

At midday Carine arrived. Cups of tea in hand, they regarded the study, and pooled their ideas for its future. Fitted units along two walls sporting lots of low cupboards would be in pale oak, with cream china handles, and there would be two knee holes for work chairs – two in case Claire wanted to work on the second wider work surface for architectural planning. Bookcases overhead would be in the same material, sized according to Emily's architectural tomes and other books. Lights under the bookcases would provide atmosphere, and ease evening work. The walls would be deep red, the flooring wood, pale like the units. One wall would be dedicated to pictures, photos, and certificates. In a corner would be a dedicated coffee station, tiny sink, and table-top mini-fridge. And the windows would be clothed in cream shutters. Workmanlike. Workwomanlike. But also exciting and inviting.

"Thanks, Carine. I'll work in the office in town while all this is going on. When can it begin, do you think?"

"How about the first week in June?" suggested Carine. "Then it should be done for the late autumn."

"Great. I'm really excited about it."

The two women stopped to talk for a few minutes on the doorstep. Emily was an old friend as well as a client; they had met at school drop-off years ago, and had kept in touch.

A low-slung dark green car appeared on the drive, was parked expertly, and a tall young man jumped out.

"Xander!" called Emily, running up to him and giving him an enveloping hug. "We weren't expecting you until this evening!"

"But it's great to see you," she added quickly.

"Hi Xander! See you, Emily," called Carine, sliding into her car, as Emily and her son waved her off, and went into the house.

"Mum, I just have to make a few calls," he shouted down.

"OK I'll be in my study, and I'll put the coffee on!"

Fifteen minutes later, the calls behind him, Xander appeared at the study door. "Let's go down to the kitchen," said Emily.

"No, I'm happy staying here," said her son, plumping down on the easy chair and putting his feet up on the desk. He'd spied the mugs next to his mother, filled up from the old machine in the study.

"How's Carla, and how's work, and is it brilliant to be off for half-term?"

"Carla is fine, just running all the time to keep up with the business. School is OK, though I'm still on the lookout for a change. Half-term is just perfect. Looking forward to the concert with Jamie tonight, and I can stay until lunchtime tomorrow if that works for you?"

Emily gazed at his lovely face, so like Luke's, his lazy hair flopping over his forehead, and his easy smile. *Carla is a lucky girl,* she thought, *to be married to my wonderful son.*

"How about the Head of Department job? Is that still a possibility?" Emily remembered the heart-to-heart they'd had on a former visit after Jonathan, the former department head, had left. Should Xander apply? Would the school simply opt for an outsider? Even though Xander was confident he could do the job well, he wasn't convinced that the Head would appoint him. "Yes, I did apply, and I was short-listed. A formality really; they had to short-list me. The lucky person was Farhana. She's lovely; she started at the beginning of term. She's taught maths for ten years, in three different schools, and impressed everyone. I did my best, but she won." He smiled with an air of resignation. "So I'm definitely looking elsewhere, but it's not urgent."

"I'm sure the right job will emerge," said Emily with conviction. "Just keep your ears and eyes open for opportunities. I know you do a brilliant job in that school."

"Lily's coming for a meal on Friday," she said, sensing that Xander didn't want to dwell on his professional life.

"Sorry I'll miss her! How's the gallery doing?"

"I don't really know. When I last heard, they were selling a fair amount. The exhibition last spring was incredibly successful, when they featured that new artist from France. He's not purely a representational artist; he has a touch of the quirky, a saving grace really. We nearly bought one of his works, but when we'd eventually agreed to buy it, someone else had got in first."

"She's so lucky, working in an area that she's passionate about. As I am," he quickly added. "I must call in to see her when I'm next down here. Sorry it's such a rush this time."

"Yes, she'd love to see you. Now I really must get on with some architecture and design. Would you like lunch here? I can rustle up a sandwich."

Xander got out of the squashy chair where sleep had just started to kick in. "No, thanks. I'll stroll down to the village and grab something there. Are we eating at six-thirty as usual? That will work well for getting into town later."

"Yes, six-thirty it is. Have a great time!" They kissed, and Xander ran downstairs, with the exact same pattern of footsteps as his mother. *How strange*, thought Emily, *that footstep patterns run in families.*

***

The late afternoon light was coming into the study-office in shafts. The sun seemed bright for the time of day, yet not unexpected, Emily thought, as it had been a particularly vivid sun-filled few hours. The light focussed on an eclectic group of books halfway up her bookcase: *The Frank Lloyd Wright Companion*; Gombrich's *Story of Art*; *England's Cathedrals*; Luke had given her the Simon Jenkins book for Christmas a couple of years ago. It would have been so tempting to down tools and dip into it. But she really wanted to finish Draft Two for Maddy and Tom. She sipped tea from her favourite mug, the old and not very expensive one that she'd alighted on a few years back, in a second-hand shop in Westerham. She liked the shape, tall and elegant with a firm fluted base, and the pattern – geometric in blues and greens, yet delicate rather than angular. Not flowery, but attractive in an old-fashioned way, with nothing harsh about the design. The pattern continued on the handle. The mug had simply appealed to her, and a hot drink from it was always more enjoyable than from the others. It was just a mug, but it brought a little bit of joy into the everyday.

Why did some items, designs, clothes, views, rooms, buildings appeal more than others? And why did those same items have a totally different impact on other people? These thoughts were ones Emily wrestled with in her work as well as privately, the whole area of subjectivity. Why didn't Luke like that dress she'd bought recently, the one that she'd been so thrilled to find in the local boutique? Did he have a different image of her to the one she herself held? Why did clients not jump up and down when she made exciting suggestions about their home extensions? Why did some people love 1960s architecture, while others – the majority, she believed – wanted it all razed to the ground, and speedily?

This was where an architect had to be an amateur psychologist as well as a professional creator of new structures. And Emily had shown herself to be brilliant at capturing clients' visions so that, often against her own wishes, she was able to create what she liked to call a "happy place" for each one. Or rather, for most. There were always some clients predestined not to be pleased with the end-product. Those, she would rather forget.

Emily hoped Maddy and Tom would like the new version. The kitchen would take up two-thirds of the extension, with the study-cum-spare room adjacent to it, both of them having wide full-length views onto the garden. An internal wall would divide the two spaces, but the final six foot next to the patio would comprise a glazed movable wall, providing a glimpse from each onto the other room, but affording privacy and sound-proofing for the study when needed. A wooden floor-to-ceiling blind would provide total privacy between the two when the room was being used for guests. Both rooms would have bifold doors onto the patio. "No Crittall windows," said Emily to herself. Crittall seemed to be everywhere: in house extensions featured in the media; in her professional journals; even the houses of some of her friends boasted these. She could see the attraction, mentally paying brief tribute to nineteenth century Frances Berrington Crittall. She acknowledged that industrial style was in vogue at the moment, but she personally didn't like those steel dividers, preferring uninterrupted glazed views.

She then concentrated on interior details, most of which she would hand over to her project manager for implementation. Since the house was on Church Road, as a nod to the name, a wooden pew with a high back would be built onto one wall of the kitchen, with benches on the other side, all comfortably cushioned; the floor would be in the same wood, and some kitchen units would be individual standalone items; for this particular project Emily wanted to avoid streamlined modernity. A quasi-old dresser would be created, and a fireplace. There would just be room for a small shower room at the back of the study, and a smart sofa bed would line the opposite wall to the desk. "A really good sofa bed," stipulated the design. This should be a comfortable space which guests would line up to return to, not one where they tossed and turned all night because of a cheap and crippling mattress.

The front door opened and slammed shut. Luke! What was he doing home so early? "Hi!" he lobbed into the house, not exactly sure where Emily was.

"Up here still. Come and join me. Coffee!"

"Decaf," she added, remembering his aversion to the real thing after midday. She heard him bounding up the stairs. But quite different to Xander's ascent. How extraordinary that there was something distinctive about each group of footsteps.

Luke's lovely face rounded the door, and she got up to embrace him. This was her friend, lover, co-parent, her friend, her very good friend. The love she had for her husband was powerful and delightfully, the feeling was mutual. "Why home so early? Back to work here?"

"No, I'm finished for the day," he replied. He sat down, gratefully accepting the coffee. Luke was quite silent, sipping his drink. He usually asked about her day.

"Is something wrong?" Emily asked.

Luke took another sip from his mug, and looked out of the window. He stood up again. He lifted *English Cathedrals* off the shelf and leafed through it unconvincingly.

"Not exactly wrong. But I have a feeling you won't like it."

"I'm going to retire," he continued, in a clear definite voice. "In six months' time".

"What? You're not ready to retire. What about your clients? The firm. The partnership. Your work which you love."

"I've completely decided. It's what I want to do. I've had enough of the law. Yes, I'm enjoying the cases I have at the moment, but to be frank, for a while I've been feeling jaded with the job."

Knowing Luke, Emily suspected she might be facing a losing battle; however, she pulled out her best attempt at ammunition. "But it's not as if you work in M and A, or a really lucrative line of law. I thought you'd work until you're seventy, as we'd discussed, maybe dropping down to three or four days a week in your sixties?"

"Look love, we've got enough to live on, we've helped the children as much as they need, and I'll have a very good pension. I'll get my partner buyout. You can decide what you want to do, to keep working or retire too. I leave that completely up to you."

Emily became quiet too. She wasn't quite sure how to handle the situation.

"What will you do?" she asked softly.

"I have no idea," replied her husband helpfully, declaiming each word very slowly. Seeing her concerned face, he added, "I'll pick up French again."

"That will be very lucrative," retorted Emily.

"Oh, and I meant to say that I've invited an old friend here for a drink at the weekend, early on Sunday evening. I hope that's OK," said

Luke, abruptly changing the subject. "Do you remember that book launch I went to? It was weird. A couple sat next to me, and all the time the author was talking, I was thinking that I knew the man. I couldn't think who he was. But then at the end of the talk he spoke to me, and as soon as he said that he used to live in Germany, I realised that it was Ben."

"Ben?" said Emily.

"Yes, Ben who married my old girlfriend, Claire. I'm sure I told you that she broke off the relationship with me, and went off to Germany to marry Ben, who had a lectureship there. Well, at the book reading he was with someone called Nicola. So I guess the marriage didn't work out. I didn't like to ask. But we had a nice chat about the book and about his new job at City University, and so I invited him for a drink. I invited Nicola too, but she'll be away for work next weekend."

"Absolutely fine," replied his wife. "But let's not avoid the R conversation...."

"I'm sorry to have given you a shock," said Luke. "Let's talk about the future tomorrow, after Xander has left. We can have a cosy supper together, and dream up all sorts of exciting possibilities."

"Agreed," said Emily. "And I'm latching onto the 'exciting' bit."

They left the room and Emily closed the door on work for another day. Down to food preparation, and a meal with her husband and son. She walked, rather than ran, down the stairs, past the family pictures descending in a row to the ground floor, and pondering the future.

CHAPTER FOUR

Lily's Drawing Room
July 2013

Emily rang the doorbell. Luke shivered. "It's cold today." He had a pullover slung over his shoulders, but he was basically simply wearing a long-sleeved shirt with his cord jeans.

The door was answered promptly. "Mum!" cried Lily. "Dad!" Hugs all round as they crowded into the hallway.

How brilliant to see Lily smiling so broadly, thought Emily. She was overjoyed that her daughter's life had taken a major upturn.

"I simply can't believe it," Luke had said, on the night of Archie's visit just four months previously, as they'd got ready for bed. Both had noticed the attraction between Lily, and Luke's old flatmate. Lily had sidled into the room at the beginning of the evening wearing her green work dress, hair loose and flowing, and Archie had stood up to greet her, simultaneously intrigued and impressed at this transformation from the awkward teenager he'd last met in the late 1990s, to stylish adult in the prime of her life.

"Less of the Victor Meldrew," smiled Emily, referencing the doom-mongering character. "In a sense, we might not have been there tonight. Did they even notice when we said 'goodnight', and came to bed?"

"I'm all for Lily finding happiness, but surely not with my friend, who remembers her as a babe in arms in his student flat, who's nearly twenty years older, and has a failed marriage and other failed relationships behind him."

"A marriage that's long in the past, a friend who is unattached, who looks maybe ten years older than Lily, but certainly not twenty, and two people looking for happiness. And although Lily doesn't look more than early thirties, she has an appealing maturity and sophistication." She added: "At least with Archie, you would know what Lily is getting. Better the devil you know...."

"Well, she's your daughter, darling, and you know her better than most. Let's see what happens. Maybe it's nothing. Just an enjoyable evening together."

Four months on, and Archie had moved both to a brand-new post in London and to a new home with Lily. The transition had been remarkably swift, and very Archie. He used all his best contacts to secure the new job, and had been surprisingly fortunate in finalising their house purchase of choice. The Victorian house they'd just moved into in Archway had class, and history, and was now the subject of all conversations with the couple. Along with their wedding, due to take place in September. The enjoyable evening together had morphed into a life-affirming commitment.

"Come into the living room. I've put the fire on. You wouldn't know it was July. It's colder than it was in June."

"Great," said Luke, rubbing his hands in pleasure. They followed Lily along the tiled hallway.

What he and Emily first noticed was the bay window, welcoming, light-filled, and looking out onto a forty-foot garden. It was draped in light yellow curtains, long and flimsy. Then they admired the art-filled walls, featuring some familiar works and others they hadn't seen before.

Yellow roses picked from the garden, one blooming and two healthy-looking buds, spiked their way out of an old glass vase on the mantlepiece.

"It's beautiful," said Emily. "It's very you. And very Archie." She'd seen the room before, but not with furniture and paintings installed.

Luke recognised some of the works from the gallery. He was now semi-retired from the law firm, a new phase which Emily was slowly getting used to, and was enjoying his Wednesday afternoons looking after the gallery, giving Lily some time away from work. He'd picked up a little knowledge of the art world over the years, but now dedicated regular time to informing himself, so that he could be of some intelligent use when tasked with being in charge.

"This is my favourite room," said Lily. "We have plans for it. We'd like to bring more colour into the walls, maybe wallpaper, and sort out the furniture. We just love to relax here in the evenings."

Luke took in the period fireplace, its tiled inserts, the two alcoves, picture rail, and cornice, and was supremely happy to see his daughter settled in this inviting, even friendly place. Could a room actually be friendly, he wondered? And yet that was the main adjective he would apply to it. Who had lived here before? The room spoke of previous families, different generations who had sat here on rainy days, in the sun, in happy times and sad, with their parents, babies, friends, laughing, listening, debating, loving.

What was it about a room which instantly spoke to him on entering, he asked himself? He often had that experience of being transformed, enriched, on walking into a new room for the first time. He'd felt it last week, on a visit to the Museum of Cambridge, when moving from what they called the 'Guest Room' (which didn't have a bed...), into the 'Dining Parlour'. The room was spacious and long, and there was a fireplace immediately opposite the entrance, with a dining table and chairs in front, and a long map over the mantlepiece. The ceiling was low, the floor wooden and uneven, and there were items of ancient furniture scattered all over the room, with helpful explanations. "What a great room," Luke had exclaimed on entering; he had spoken without thinking, an instantaneous reaction. No, not "entering;" he hadn't entered the room. He had met it. It was the beginning of his relationship with that room. Which meant, he reflected, that a room could indeed be friendly. And the second name of that particular room – "Parlour" – spoke to that friendliness. This was indeed where people would speak, "ils parlaient," and they would form relationships, and where warmth would be created, as they interacted and ate and drank together. Indeed, a room could be friendly, exactly as Lily's living room was, this room that he'd just encountered.

"Archie will be here soon. He's seeing patients this morning." On Saturday mornings Archie frequently worked at the nearby private hospital. It was useful and rather lucrative additional income, but he also enjoyed the change from his weekly workplace. "What would you like to drink? Coffee, tea, cold drink?"

Coffee promptly appeared; it had already been brewing. They sipped from shapely glazed mugs – purple for Lily, mustard for Emily, and jade for Luke.

"How are plans for the wedding coming along?" asked Emily tentatively. She spoke tentatively because subtle friction had surfaced over who performed which roles on the day. Luke was due to walk Lily down the aisle, yet it was an uneasy plan. Everyone was aware of the absence of Lily's real father, and Lily's request to Luke to "give her away" had been business-like rather than warm. Emily was aware of the sensitivity; she felt it deeply.

Archie had simultaneously asked Luke to be his best man, a role which clearly wouldn't dovetail with being father-of-the-bride. Typical Archie, he hadn't thought through the plan, and asked Luke spontaneously, soon after the engagement. Once he'd realised the impossibility of Luke playing both roles, he'd rung him up to say that Mike, the medic he'd shared the Lothian Road flat with after Luke had left, would be happy to act as best man. Mike had played this role for Archie before, when Archie had married Polly, so he had been through a sort of dress rehearsal.

"All good!" replied Lily. "Dress bought, bridesmaids sorted, venues all seem OK. Did you find an outfit, Mum?"

Emily seemed vague. "I'm working on it, but not making much progress yet. Ask me in a month's time."

She had loved accompanying Lily to choose her wedding dress. It was a highlight, and a rite of passage that she'd treasured. Yes, she would secure her own outfit eventually, but it was a minor matter compared with the bride's dress.

The door slammed shut. Archie was home. "Hi everyone!" He breezed into the room, and embraced everyone, including his fiancée who he'd seen just hours before. "Let me grab a coffee."

"He's early. I wasn't expecting him until twelve," said Lily.

"I had a cancelled appointment at eleven o'clock," volunteered Archie as he returned. "Irritating, but it gives me more of a weekend. It's great to see you."

Luke was still getting his head round this scenario of his oldest friend marrying his daughter, but he told himself to get over it, and get used to it. This wasn't going to go away, and their love for each other was really – resplendent, he decided. Yes, resplendent was the perfect descriptor. Their love lit up the room.

"How was your week? Are you satisfying your clients' demands, Emily, and are you luxuriating in your imminent retirement, Luke?"

As he talked, Archie was walking over to the drinks cabinet in the corner of the room. He busied himself briefly, and came back with a tray of glasses and a bottle.

A pale sun had appeared; it didn't exactly qualify as July sunshine, but its mellow glow enhanced the uplifting colour of the curtains.

"My week was great, thanks" replied Emily. "And that looks like a celebratory bottle you're holding, Archie. Are we tasting for the wedding?"

"Close," replied Archie. "But wrong. Lily, over to you."

Lily unfolded herself from the wing chair by the fire, and sat up with a broad smile. "I'm pregnant!" she proclaimed, in a most un-Lily-like very expressive tone.

There was a brief silence in the room. Then, "Lily!" exclaimed both Emily and Luke together. "Brilliant. Brilliant." "A grandchild," continued Emily dreamily. Multiple embraces followed, all round the room; it was almost a group hug. "Timings please," requested Emily.

"I'm due in February, so hopefully I won't need the wedding dress adjusted, or maybe only slightly. We haven't told a soul yet, and don't plan to, if we can keep the secret, until the wedding. I'm only eight weeks still, so it's very early days, but we really wanted you both to know."

Luke was thinking to himself again. So my friend's child will also be my grandchild. OK, that's fine, though it feels a bit weird.... This child will call Archie 'Daddy' and me 'Grandpa'. He or she will look at me and think, "Why is my Grandpa best friends with my Daddy?" "Get used to it, Luke," something in his head was saying.

Archie had his arm flung over Lily's shoulder as she sat back in the chair, somewhat to Emily's surprise, sipping champagne. "I'm thrilled!" he beamed. "So am I," echoed Lily. "It's just the right time for me to have a baby. I'll be thirty-five when it's born."

"Let us know if you need any help," said Luke. "I mean more help than help with the wedding. Let us know if you'd like us to do anything as you prepare for the birth etc." He wasn't quite sure what "etc" meant, but he added it just to sound helpful.

"Thank you! I'm just over the moon," replied Lily.

"It's a brilliant house for a baby," added Emily. "You have so much space, and a great garden for him or her to play in. This is a beautiful room; I really like it," she continued, addressing Archie.

Luke added, "I definitely think it's a drawing room, not a living room, Archie. Maybe that has a more formal ring, but the architecture of this place lends itself definitely to a withdrawing place. Architraves, cornices, picture rails, high ceilings. You can withdraw here from the fuss of the everyday, maybe even from a crying baby."

Lily frowned. "The crying baby will be here, with us!" It wasn't really intended as a rebuke, but Luke got the not-so-subtle message.

"Of course. Of course. The baby will be withdrawing too." At that point his mobile rang. "Sorry, I'll quickly take this. I'm waiting to hear about an appointment tomorrow".

The corridor was well sound-proofed by its heavy wooden doors. Luke closed the door firmly and answered the call. "Hi Ben. Looking forward to seeing you tomorrow for a drink!"

"Luke, I'm so sorry but I'm going to have to postpone our drink tomorrow evening. Nicola has heard she can have a small procedure she's been waiting for, early on Monday morning. Cancellation at the hospital, so she got lucky. Can we meet another time?"

"Totally OK. Sorry to hear about the operation, but it's great Nicola got a slot."

"Yes, you have to take these windows when they happen. Hey, it was good to see you at the book-reading. Let's meet another time!"

"Yes, let's do that." Luke hesitated. He was so over-eager to hear what had happened with Claire, to know where she was now, that instead of closing the conversation there and then, he uncharacteristically spoke without thinking. "Hey Ben, I'm sorry it didn't work out for you and Claire."

There was a sudden silence. Then Ben spoke. "Didn't you know, Luke? Claire died. She had breast cancer. It was terrible. We thought they'd caught it, but the treatment just didn't work. She died ten years ago. I'm so sorry you didn't know."

There was another silence. Luke was taking in the news, and doing his best to understand that it was real. Claire didn't exist any more? He'd always had a subconscious feeling, no actually a belief, that one day he would see her again. Not to marry her, or to have a relationship. But he'd been sure that there would be another conversation with Claire, another sight of her lovely face. And now Ben was telling him that this wouldn't happen. Ever.

"Ben, I am so so sorry. No, I had no idea. How terrible for you. My apologies for bringing back painful memories." He spoke very slowly, and now couldn't find any more words. He felt cold and slightly unsteady.

"We had a child. A girl. Johanna is twenty-eight now, and living in Manchester, a working lady. It's been hard for her, but she and Nicola have a good relationship, which helps a lot."

"Lovely," said Luke at once knowing that he'd chosen the wrong word. He wondered if Johanna looked like Claire, talked like her mother, walked like her, had the same smile.

"I've got to go, Luke. Let's talk in a few weeks. And I'm sorry you hadn't heard the news."

The News. Luke put his phone away thinking this was a weird way to describe someone's death. Like a bulletin in the media. Tonight's News.

He composed himself as best he could, and went back into the room.

"That was a long call," commented Emily, looking vaguely disapproving. Then she was aware of his subdued expression. "Bad news?"

"Yes actually, but no-one any of you know. I'll tell you later." He smiled at Lily. "How's the pregnancy going, love? Are you suffering at all? Sickness? Tired?"

"I'm having early nights, and that seems to keep me going, thanks." But Lily's expression was concerned. Like Emily, she could sense the unease.

"Lunch?" said Archie. "It's all cold, but rather tasty, and there's lots to eat. Let's go into the kitchen."

The sunlight had disappeared. It felt cooler in the drawing room. "Yes, that sounds like a great idea," said Luke. "Lunch, and maybe another drink, will be very welcome."

CHAPTER FIVE

Riverside Gallery
September 2013

Lily was *en route. En route* to her wedding. Luke was driving, and Emily was in the back. *I am about to marry a man nearly twenty years older than me,* Lily was thinking. *When I'm in my mid-sixties I might be a widow. Or earlier. Or else I will be looking after frail him.* She brushed all these thoughts aside, and determined never ever to indulge in them again. Upbeat thoughts took over. *It's also highly possible that this healthy-living doctor will live well into his nineties. Who knows what's going to happen?* she countered to herself. *I really love him,* she reminded herself, *and I will remember this day for ever.* Her feelings for Archie totally superseded all her past romantic attachments, and she was as happy as she'd ever been.

The early-morning sickness that had plagued Lily for several weeks was thankfully absent today. Emily thought her daughter, with a bit more colour in her face, looked delectable in her off-white silk dropped-waist 1920s dress, with a shiny poker-straight blow-dry, and a riot of small white flowers dotted randomly on the diaphanous long veil cascading down to her waist. And typical Lily addenda were the touches of blood red – in the five flowers on the veil, her deep crimson shoes, and the occasional red roses in her bouquet.

"Thanks for all your help with the wedding, Mum," Lily had said the previous day. "And for bringing me up. And I'm really pleased that Dad is going to give me away." It was a brief speech, but incredibly touching; it brought huge relief to Emily, and a gentle melting away of recent tensions.

Luke was driving very carefully, in fact almost oddly, taking corners extremely slowly, and being ultra-vigilant of the speed limit. He was determined to get his daughter to the church safely and legally, as well as on time. He was totally silent, mainly caught up in the significance of the day. But annoyingly, work was also on his mind. A new case, working in tandem with a French lawyer, had in recent days become more complicated, and as it was his final main case before retiring, he was keen to pull out all the stops. However, he hadn't foreseen the latest problems.

Ahead of them was the car carrying the bridesmaids, driven by Xander. Jessie, Carla, Archie's niece Amanda, and Naomi, a university friend, just about fitted into the vehicle, following much careful arranging of dresses as they climbed in. Emily had been on hand to smooth over the final dress, which happened to be Jessie's.

The wedding was to be in a nearby church. Lily and Archie had both made abundantly clear that they "weren't religious" but that they loved the idea, the romance, and the setting of a church ceremony. Jessie privately thought this a bit ridiculous. In her straightforward way, she wondered, if the couple didn't have any spiritual ties then why did they particularly want to marry in a church? She guessed it was the atmosphere, history, and architecture which attracted them. However as Jessie herself was what people would popularly call "religious", she was looking forward to a service which nodded to God. At the same time she was inwardly fighting personal heartache, after her recent break-up with Jeremy, which was very public news in the family. Ever practical, in no way did she want this to mar the day for others, or for herself. So like her sister, Jessie pushed negative reflections to the back of her mind.

"It was a lovely service," commented most people afterwards. *As people do at weddings, and as people do at funerals too*, thought Xander, listening with amusement to the standard polite though heartfelt comments. Nothing had gone wrong. The clergyman, a young curate drafted in because the vicar had suddenly been taken ill, handled the service with impressive ease (he told Xander later that it was the second wedding he'd taken), and the marriage ceremony, music, readings, and short address passed off without incident. Lily and Archie lived the occasion as though in a dream. Was this really their wedding? It seemed so like other people's weddings, and it seemed unreal to be the central characters.

In fact the two people most affected by the service were Luke and Emily. "How can two people ever really understand that gigantic moment-in-time commitment?" they asked each other that evening. "Blink and you might miss it. One moment you're single and free. The next, after a few publicly uttered words, you are deep into a lifelong commitment," philosophised Luke.

"It's utterly amazing," continued his wife. "You only totally understand it each day, each month, each year, each decade, as the marriage becomes deeper, richer, more precious," said Emily. "Lily and

Archie won't realise this for years. Neither will Xander and Carla." And as she spoke, as someone who didn't ever take her happiness for granted, Emily wasn't unaware of the countless thousands who didn't have that experience of a successful marriage. She was blessed – or cursed, whichever way one viewed this personality trait – with an ability to empathise and try to understand, and even attempt to improve, the lives of others, rather than only to pity them, move on, and forget.

Riverside Gallery was all they had expected, and more, and even still more. As godfather to Fergus, Tina's son, Archie had kept in regular touch with his father Ricky. What neither Luke nor Archie knew in the 1970s, was how wealthy Ricky was. He "came from money"; his father owned a sizeable advertising company. Hence Ricky's career in advertising, which had blossomed largely thanks to a combination of his father's good advice and significant funds, as well as Ricky's own ability. Alongside that business, he had opened an impressive gallery, managed by Fergus who, having grown up in Germany, now resided in London.

The gallery was housed in a converted warehouse by the river. A couple of "wedding buses" had been organised to offset parking problems. The building was impressive, completely adjacent to the Thames, red-brick, on two floors. Archie and Fergus welcomed everyone at the door, pointing them onwards to stylish waiting staff proffering drinks on trays. Artwork, an eclectic mix of contemporary and more traditional, Fergus's preferred *mélange*, was either on walls facing away from the light, or in well-designed alcoves offering equal levels of protection from sun and daylight. All walls were wood-panelled. Deep windows enabled great views of the river. Some had been converted into doors, and were flung open onto iron balconies. Round tables, resplendent with long red tablecloths and white flowers, were dotted around the gallery's three rooms. For a September day it wasn't bad. It was in fact a rather golden September day. The deep blue sky and slight crispness in the air suddenly reminded Carla, who was from New York, of that day on 11th September 2001, when pictures of a cloudless blue sky were flashed around the globe on that terrible morning when the world changed. She didn't like the thought; unwittingly replicating Lily and Jessie's upbeat turnaround thoughts Carla at once chased it, and started instead to socialise.

"Congratulations!" she shouted above the noise, to Lily, her sister-in-law. They hugged, though not quite as warmly as might have been expected. In some ways they were too similar, and this hadn't made the relationship totally straightforward. Quirky, determined, and business-like described both Lily and Carla very accurately. Carla's florist's business had her distinctive creative flair, just as Lily's gallery mirrored its artistic owner, creating a gentle rivalry which was at the crossroads of either jealousy or co-operation. Luke and Emily knew which way they would like this to go; it was a tension which they dearly wanted to see resolved. "Let's have an all-bridesmaids' hug!" cried Jessie, as she, Amanda, and Naomi gathered them all, including the bride, in a warm embrace, lighting up a brief moment of tepidity which no-one, not even conflicting personalities, wished to darken this day.

The meal was all that fitted with a celebration. Too many courses, wonderful food, sparkling wine and sparkling conversation, afternoon sunlight part of the menu, all washed down with coffee and wedding cake. Family, friends, and colleagues feasted together. Duncan and family were there, Emily's elderly parents Sylvia and James, Archie's mother Fiona still in fine fettle, other siblings, cousins, dear friends, Fergus's father Ricky and wife Jane, Lily's arty friends, Archie's medical team – and Tina.

"How could I not be there to see your daughter married?" she exclaimed, hugging Luke and Emily simultaneously. "And hosted by my son!" When all had had their fill, everyone gathered in the largest gallery where additional chairs, sofas, and luscious floor cushions enabled the assembled gathering either to sit or recline. Luke made a suitable and sensitive speech, carefully avoiding the descriptor "Father of the Bride"; he also couldn't quite bring himself to welcome his "new son-in-law" into the family, resorting instead to humour. "Little did I know, when we shared a student flat, that my flatmate, a medic, would in time enable himself to become my son; such are the wonders of modern medicine." Cue much laughter and cheering from his audience. He also talked up Scottish success, using Andy Murray's recent Wimbledon victory as a comparator to Archie's great medical skills, and skills at sourcing an excellent wife, all thanks to Scotland. Cue more whoops, mainly from guests in kilts. Mike followed with a series of traditional Best Man jokes, some of which, as time-honoured ones, he'd used decades ago at Archie's wedding to Polly.

"I can safely say that I don't know a kinder doctor," he said, looking warmly at Archie. "Who will I'm sure be the kindest husband. And – permission of bride and groom, I have the privilege of divulging this – the very kindest father – in just over five months' time."

Every female eye, and a few male ones, flitted to Lily's stomach, so carefully hidden under her flapper waist. And the room rang with loud applause, as Archie beamed at his wife. Lily beamed too. What a day. And she hadn't felt sick at all. "Yes, we're very happy!" she wide-mouthed across the table to Amanda, who was blowing endless kisses to the expectant mother. Archie followed with a brilliant speech, making the most of the dramatic announcement, which he'd preferred to task to Mike. At times a sensitive soul, the last thing Archie wanted on his wedding day was to cry, even if they were tears of joy. Not a good look for a dashing groom.

The gallery was darker now, as the sun set. Tall candles illuminated carefully selected areas, mostly corners and key tables. Dancing would be in the Twentieth Century Gallery. Luke elected not to dance for the moment, relaxing instead with Xander at a corner table. "When's the interview?" he asked his son.

"A week on Monday. I'd really like this job. I know I'm young, but I can do head of department. I'd like to drive the vision for maths in a good school."

"Well, I really hope you get this one, after the disappointment earlier in the year."

"I'm looking forward to the interview. I have a good feeling about this one."

Xander had always been determined; he wouldn't ever interrupt a task halfway through, not for food nor leisure nor boredom, until that task was complete. He'd been a determined child, toddler, young boy, and teenager. Determined to do well in everything. And he did. Wonderful 'A' levels, first class degree in maths, early and very happy marriage, success as a teacher at a difficult school. Luke was slightly in awe of his son, and terribly proud.

A loud noise came behind them, the sort totally inappropriate for a stylish wedding. It sounded like someone screaming. In anger, not in fear. It also sounded very American. They both jumped up, the other occupants of the room looking equally alarmed.

"Sounds like Carla!" said Xander with a panicked look. The noise came from the corridor, near to the gallery entrance. In the corridor they found a distraught Carla, and an equally distraught woman standing nearby.

"They are in no way trashy!" shouted Carla to the silent, red-faced woman. Luke had never seen his daughter-in-law in this state before.

"Get her out of here. Now," he directed, as simultaneously Xander was doing just that.

"Come on, Carla, let's go home," urged Xander.

"My flowers are never ever trashy. I've never been so humiliated."

"Who is that woman?" Luke asked Archie *sotto voce*. The groom had skilfully and suddenly appeared, having quickly closed all doors leading to the corridor. "Wife of my colleague from Edinburgh," he muttered. "Not careful with her words. Probably had too much to drink, and said something stupid."

Luke went into disaster management mode. Thankfully Xander and Carla had gone. "I'll handle this," he said to Archie, "go back to your bride!" He spoke soothingly to the crimson-faced woman. "There's a comfortable chair in the Red Gallery. Let me take you there. I'm so sorry that you've been shouted at. Shouting has no place at a wedding. Let me get you another drink."

A drink unadulterated by any alcohol, he thought to himself. Trying not actually to push her, he ushered her out of the corridor, using all the charm he could muster, and to his surprise she acceded. He added, "I'm Luke, father of the bride."

"Yes, I know. You made that great speech. I'm Maggie." She didn't sound too drunk, just a little slow in her speech. To Luke's relief, he spotted Emily in the same room, chatting animatedly with her sister Caroline and husband. "Apologies Caroline and Mark, Emily, emergency mode, may I introduce you to an Edinburgh friend of Archie's!" They knew the couple well enough to take the liberty, and he would explain later. He got Maggie an orange juice, and having quickly whispered, "She's drunk, Carla shouted at her, please pacify," into his astonished wife's ear, abandoned her to Emily, and sank into a chair next to Mike in the Portrait Gallery.

"What was that all about?"

"Please don't ask. Let's talk about something different," replied Luke, cradling a fresh drink, and enjoying the peace of a new room with its classical music background. He winced as he looked at the floral arrangement on the table. Carla had gone for huge blooms – hydrangeas, lilies which were clearly so appropriate, and roses, all white – admittedly dramatic but in no way could the displays be called "trashy". He understood how Carla's artistic sensibilities had been injured, no doubt slightly fuelled by alcohol.

Mike's wife Lorna was chatting to Tina on the other side of the room, catching up on lots of news. There was an interesting work of art behind the two women; it was circular, featuring a Janus-style bust, one face white and one face black. But they didn't look out to the right and left. They looked out diagonally, so that both faces were visible, rather than profiles. *The Portrait Gallery,* reflected Luke. "Do you know anything about French property law?" he asked. Mike was a law lecturer at Edinburgh University. Yet aware how different even Scottish law was from English law, Luke didn't have high hopes that there would be a helpful reply.

"Not a lot. Why?"

"I'm on my last case before retirement, and was hoping it would be an easy one. No chance. I'm representing an English woman in the middle of a divorce – that bit's not my case of course – from a French man. She's aristocratic up to her eyeballs, and extremely awkward. And the property is massive. And in Paris. On top of which this woman is seriously depressed. The case is delaying my retirement, which doesn't thrill me. I'd hoped to be gone by next month."

"Can I get myself another drink?" was Mike's first response.

"That's the way I feel about it!" said Luke, laughing as his tension over the recent incident began to lessen.

"Well," began Mike, collapsing into a chair, white wine in hand, "I know a little. Sounds as though you have a tricky client. But aren't they all?" he smiled in a conspiratorial way. "Is there a *tontine* clause in the title deed?"

"Yes, I clarified that at the outset. So both of them have to agree to the sale, unless they agree to revoke the *tontine* clause, and transfer the property to just one of them. That's not going to happen, as they both want as much as they can get. The problem is getting them to agree on the terms of the sale. If they can't, we can't apply to the court for an order for sale, and we'll have jolly deadlock."

"I guess you're working with a French colleague?"

"Yes, a woman in Paris who's got a good lot of experience of these kinds of deals. She's at an established law firm. I'm going over to meet her next month, along with Philippe and Sophie."

"My sense would be that a gentle but thoughtful approach to both parties should bring mutual consent about the sale, but in good time. Sounds as though this needs careful handling."

"Wish me luck," smiled Luke, finishing his drink. "Thanks. If you have any further thoughts, please let me know. I should attend to the bride and her mother now. And you may be needed again as Best Man." He was aware that some traditional wedding pranks were being plotted.

He found Emily in the Red Gallery, still talking to Maggie. She looked up with a slightly accusatory expression on her face. "We missed you," she said. "But Maggie and I have been chatting about Edinburgh. She's been living there much longer than we did, and knows all the best places to eat and go to the theatre."

"Great wedding," added Maggie. "I loved your speech," she told Luke once again. "You make a fantastic Father of the Bride."

Emily thought Maggie was getting slightly over-friendly in her tone, reiterating compliments to Luke, and she really wanted to spend some time with her husband at their daughter's wedding. "Maggie, we'll see you later. I'll see you again before you leave."

"What on earth did Carla say?" she asked Luke as they walked away. "I've never known her be rude to people. And I'm sad that Xander had to leave too."

"She's quite strong-minded, and I think she'd had too much to drink. But Maggie must have fairly had a go at her, to provoke such an outburst. Xander will tell us I'm sure."

The wood panels on the walls made this venue rather special, they both thought, wandering through the galleries speaking to their guests. The panels were an odd but satisfying combination of cosseting homely warmth, and stately grandeur. Food and drink were still plentiful, copious amounts of cheese, fruit, and biscuits having succeeded the lavish wedding breakfast. Groups of guests had self-divided into young and older. Lily was laughing with some of her girlfriends, Archie by her side. Fergus was with some artist friends. Tina, convivial as always, was working the room in her inimitable way, of course looking older than her student heyday in the late 1970s, but still glamorous. Emily's parents and Fiona were with a seated older group by a window, partly gazing at the lights on the other side of the river and partly watching younger groups chatting nearby.

"And look at our other daughter," said Emily. In a corner, seated by a small round table and conversing earnestly, were Jessie and a young man.

"Is that...?" began Luke.

"Yes," confirmed Emily. "It's the curate, Andrew. Archie invited him because he was so charming in the pre-wedding meetings, and also he comes from Scotland. Plus apparently his mother is a doctor. Lots of connections."

"Our daughter and a curate," said Luke. "Do curates marry?" he added, trying to be casual but in effect succeeding in sounding fearfully premature.

"Of course they do. You're getting mixed up with Catholic priests."

"He seems a nice chap. And attractive."

As they spoke, a ripple of laughter broke out from Jessie's table. It was good to hear. Her tears following Jeremy's rejection had made the last few weeks very hard for Emily as well as for Jessie. How extremely refreshing to see her enjoying herself. And to know the conversation wasn't totally earnest.

CHAPTER SIX

Les Erables
October 2013

The house, which dated back to the late nineteenth century, but seemed much older, was filled with antique furniture and other interesting features. Its rooms were vast, with large windows looking out over the garden. Many of the rooms were wallpapered, in delicate pictorial and occasionally floral styles; sight of these confirmed to Emily that she was really in France. The house was in a quiet rural village not far from Paris, and all the family were due to be there at some point during the two weeks in the second half of October. They had shared the cost between them, Luke and Emily paying the lion's share; Lily and Archie would join on their way home from honeymoon. For all, following a busy summer, and with wedding organisation behind them, it would be a welcome chance to relax.

The garden of 'Les Erables" was rambling, with green areas, statues, half-abandoned flower borders, and a run-down tennis court. Inside there were huge dried flower arrangements, family pictures, linens, candelabras, hand-painted crockery, coloured wine glasses. And there was a spiral staircase, challenging for those carrying too much or in a hurry, but charming nevertheless. Luke and Emily arrived promptly on the first Saturday. "It's beautiful!" she'd exclaimed as they parked in the drive. "What a peaceful setting." Although it was early evening, it was just warm enough to sit outside, and they collapsed into welcoming garden chairs on the long, wide terrace, enjoying the gentle light from overhead lanterns.

"Please don't work too much on this holiday," pleaded Emily, as before unpacking they sipped a refreshing drink of *sirop,* conveniently discovered in the vast kitchen fridge.

"I'll try not to. But this case is bothering me. It's not straightforward, and it's important I get it sorted before I finally retire next month. I will have to go to Paris one day, and I might have one meeting with Sophie here."

"OK, understood. But let's get some family things in the diary to fill the other days."

She gazed at the garden. "It's so therapeutic. I could stay here for two months, not just two weeks. I'd like to hide away here."

Less therapeutic was the unpacking of cases and bags, storing supermarket purchases in cupboards, fridge, and freezer, getting to grips with heating, hot water, security, and internet connections, and attempting an impromptu meal before settling down for the night. Jessie was due the following day. "I'll pick her up from the station," offered Emily. "I can have a look at the town at the same time."

"What was that letter all about?" asked Luke, as they finally turned in. Though extremely tired, he was curious to know who had sent the fairly thick letter which had arrived yesterday, its handwritten envelope anachronistically addressed to Ms Emily Holdsworth. No-one had sent a letter similarly addressed for decades; she'd become Emily Wentworth on marriage, and the addressee harked from a different era. Their long journey here hadn't been the time to ask. Now probably wasn't a good time either, but curiosity got the better of him.

"A really strange letter," replied Emily, sitting in pyjamas on an elegant pale turquoise upholstered chair. "I hardly know where to start."

She sighed.

"It's actually, unbelievably, from Jimmy Smith, Lily's father. It was quite a shock to receive."

"How on earth did he find you? I thought he scarpered after you got pregnant, and hadn't been heard of since."

"Apparently he contacted the Edinburgh University alumni office, who agreed to forward his letter. I find these alumni departments really irritating, snooping on people long after they've left. Apart from the top line which Jimmy's written, the handwriting on the envelope is from someone in that office. He's sent me a long letter about his life since we last met. It seems that he works in publishing, coincidentally given Lily's work, in art books, the sort you see on coffee tables, which he says are still selling well despite all the cutbacks in publishing. He hasn't had children, and is suddenly keen to know about the one child who's his. I guess it's a case of *anno domini*."

"'The one child who's his.' Really his? Only biologically I think, and therefore to my mind, and in my very personal experience, rather tangentially. I know Lily way better than he does. He doesn't even know her sex or name."

"I'm terribly torn. I don't know what to do. What I'd love to do is forget all about the letter. But I can't rid myself of a duty to Lily, that she has a right to be in contact with him. I'm thinking maybe I should meet him, and then make a decision after I've done that. What if he's really horrible now? His actions in 1978 weren't too impressive. What do you think, Luke?"

Luke experienced a mixture of internal reactions. The first was extreme annoyance, that this person who hadn't taken the slightest interest in Emily's elder daughter, who hadn't even stayed around for the birth and, even worse, had suggested that she be aborted, should have the cheek to get in touch thirty-four years later. The second was the actualisation of what he'd always known, that he, Luke, wasn't Lily's father, and that he wasn't really about to become a grandfather. But the most overpowering reaction, which was surging up inside him, and threatening to disturb the peace of the vacation, was great anger at the aggravation this was causing to Emily, and would continue to do. It was an interruption to their life, and one they could dearly do without.

"I'm so sorry," he said. "This is very difficult for you. It's highly inappropriate for him to make contact after this length of time, especially after he abandoned you right from the start. How does he even know that you had the baby, and didn't follow his heartless advice? I guess that based on what he remembers about you, he's taking a chance that you loved your baby from the moment you knew you were pregnant and never diverged from that."

Emily sighed again. And then suddenly, she cried. Emily rarely cried. She spoke between sobs. "I feel so bad for Lily. And for you. You are the most loving father to her, and now we're being sabotaged by Jimmy. Totally selfishly."

"Sabotaged is a bit strong, love. But this is hugely emotional for both of us, not to mention Lily and Archie, if they ever hear about the letter. Let's sleep on it. No point in worrying about it tonight. The ball's in your court, and you can take your time to answer it. That is, if you decide to answer it at all."

The subject was dropped for the moment. Luke eventually slept well, but Emily woke up several times, and her first thought each time was of Lily and her father.

***

The weather the following morning was all that they'd expected of a French holiday. The sun shone, the air was mild for October, and the birds sang. "Idyllic," they agreed, "almost too idyllic to be true." Emily picked Jessie up from the nearby town at eleven o'clock, and they relaxed together, enjoying the house's space and light.

Ben and his family were due to stay with them overnight on their way further south into France. Having met him for a drink in the summer, Luke decided that he rather liked this man who had married Claire. They had the same sense of humour, a few interests like cricket in common, and there was a strange sense of family through their past relationships with her. Luke was still in shock at Claire's death, and somehow it helped him to hear little snippets about her from Ben. Though he didn't want any kind of romantic references; that would be painful territory. He hadn't yet met Nicola or Johanna. Like her husband, Ben's wife worked in the Cass Business School at City University, and was well on the way to being appointed one of the University's Pro-Vice-Chancellors. Johanna was an associate solicitor in a small law firm in Manchester; having offered to act as mentor, Luke was pleasantly surprised when Ben let him know she would welcome his advice. And thankfully the house boasted enough bedrooms that the

Wentworths could easily accommodate three extra guests.

Ben and family arrived one hour after their estimated time because of a late ferry crossing, having alerted their hosts by phone. The food was ready, a tempting salad with chicken and fresh greens from the local market, spicy dressing, selection of breads from the *boulangerie,* local cheeses and to finish, a splendid strawberry *tarte* from the *pâtisserie.* Emily immediately liked Nicola. She was apologetic about their late arrival, warm, intelligent, with an excellent sense of humour, and easy to talk to. "I met Ben a few months after Claire died," she told Emily. "I hope I was a help. He was totally lost, and was finding it hard to look after Johanna."

Johanna, due to meet up with her partner Anthony in Montpellier after a few days' holiday with her parents, clearly had a good relationship with her stepmother. It emerged that they went to the theatre and cinema together, and often shared new recipes. During the evening they both regularly mentioned Claire, without tears or overt sadness, but appropriately honouring her memory, gifts, and attributes so that Nicola, despite not having known Ben's first wife, was seamlessly included in that remembrance. After dinner Jessie and Johanna went for a stroll, leaving the older adults alone.

Luke chatted with Ben over an after-dinner drink. "Claire was a wonderful person," confided Ben. "She had a strength which I wish I'd inherited after her death. I loved her and I admired her. The admiration was almost more important than the love."

"I'm really moved to hear that. We only had a short time together, and I think it was interrupted mainly because she met someone called Ben." Cue gentle smiles from both. "But she was an impressive individual. Here's to her memory." In silence they drained their glasses.

Luke was intrigued to meet Johanna, who he had expected to look a little like her mother. To his disappointment, but quasi-relief too, she looked exactly like Ben. The only similarities to Claire were her smile, and a slightly quizzical look when puzzled. She was enjoying law, but welcomed the chance to discuss some trickier aspects with a seasoned practitioner, so she and Luke stayed up chatting once she got back from the walk with Jessie.

All were up early the following day. The guests wanted to make a prompt start, and Luke was due to travel to Paris to meet with the solicitor, and with Philippe and Sophie. Emily and Jessie welcomed the chance to spend a day together with nothing particular on the agenda. In fact, in the end Jessie spent a lot of the day dozing; her work was intense mentally and physically, and a relaxing holiday was much-needed, especially before Andrew joined her in a few days' time.

Luke arrived back promptly at seven o'clock looking tired and hungry. "It's all ready," was Emily's welcome greeting. "Come and tell us how you got on."

"A good journey until I hit the *périphérique*. It's the mother of all ring roads, but amazingly I got to the law firm in time. Dominique, the French solicitor, is superbly capable, and had the meeting all organised. But Philippe was late, which wasn't a great start. Sophie is so edgy, and she was drumming her fingers on the desk all the time until he arrived."

"Forget about it now, Dad. You're on holiday! Tomorrow you can do what I've been doing all day. Sleeping, and then more sleeping...."

After the meal Luke took Jessie's advice a day early, and dozed on the *chaise longue* in the spacious *salon* while the others read. He woke up to the ringing of Jessie's mobile. "Sorry, it's Andrew. I'll take it outside."

"Is everything OK?" ventured Emily. "I know you can't tell me any details."

"It's not straightforward. People! Legal cases would be so easy if personalities weren't a factor. I'm afraid I've arranged for Sophie to come here for a short meeting on Wednesday morning."

"That's OK. You did warn me."

They were silent for a few minutes. Emily gazed at the *armoire* in the corner. You would simply not see an item of furniture like it in England. Unless of course it had been imported from France. She loved its size, its solidity, the decorated panels. And the lamp next to it, with an ivory-coloured lace shade, complemented the antique style. She'd had a look inside earlier today, finding a real mix of items – blankets, a few board games, old-fashioned wooden tennis racquets, in fact exactly what you'd expect to find inside a French *armoire*.

"I'm glad that Lily arranged to see Carla," she remarked.

"That was difficult for Lily. I was impressed by the way she handled it. Especially so soon after the wedding."

"That's Lily for you. She's very practical and quite business-like, and I guess she wanted to clear the air before they left on honeymoon. When Carla saw me afterwards, she said she'd really appreciated Lily's kindness."

"I still can't understand why she flew off the handle so significantly at the wedding reception, and so publicly. It must have totally spoiled the day for Xander, having to run off home and miss the final festivities."

"I've told you, Luke. It was a combination of things. I would have felt the same. She and Lily aren't very close anyway. And then it was

Lily's big day, everything was focussed on her, including the dramatic pregnancy announcement. But the big trigger was that tactless remark about the wedding flowers, which I know Carla had spent no end of time on; it was absolutely the last straw. I feel deeply sad myself as I think about the whole build-up."

"Yes, I understand all that. Let's hope that the peace-making chat between her and Lily has done the trick and we'll have no more scenes like that the dramatic one with dear Maggie, the over-friendly guest from Scotland."

Jessie reappeared, smiling. "Andrew sends his love, and he's looking forward to seeing you both on Monday."

"He'll be ready for a rest, after the vicar's holiday," commented Luke. To him, as a complete non-churchgoer, the thought of being a young curate ("vicar-in-waiting", Luke called it) in sole charge of a parish, with its varied activities and complex needs, terrified him. *But Andrew has those skills, and the training,* he reminded himself. It would be good, next week, to spend a few days with Jessie's boyfriend, who seemed very nice, but whom he and Emily didn't yet know terribly well.

They sat in silence for a moment. "This room is special, and so is this moment," said Jessie spontaneously. She looked at the terracotta painted walls, full-to-overflowing bookcases, two alcoves with their cameos and tall tables, the four arched windows, pale linen curtains, and absorbed the stillness. Then unexpectedly, she proclaimed, "I am sitting here quietly and I'm totally present in these few minutes in time and, do you know, these few moments are utterly stand-alone, neither in my past nor in my future. And although I'll be in this room again, just sitting here with you now, dear and quite unique parents – it's an entire one-off."

Emily was quite overcome, and Luke showed no emotion. Although a medic and a scientist, Jessie could also be a bit of a philosopher, and at this particular moment her thoughtful side came to the fore somewhat dramatically.

"You think I'm nuts," she continued. "You think, that I think, that I'm in a romantic movie, talking like this. But I really want to treasure this moment in time, this place, this part of my history. Yes, I know it's only a room, and I can hear you thinking precisely that. But right now it's also a comfort blanket, an indulgence, a luxury, and even an adventure. It is material, yet although material, it's not totally devoid of the spiritual. This is a joyful moment."

Emily was glad her daughter had inherited something of her architect's appreciation of place, and she understood her sentiments. "I agree," she replied. "And we're so glad to have you here with us." She crossed the room and gave her daughter a quick hug. "I think that with your meditative bent, you're ideally suited to having a curate for a boyfriend," added Luke. They all laughed and there the philosophising ended – for the moment.

Later that evening Emily sidled into the kitchen where Jessie was preparing her bedtime treat - a furry hot water bottle. A house of this size warranted it, especially now that autumn had kicked in.

"Do you like Andrew?" she ventured, treading carefully.

"Very much," Jessie responded readily. "We're what I'd call kindred spirits, you know. I'm so lucky to have met him. He's much more my type than Jeremy." She paused. "You know I was so upset when he ended it with me. But I guess it was for the best in the end."

"I'm glad that you've met Andrew," responded her mother softly. "So very glad." Her daughter's happiness was infectious, and Emily was glad to share in the joy.

Two days later Sophie arrived for the meeting with Luke. She was fifteen minutes early, and as Luke was still in the shower, Emily let her in, and ushered her into the smaller living room. She'd prepared coffee beforehand and briefly settled Sophie into the room, before leaving her and Luke to their private meeting, which lasted precisely one hour. Luke saw her out. So all that Emily saw of her husband's client was a brief two-minute greeting. Yet she was shrewd in her observations of people on initial meeting; you could tell so much at first sight even if some assessments might later be disproved. Dress, gait, stance, facial expression, voice, accent, conversation – all were indicators.

And Emily's immediate observation was of a somewhat deflated and exhausted person with little interest in how she looked, or sounded, or spoke; yet she also detected a hint of steeliness, and a whisper of entitlement. This woman was definitely in the midst of an inner battle. A driver had brought Sophie from Paris, and he was dispatched with a brusque request to return in an hour's time. *Why didn't Luke meet her in Paris?* she wondered. But later on her husband related that Sophie preferred meeting in the relaxed surroundings of his home-office, rather than at a firm or in a stark hotel. She had very definite ideas, and in her state of mind, he was keen to do all he could to ease the situation.

To Emily's surprise, Luke seemed more cheerful after his client had departed. "That went quite well," he commented, not wanting to divulge too much. He'd agreed with Sophie that the sale would go through fifty-fifty, and he hoped that Dominique would agree the same with Philippe. It was clear that Sophie needed the money. Her background was wealthy, but her parents, who were what would in the past have been called landed gentry, had lost a lot of money through foolish decisions. Her two children would remain in France; it was their country of birth and schooling. But Sophie wanted to return to the UK, and start a new life there. Luke's advice was to accept the fifty percent offer, and not to hold out for more. Being central in Paris, and with six bedrooms, the house was worth a lot, and so the pay-out would be substantial. He was a little concerned about her state of mind, and could see how Philippe was a driving force, to the extent that Sophie was cowed and mentally beaten down. *How did they ever get together?* he mused.

But now the meeting was over. Luke was skilled in compartmentalising his professional and private lives; soon, with his retirement from the firm, that would be a whole lot easier. For now he could forget about work, and enjoy the holiday. Though Emily's letter from Jimmy was constantly on his mind, somewhat dulling that enjoyment.

"Who's up for *crêpes*?" suggested Luke a few days later, and in relaxed holiday mood, after getting up well past his usual time. Pancakes were a key feature of their family holidays in France, and he was determined they wouldn't be forgotten.

"Yes, let's celebrate Xander and Carla's first day with us!" agreed Jessie as they breakfasted lazily on the terrace, awaiting the imminent arrival of their two extra guests. Half an hour later, the couple were parking their car in front of *Les Erables*. "You have the best bedroom; Carla will love the view of the garden," enthused Jessie as she embraced her brother and his wife. Xander looked like someone on the verge of enjoying a holiday – tired but also expectant. They'd driven straight from the early morning ferry.

"I always relax the minute I'm on French soil," declared Carla. "Less traffic, sunshine usually, and the daily promise of *croissants* and *café au lait.*"

"Yes, let's go to the *crêperie* for lunch," they agreed.

A long lazy lunch later, following on from the lazy *petit déjeuner*, all were back in the *salon* at *Les Erables*, drinking peppermint tea and making the most of the comfort. The room looked totally different in the early afternoon light. The sun came and went on a whim today, as the weather flirted with them. There had even been some rain earlier on. When the sun was out, it was bright, and highlighted one of the sofas, upholstered in deep terracotta velvet, its high curved back standing out vividly against cream flowing drapes in the background. "I could paint that," said Carla sleepily. She loved to draw and paint in her spare time. "I could capture just the sofa, and the curtains, all the shapes." She yawned and leaned against Xander, and went to sleep.

"Any news from the application?" Emily asked him tentatively. The job Xander had discussed with Luke at Lily's wedding, the one he'd had a good feeling about, hadn't worked out. So yet another application was in process. This was the fifth one. Xander was tired of making applications, creating a slightly different *persona* for each one, and taking care not to kill an application by stupidly replicating the previous school's name in the form he had to submit.

"This one has what sounds like a very committed department, mostly young, and creative too. They've set up a weekly Maths Club which seems to be very popular. Anyone who can successfully join the words "maths" and "club" has my vote."

"The interview is a week on Tuesday," he added.

"We'll be thinking of you. This job has your name on it," declared Jessie.

"Luke, is that a work message you're looking at?" said Emily suddenly. Although concerned for her son, at the same time she noted a characteristic frown on her husband's face, and heard the accompanying sigh, which usually heralded bad news.

"Really bad," he told the assembled company, including Carla who had now opened her eyes. "I can't divulge details of a case, but this bit of news is OK to share. Though not to spread." He looked threateningly at them all. "Sophie, my client who visited here the other day, seems to have totally disappeared. The driver dropped her at her rented flat in Paris on Wednesday evening, and she hasn't been seen since. She's not at the flat, not answering texts or phone calls, and her children are worried sick."

"She looked so dejected. She didn't look like someone who would have the strength to disappear," said Emily.

"Well until we hear further news, this kills our case dead. How worrying for them all. I'll just have to wait and see what happens."

Jessie spoke. "It's truly terrible, Dad, but as I said on Monday evening, you absolutely must enjoy your holiday. Sophie is your client, and not a member of your family. I'm going to put a ban on you looking at your e-mails. Can't you set an "Out of office" message?"

Luke managed a smile at his daughter's parental manner. "OK, no more references to work," he agreed. "Let's hope that Sophie reappears very soon, and I can wait on the news until we're back home."

The rain returned, heavily this time, making any *sortie* either impossible or very soggy. "How about a game of Monopoly?" he suggested to the family gathering.

CHAPTER SEVEN

Peacehaven Care Home
October 2013

"So when did you definitely know that your husband was a murderer?" Alice asked Pauline, as they sat looking at each other in her room at Peacehaven Care Home, Alice with her I-Pad and phone making a recording, and Pauline calmly sipping a tepid cup of tea. She had already related the whole sorry tale, but Alice was delving into details, and also wanted to be absolutely sure that she'd heard correctly. And as this was Alice's first oral history interview, her mother Felicity was sitting in, relaxing in a chair near the door, and being her usual circumspect legal self, though inwardly gaping at the revelations.

Felicity's "good idea", as excitedly outlined to Emily, hadn't been welcomed by the matron in her mother's care home. And at the second place she'd tried they were equally unimpressed. But the matron and staff at Peacehaven saw the wisdom of the idea, and were enthused by how it might open up the lives of their residents. So four interviews had already taken place, some done by sixth formers, and two others by history students in the first year of their degree. Signed agreements had been drawn up, with exact parameters, in the hope of avoiding misunderstandings or disappointment.

"When he came home in bloodied clothes, and then I heard about the boy's murder, two days later," Pauline replied in her matter-of-fact manner. "He came home really late, around one-thirty in the morning, which wasn't strange, as he was often out late with mates, drinking at their houses, or just walking around the town, always drunk. And I found his clothes the next morning, just dumped on the kitchen floor. You'd think he'd have had the sense to put them in the washing machine. But that was always my job."

She stared at Alice and then at Felicity.

"I couldn't ask him, and I couldn't go to the police. He would have beaten me up. He knew that I knew. Oh, I know he knew. He left me a couple of months later, but I still didn't tell the police. I was still scared he or his mates would come to get me. But I was sad about the boy. He was only fifteen I think, and he'd got into an argument with Billy and his mates. They never got a conviction for the murder."

Felicity cleared her throat. She hadn't wanted to interfere with Alice's interview, but this was more than a straightforward common and garden oral history chat. No-one could argue that it wasn't oral history, but it was significantly more dramatic than they'd anticipated. "How long ago was this?"

"Ten years?"

"How would you feel about him being reported now, now that you're in this safe home, with people on duty all the time, and good security?"

"I'd definitely like that," replied Pauline. "Why do you think I told you about it?"

"I'm a lawyer, and I could speak to the right people, to see if they can find your ex-husband. Would you be happy to give more details to a police officer?"

Pauline beamed. "Yes, I could tell them everything."

For a brief moment Felicity wondered if the whole story had been made up, as an attention-seeking ploy, but what she'd heard from Pauline as she related the tale to Alice had been pretty convincing, and for her to name someone for murder as a ploy would be a crassly self-destructive action.

"I'll ask someone to come and see you. And I won't tell anyone else about this conversation. Please can you not speak to anyone else about it."

"I've kept quiet for ten years, so I can keep quiet again."

"Alice, was there anything else you wanted to ask before completing the interview?" asked her mother.

"No, I've got all I need. Thanks so much, Pauline. We'll be back in touch."

"Thanks. Nice to see you," replied Pauline, rising from her chair with difficulty as they reached out to shake hands.

"Let's go and sit in the conservatory," said Felicity to her slightly shaken daughter.

The home was newly built, and boasted a small addition to the main dining room, known as the Conservatory. It looked out onto a well-tended central garden. Felicity was impressed with the building, and general atmosphere of the home. It appealed to her much more than her mother's residence. Should she think of moving her mother, thought Felicity? Floral arrangements were always fresh; several were dotted around the main areas. And the entrance area was welcoming, with none of the sad odours which often permeated the main corridors of nursing and residential homes.

"Well done on the interview, and for keeping calm. A real baptism of fire. Of course don't use any of the story about Billy. We'll have to hand it over to the police. But you can put the rest of her story together. She's had an interesting life; her experience working in a supermarket for all those years, and moving up the ladder to management, is interesting from a social history aspect, and she can tell a story well."

"I enjoyed it," said Alice. "It's fascinating hearing about people's lives, especially about women and how their roles have developed. I'd like to do another interview sometime."

"Let's leave it for a few weeks, and see who else would like to take part."

Felicity was excited about the project, though disappointed it hadn't been instigated in her mother's home. So far they had four accounts, all of around a thousand words, already approved by the participants, and she foresaw an interesting volume, albeit most likely a thin one compared with most publications. She hoped the project might be a model for other homes.

"Here's your tea, my love," she overheard as she walked past a room on her way out. Felicity immediately bristled, almost visibly. She'd heard her mother being addressed in the same way, and didn't like it at all. It was fine if a resident was happy to be called by a "pet name", but not otherwise. She was aware that some staff in homes thought it was caring to address their clients like this. But Felicity felt it could be disrespectful, and dearly wanted residents to have a say in the matter. She would have a think about whether or not, and if so, how to address the issue.

Alice caught the bus into town to meet friends for a couple of hours, and Felicity sat in her car pondering. The front of the home was carefully thought through. A mock Georgian façade was flanked by two *buxus* shrubs in giant pots. A lawn lined with a tiny and very tidy hedge surrounded the frontage. And the name – Peacehaven – was carefully inscribed over the entrance.

Felicity thought about her lunch with Emily the previous day. Her friend had confided about Jimmy Smith's surprise letter. "You're the only person apart from Luke, and eventually the family, that I'm telling," she said. Felicity's ex-husband was a former colleague who'd disappeared ("run off" sounded too seamy) with a fellow lawyer from their law firm. The couple had married and moved north where they now worked at the same firm, but in the Manchester office. So Felicity understood what it was like to be a single parent to a daughter. Although Emily wasn't single, in this case she suddenly felt very much alone. Luke certainly wasn't going to accompany her to meet Jimmy. Both she and Felicity had extremely absent fathers to their daughters.

"I think your plan, to meet him and then decide what to do, is absolutely right," advised Felicity. "It's important you assess him, as it were, before even breathing anything to Lily about him having been in contact."

"I certainly don't plan to meet with him before the baby is born, which is three months from now. The thought that Jimmy and I will jointly be first-time grandparents doesn't exactly thrill me. I'm tempted not to tell him that Lily's married when I do see him, nor that she has a baby. I know that sounds dishonest, but I so want to protect Lily, especially at such an important and fragile time in her life. And I really feel for Luke. He's hurting a lot at this horrible development."

"Try not to worry," said her friend. "Jimmy lives a long way from you, so he's not going to crash into Lily's life in any major way. Maybe he just wants to meet her, to see what she's like, and may not want much contact after that. And her wishes need to be considered. It's possible that she'll simply refuse to see him."

"That's a strong possibility, given his decades-long lack of attention, and his abandonment of me and her right from the start," reflected Emily.

"I'll be thinking of you. Please let me know when you've made contact with him, and when, if at all, you're due to meet up."

Felicity watched a couple park their car, and press the entrance code for the main door. It was after five-thirty, and only electronic entry worked after office hours. A member of staff came out shortly afterwards, and made her way to a car behind Felicity.

She suddenly remembered that she'd left her other bag, the one with some food shopping in it, in Pauline's room. *How infuriating,* she thought. *I'll have to go in again. Hope someone comes to the door quickly.* After almost a five-minute wait, Felicity was admitted, explaining to the flustered staff member why she'd returned. It was clearly an inconvenience to come to the door to let her in. She described Pauline as a friend, hoping she'd be able to make her own way to the room on her own, and her tactic worked. She crept along the corridor, aware that some residents might already be asleep.

Pauline was one of those. She was dozing in her chair, not yet in bed, but clearly exhausted. There was Felicity's shopping bag, exactly where she'd left it, just behind the door. She reached in gingerly and grabbed it, then retreated back along the corridor. Halfway along she heard a voice, in one of the side rooms. "No, you can't do that. Stay where you are!" The voice sounded cross and harsh. Concerned at the tone of voice, Felicity sidled up to the half-open door and listened, simultaneously making sure that no-one was watching from the corridor. Through the doorway she could see an elderly man half standing up from his chair, and reaching out for something. Then she saw a carer grab hold of him, and push him back onto his seat, forcefully. The man looked frightened. "I just wanted to get my book," he quavered.

"Don't try to do that again, you silly man. I'll do it for you."

Felicity was appalled. She seethed inwardly, but controlled herself. There was no-one else in the corridor, but there were voices in a nearby room, and she was aware that the carer might exit the room at any moment. So, doing the most judicious thing in the circumstances, she quietly crept back along the corridor to the exit, let herself out, and quickly drove off, taking in what she had just seen.

All the way home Felicity reflected on the episode. The behaviour she'd witnessed was clearly completely inappropriate and shocking. She wondered if it was unusual, or the normal pattern when no-one was watching, either for that particular carer, or for others as well. She completely understood the frustrating nature of the carers' work, but in no way did this excuse them for impatience, rudeness, or even downright cruelty. Felicity wanted to act in the best interests of the residents, and decided that cautious observance over a period of time was the best way forward, ahead of action. She wanted to speak up, but needed solid evidence for her complaint. She would discuss it with Emily, whose wisdom and confidentiality she greatly respected.

Alice was home when she got back, looking tired. "Let's have a pizza, Mum, and a Coke and curl up on the sofa together watching something light."

"Great idea!" Felicity was more than ready for something light-hearted, after the stress of the last thirty minutes. "Ham and pineapple pizza? You get the Coke, and choose a film and I'll heat up the pizza. Let's forget about care homes, and murderers, and oral history. Let's chill."

CHAPTER EIGHT

Orangerie, Xander & Carla's Home
November 2013

Lanterns dotted around the room lit up different areas. Carla surveyed it all: a tall vase with huge pale pink roses, a shelf of gardening books, a trio of family pictures, an illuminated glimpse of the arch into the garden. The Orangerie, as Carla and Xander had rather grandly named it, was bijou but somehow grandiose at the same time. It was a small but lovely glazed extension to their terrace house in Reading, created by a previous owner, someone clearly with a bit of a Joseph Paxton fixation. Basically it was an iron-framed greenhouse added onto their home, modelled on the Victorian style, and with a decorative roof highlighted at night by two low-hanging chandeliers with dim bulbs. Xander and Carla loved this place, and it was where they'd chosen to celebrate his thirtieth birthday this evening, and his new job as Head of Department at St Joseph's School. A double celebration. The extension was perfect for showcasing Carla's floral displays, usually at night. By day the room was too hot for flowers; they would droop rapidly and wilt before their time. So before going to bed Carla would ensure that the floral arrangement *du jour* was safely transferred to their living room, where it would be safe from early morning sun.

The oval table was set for eight. Eight dark red velvet chairs. Eight lace napkins. Two candelabras on the table. "Enchanting," declared Emily, arriving first, at seven o'clock, having come by train. Luke was due to drive there later, after a work meeting. "Happy Birthday!" She hugged her son. "Presents later, when we're all here."

"Thanks, Mum. Would you like a glass of champagne? Or mulled wine, as we're heading into winter?" She chose mulled wine; it was chilly outside, and a bit foggy, faithfully reflecting November's traditional image. Lily and Archie were hot on her tail, arriving just minutes later in their four-by-four vehicle, Lily now blooming, her baby bump noticeable under a tight dress. Carla emerged from the kitchen, and she and Lily embraced warmly. This was good to see, thought both Xander and Emily.

"How are you?" she asked Lily. "Are you well?" Carla was determined to make an effort, and deepen the relationship with Lily.

"No more sickness, which is good. But I'm quite tired every evening. Forgive me if I don't sparkle all through the meal." She appreciated the understanding smiles on everyone's faces. There was a loud knock on the front door.

"That'll be Jessie and Andrew," predicted Xander. In fact it was his father, the meeting, by mutual consent of all the partners, having ended promptly.

Carla was looking at her watch, and kept popping back into the kitchen and then back to the drinks party again. She had a look out of their front window, but no sign of Jessie and Andrew. She looked at her phone; no messages from them. She stirred the soup several times. Then there was the sound of people arriving, and increased volume of conversation.

"Hi, Jessie and Andrew!" She kissed them both. "We can eat! Please take your seats."

Andrew had been held up by a visit from a distressed parishioner, and apologised profusely.

"Not a problem," responded Xander. "Have a drink." He wasn't clear why they were sitting down so very promptly after his sister's arrival, but guessed it was something to do with food that was more than ready to eat. Getting food right for a group of people was challenging, especially when arrival times were staggered.

"Just sit where you like," was the instruction. "I'm bringing the soup through now."

"Let's sing to Xander," said Lily loudly, above the chatter. "Happy thirtieth, little brother!"

"I can't believe I am so old," replied Xander, not thinking in the heat of his birthday euphoria that the comment was insensitive for the majority – each apart from Carla being older than him, and some considerably so.

"And well done on the new job," added Andrew, as everyone tucked into curried parsnip soup. "It sounds like a super school, and a great opportunity. I've heard a lot of good things about St Joseph's; I actually have a friend who used to teach there. Amazing coincidence."

"That's good to know that you've heard positive things, Andrew. I'm incredibly excited about it. OK so it's simply maths and children muddled together, but that's precisely why for me, it's exciting! I absolutely love maths, and I want to enthuse these pupils, so that they can have a lifelong commitment to the subject, just like me. It doesn't have to be an integral part of their job, but it should be a skill they use regularly, and that brings satisfaction and joy."

"The joy of getting the answers right," smiled Luke. "Did you say all this at your interview? If so, I can see why they offered you the post."

"Well, here's to the new job – which incidentally pays better than the current one – and here's to our thirty-year-old Birthday Boy!" Carla winked at the family following the reference to salary, and raised her glass.

"So when's your trip to the US, Carla?" asked Archie, after the toast.

"Two weeks' time, at the beginning of December. I'm going to stay with Fleur for a few days, then with Mum and Dad. "

"You didn't tell me the florist you're going to see is called 'Fleur'. How weird is that?" commented Xander, rolling his eyes. "Was she given the name because her parents thought she'd go into floristry, did she set up a florists' business because of her name, or is it just a bizarre coincidence, or even an attempt at a joke?"

"Slight coincidence, yes, but Fleur is actually her second name. I think her parents were great John Galsworthy fans, and wanted a Forsyte name for their child. She sounds an amazing professional. Apparently she regularly does the arrangements for the Waldorf Astoria, and for some society weddings. I'm looking forward to picking up a few tips."

"Here's another coincidence. I'll be in New York then as well," said Luke as he finished his soup. "The firm has arranged a grand dinner for my retirement for a selection of our UK and US partners, and we'll celebrate at the Yale Club on December 8th."

"We must meet up! My dad's going to take me to lunch at the UN. Maybe you could join us."

"That would be great. I've not been there. But don't worry if it doesn't suit. Let's play it by ear."

Carla and Xander cleared the soup dishes and reappeared with lasagne and salad. "Vegetarian or meat? Let me know which you'd like," she said as she prepared to serve the main course.

Lasagne was followed by a superb birthday cake from a local firm, followed in turn by the opening of presents. "Great gift, Mum and Dad," beamed Xander as he held up a new cricket jumper. "Just right for next season. And thanks for my favourite aftershave as well."

"I'm aware that it's a completely unseasonal present for November, but the cricketing year will be with us again before you know it, and I heard you needed a new one," said his father. A knowing smile was exchanged between Carla, and Xander's parents.

"And what a brilliant present from you all," he exclaimed opening a joint gift from Lily, Archie, Jessie, and Andrew, a year's subscription to his favourite sporting magazine, together with two tickets for *Jeeves and Wooster in Perfect Nonsense* in the West End. "I've heard excellent reports, and Stephen Mangan as Wooster has had brilliant reviews. Thanks so much."

The birthday evening ended with group photos to mark the occasion, one with the five Wentworths on their own, and another of the three young couples. As ever with groups choosing the right backdrop, there was much discussion before agreeing on the living room fireplace with its prized overhead picture of Mount Vernon, bought on the couple's honeymoon. In each picture Xander beamed in its centre, sporting his thirtieth birthday badge, with Carla in her pale pink dress on his arm.

"A truly happy family occasion," said Emily sleepily as they drove home. "What a lovely meal, and everyone was on good form."

"Less stressful than our other recent meal out, my love. What was it about that evening with Ben and Nicola that didn't click?"

Emily was thoughtful. "It feels bad to say it, and I'm sorry if this upsets you, but it seemed almost as if it was Claire who intruded into the dinner. I know it sounds odd, but it felt as though her ghost was hovering."

"Her memory will inevitably be a factor in our relationship with the Armstrongs," agreed Luke. "But what was it specifically that gave you that feeling?"

"Oh, a real eclectic mix. Of course, your former involvement with her, the characteristics which you told me Johanna has that remind you of Claire, Ben's marriage to her and – sorry to say this – but the way Ben kept looking at me was disturbing. You said when you met me, that I reminded you of your previous girlfriend. Was he thinking the same? I didn't like it. Am I Emily, or a quasi-reincarnation of Claire?"

"Darling, you are absolutely your own person. There is no way that you are any kind of replacement for a lost love. Absolutely not. Definitively not. And I'm sorry I ever mentioned seeing Claire in Johanna; that was thoughtless of me. Maybe it's best if we don't meet with Ben and Nicola for a while."

"Thanks, that makes me feel a whole lot better." She paused. "I do like Nicola. Maybe I'll meet her casually a few times, and we could resume our dinners *à quatre* later on."

Emily changed the subject, as she was wont to do on car journeys. "I've been thinking about Jimmy's letter. I'm going to write back to him suggesting we meet in the spring, but not fixing an actual date for the meet-up yet. I can't face it before the baby is born, and I'd like to be on hand after the birth in case Lily needs help or support. But by March I could free myself up to see him. Sadly I've come to the conclusion that I just have to do this, to be fair to Lily. Are you happy with that way forward?"

"Yes, I agree that that's a wise decision, despite the trauma it will likely bring to you, probably to me as well, and most definitely to Lily, depending on what Jimmy is like now, and what he's looking for."

Emily continued in a low voice, speaking slowly. "Being fair to others is so important, especially to people you love. And I did bring all of this on myself by having the relationship with Jimmy when I was a bohemian student. As did he, of course. We do share the responsibility of having brought a child into the world."

Luke was silent. He didn't quite know how to respond to Emily's inner thoughts being voiced with such depth of emotion. They were silent for some time.

"I'm pleased with my study refurbishment." She moved to more mundane matters. Mundane for others, but special for her. "Carine has done it just as I wanted, and it's made a huge difference to my work at home."

"I'm glad," replied Luke, half-thinking about work the next day.

"Is there any word about Sophie?" Emily asked, switching subjects once again, and knowing of his ongoing concern about the case.

"Not a hint of where she can be. Apparently one suitcase was taken from her apartment, and a few clothes, but she didn't take her car. Her children are distraught, and Philippe is a mix of sad and mightily angry; I would say the anger overshadows his sorrow. Dominique is keeping me informed."

"What will happen if she doesn't turn up?"

"After a period of time – I can't remember the exact length – the house will simply be sold with Philippe as sole owner, and I won't have much more to do with the case, apart from receiving my fees for work done thus far. I have a call with Dominique on Friday; I'll hopefully know more then."

"I'm so sorry. It's a sad last case, and a frustrating one."

"It's a waiting game, unfortunately. Sophie was so low that I just can't imagine where she's gone, and what she's doing."

They were nearly home.

"I hope you can meet with Carla and her father when you're in New York next month. He's such a lovely man."

"Yes, though Carla confided in me before we left that she's worried Giovanni's in some financial difficulty. His role at the UN is significant, and he can't afford to be involved in anything shady."

"I can't remember what his role is exactly?"

"He's second-in-command. Deputy Permanent Representative for the Italian Mission. All his upbringing in Italy, his studies there, and his half-Italian parentage must be valuable for his job, together with his graduate degree from Harvard. He's impressive. So if there's a financial problem he as well as Carla, must definitely be worried. Maybe if I meet with him, he'll open up a bit."

"At any rate, it should be a good trip, for you, and for Carla. Glad we're home. I have to be up bright and early for a client meeting."

"Yes, I'm greatly looking forward to the visit. I love going to the US; it always energises and excites me, and Obama being at the helm for a second term is brilliant."

The November murkiness had cleared, and the swift journey home was very welcome, each aware of their work appointments the following day.

CHAPTER NINE

United Nations Cafeteria Overlooking East River
December 2013

Both Luke and Carla were due to spend a week in New York, though only two days of their visits would overlap. Carla flew out on December 2nd, spending her first few days with Fleur. She was excited about the opportunity, enabled through Fleur's brother, who played in an orchestra in Reading with a friend of Carla's. "My sister loves to mentor young florists," Eric (of course he too had a Forsyte name) had told Carla. "Let me ask her." Carla's assistant Annabel was thrilled to be in charge of the business for a week, and it was all duly arranged.

"Just get a taxi from JFK," Fleur had e-mailed. "Come straight to the shop; you'll be here mid-afternoon." So Carla was now installed in a yellow cab, whizzing along the expressway, and doing her best to avoid conversing with the driver. She loved to meet new people, and she was sure her driver was an interesting person, but invariably, once engaged in conversation, cab drivers waved their arms around expressively, frequently employing both arms at the same time, and although she'd been raised in New York, being in the midst of fast traffic with her cab travelling at top speed still terrified Carla. And once any friendly conversations between driver and passenger had begun, even though out of genuine fear she tried not to continue them, drivers tended to gather speed verbally, warming to their topics, and so it became a lost cause, even unencouraged by a completely silent passenger. So at this precise moment Carla sat silently, absorbing the familiar atmosphere, flying past Queen's, relishing the first distant sight of the Manhattan skyline, and then delighting in that skyline coming into focus as they got nearer, enjoying the dramatic billboards, even not worrying about the obligatory traffic jam at Lincoln Tunnel, and looking forward to her time with Fleur, to be followed by a relaxing visit with her parents.

The three days, like the Expressway traffic, whizzed by. Carla was glad to help as well as observe. Exotic flowers which she would only access with difficulty in the UK, came into their own here. "Don't worry about plants you can't get hold of at home," said Fleur. "Just concentrate on shape, colour, size, and longevity." Her mentor would create wonderful symmetrical arrangements, row upon row of the same high vases filled with identical colours, or a sequence of primary colour flowers, or lines of the much-loved pastels, or some low arrangements with evergreen shrubs; she did clever things with spiky plants, and skilfully mixed other items with her flowers – candles, shiny baubles, jewels, antique books.

Carla's first sight of *Fleurs et Arbres* ("We are exactly what it says on the tin," boasted Fleur. "We bring life to your event with a mix of flowers and dwarf trees.") convinced her that she'd made the right decision in visiting. The business was situated in a converted late nineteenth century chapel, a rare gem in Manhattan, albeit not right in the centre of the island. Like Carla, Fleur had enjoyed family support to start her business which now, thanks to its success, employed ten people. The building boasted arched beams, Dutch doors, and hardwood floors, and had a twenty-five foot ceiling. It was filled with small trees, arbours, flower arrangements, most of which were built as backdrop, conjuring visitors into a state of heightened imagination. Very little was for sale in what was effectively a showroom for their wares, strategic business deals inspired by the displays taking place in conversation with Fleur and her staff. With a dizzying lofted area for Fleur's office, the old chapel was blessed with glamour, and capable of inspiring dreams. "We fire people's imagination, so that the boundaries of what we can achieve for them are limitless", was the business's strapline.

During her visit, Carla's vision was enhanced neither in the detail nor the science, much of which she knew, but in expanding her vision to envisage offering more expansive options to her clients. She already knew the importance of listening to her clients, of imbibing their dreams and aspirations, but now she was being schooled in giving them a more sophisticated choice. She spent hours in what Fleur called "the plant room", of course filled with flowers and dramatic potted plants, but its name also indicating the nerve centre of the business, its throbbing heart, theoretically mirroring an electrical plant room. She was inspired by the pictures and videos of projects carried out by 'Fleurs et Arbres' and by talking with Fleur's staff. She was impressed with their enthusiasm and artistic flair, and pondered how she could use this experience to develop her own business, 'Flowers for Life', back home.

So on December 6th, having finally emerged from jetlag and with the business side of her trip over, Carla set off for lunch with her father and Luke, full of energy and anticipation. She was now staying with her parents in Brooklyn, its newly stylish neighbourhoods a wonder as the district gradually lost its previously dubious reputation. She'd set off with her mother earlier that morning, taking the metro to Macy's where they'd had coffee and a long indulgent chat. The thirty-minute walk from there to UN HQ was welcome and refreshing after three long days' work in the city; she enjoyed the freedom of walking around, looking at the sights, admiring the architecture, looking out for bargains in shop windows, and snatching every possible sighting of floral displays. The Chrysler Building never failed to thrill her, and passing by Grand Central reminded her of its warren of walkways, and of what had felt like an almost physical shock when years ago she had first emerged into its vast central concourse to see the iconic clock, grand cathedral-like windows, and departure boards detailing super-exciting routes; you could choose Niagra Falls, Florida, or the Mid-West, as your fancy took you.

Luke approached from the other end of the street, having enjoyed the walk from the Waldorf Astoria where he was staying. It was a very cold day, but there was a clear blue sky, so if he walked quickly, and where possible kept to the sunny side of the street, he could brave the temperatures. The skyscrapers made it challenging to find a spot in the sun, but there was just enough occasional warmth, and his clothes were just weather-proof enough, to shut out extreme cold. And between the frequent blocks of high rises along East 47th there was sunny respite, especially when he had to wait for a crossing. He enjoyed passing various missions of the UN on his route. Although he'd visited New York many times in the course of his career, he hadn't ever been to the headquarters. Luke was still suffering from jetlag; in spite of well-honed techniques over the decades for combatting this, he was ever prone to waking early and not being able to sleep at night. Thankfully his celebration dinner was still a couple of days away, by when he hoped totally to have recovered.

Giovanni came from his nearby office on One Dag Hammarskjöld Plaza, a six minutes' walk. He was much looking forward to hosting his daughter and her father-in-law. It was nearly a year since he'd seen Carla; he was proud of her professional success, and didn't for one moment regret the financial support he and Anna had provided. And he liked her husband. In spite of retaining their daughter on the other side of the Atlantic after her studies in the UK, in what they guessed would be a permanent home country for the couple, Xander was all they would have hoped for in a son-in-law. And they had half-expected something of the sort when Carla went off to study in England. "She'll probably marry an Englishman," Anna had prophesied.

The three met today in the entrance of the UN headquarters, where Giovanni handled their security. The height and breadth of the building never failed to impress; it was a magnetic presence, so familiar on world screens, dominating West 45th Street, and adjacent to the East River.

"Thanks for hosting us here," said Luke to Giovanni. They'd met at Xander and Carla's wedding a few years back and it was good to reconnect.

"My office is in another building," explained Giovanni. "But I come here for meetings, mainly the big ones," he smiled. "Shall we go for lunch? I'll show you around the building later." He spoke in a gentle half-Italian and half-American accent, a charming mix. He stopped dramatically, halting them all in their tracks, to add warningly, "The cafeteria could actually be a cafeteria anywhere; it's not particularly impressive in itself, but the view is something else."

On entering the eatery, Luke saw what Giovanni meant. If it hadn't been for the amazing vista, which was its indisputable salvation, this area, a venue of such aspirational triumph for the right architect, might have warranted the adjective "dispiriting". But vast floor-to-ceiling windows with a panoramic view of the East River, of its traffic, and buildings on the opposite bank, offered a welcome escape from the dreary interior, and from the right angle, Roosevelt Island and Long Island City could both be sighted.

"It's just been 'renovated'," commented Giovanni with a wry smile. "Let's grab our food and sit by the window," he continued. Luke imagined Emily's reaction to the cafeteria, but didn't share his thoughts with their host. Seated by the window, in a corner, all three feasted on the view and, to a certain extent, on their food. "It's still finding its feet on the catering side after the renovation," added Giovanni. "But it's a lifeline for the thousands who work here; the building is a sort of lunch island, set on its own; it's a fair walk to other places, and everyone is busy, desperate to get back to their desk. So this is basically our work canteen. I'm sorry it's not more special. If we'd had more time, we could have eaten in the Delegates' Dining Room, but I have to be at a meeting after our tour of the building, and I thought the tour was more important than a slightly grander dining experience."

"I totally agree with your decision," said Luke warmly and reassuringly. "I'm looking forward to the tour, and it's just great to be here. It's a unique place, and a real honour to be hosted. Thank you!" He meant what he said. Although there could have been a tad more atmosphere in the cafeteria itself, the thrill of being in this iconic building, amongst the people who made it special, and absorbing its significant history, more than discounted being in a slightly soul-less eating area. Luke and Carla were fascinated by the range of nationalities represented at nearby tables, hearing snatches of conversation in a variety of languages, mostly unrecognisable. "There's a real buzz here, Dad. I feel history is being made as we sit here."

"It is exciting to work here, all the time. Never a dull moment," commented her father. "And you are right about history being made. Who knows what discussions are going on around us, and what decisions will be influenced by the chit-chat right now?"

"I'll be back in a few minutes." Carla crossed the cafeteria to find the restrooms.

"How is the lovely Xander?" asked Giovanni.

"He's well, thanks. Delighted about his new job at St Joseph's School, which he'll start in April. We're very pleased for him."

"He is a good man! Swell. What a great couple. Awesome. We are so happy for them." The half-Italian accent merged with retro American adjectives.

"And how are you, Giovanni?" asked Luke, hoping to get to the point. "Is work good?"

"And life in general?" he added. He knew enough people in New York not to pussyfoot around.

"Not so good, to be frank. Did Carla tell you?"

"She said there might be some financial challenges."

"Challenges! Challenges! That's a gentle word. Between you and me, Luke, I'm worried I might lose a lot of money. *Grande problema.* I trusted someone I shouldn't have, and now I owe big time. My mistake. Big mistake." Giovanni was drinking his coffee calmly and leaning back casually on his chair, his pose a sharp contrast to what he was saying. Luke poured them both some more water. Giovanni looked thoughtful, gazing into the distance.

"Can I help? I have a bit of insight, from my work."

"It's very complicated. It would take me hours to explain it all. My biggest worry is letting Anna and Carla down. And our son Giacomo."

"I have a colleague in New York who's an expert in financial fraud. I could put you in touch, if you think that might help."

Giovanni continued to look thoughtful, at the same time spotting Carla making for their table. "Even the restrooms here are a source of fascinating conversation," she commented as she sat down. The other two, still reflecting on their discussion, smiled vaguely at Carla's throwaway observation. "And thanks for the lunch, Dad. My salad was delicious, and the coffee was good too. Plus this view is stupendous."

"Let's go on our tour," declared Giovanni. "Otherwise we won't have time to do it all."

Luke was aware that he could have gone on a public tour of the UN headquarters, but this personal tour was much more special. In the vast General Assembly Hall both he and Carla, separately, stood on the speakers' rostrum, each miming making a fervent speech to nearly two hundred nations. "I am Ban Ki-moon!" declared Carla – to Giovanni's great relief, not very loudly.

The second floor Flag Hall awed them all; it felt as though they were at the centre of the world. And the artwork which most moved Luke was the mosaic, "The Golden Rule", presented by the US government on the fortieth Anniversary of the birth of the UN. It ambitiously depicted people of all traditions and cultures in total harmony. Inscribed on the surface they read: *'Do unto others as you would have them do unto you.'*

"It's from the Bible, though here it's unattributed," frowned Giovanni.

"Dad, I'm meeting Fleur for a final debrief at two-thirty, so I need to run. Thanks for a great visit! See you tonight." Carla left them, strategically managing to walk both speedily and gracefully, her long black winter coat swinging as she hurried, carrying the hat she would don once outside, and her favourite suede shoulder bag.

"Giovanni, I'm really grateful for this lunch and visit. It's a highlight of this New York trip. Thank you!"

"A true pleasure. And it's good to get to know you better."

"Let me know if you'd like to speak with my colleague James. He owes me a favour, so it wouldn't be a costly consultation. And I'd be happy to help with any additional fees. I'm so sorry to hear about your worrying issue. We've all made unfortunate financial decisions, and it's not always clear who the bad guys are. I know I've been in some hotspots, thankfully all behind me now."

"Luke, I promise to consider this possibility. *Mille grazie.* I am grateful. I will be in touch. Now you must rest before your big dinner in two days' time. Get over that jetlag. Stay up until midnight if necessary, then take a sleeping pill, and sleep through until breakfast time. No waking up at three am!"

They parted, and Luke strolled back to the Waldorf, where he was due to have a drink with a former colleague at six o'clock. He mused on the lunch, on Giovanni and his daughter, and on the happiness his son had found with Carla. They had met quite by chance, when she had organised the floral arrangements for a special conference at the Institute of Education. Xander, in his third year as a teacher, had attended. Luke remembered Xander telling him about their meeting.

"Dad, I've met this incredible girl," he told him that evening after dinner, and after some wine. His father was quite taken aback. Sons didn't normally share like that. It must have been a particularly good wine, he decided.

"Great," he replied. And then, "Tell me about her," he risked, suspecting that at such a bold question, Xander might end the conversation. Emily, to all intents and purposes deep in a good book, but naturally keen to know everything, listened raptly while ostensibly continuing to read, as Xander obligingly supplied a mini bio.

"She's American, has a half-Italian father which I guess makes her a quarter Italian, she has a degree from Queen Mary's, did a florists' course afterwards at McQueens, and has set up her own business thanks to a bit of help from her parents."

"And she's gorgeous – dark hair, great figure, vivacious, artistic, laughs a lot. I'm taking her out for dinner tomorrow."

"Wonderful," almost spluttered Luke, still not sure why he was being taken into his son's confidence so early in a relationship, in fact before it had even begun. "She sounds just perfect."

"She is," confirmed Xander, wandering out of the room and upstairs, leaving his parents open-mouthed. All of these happy memories came back to Luke as he navigated the numerous blocks back to the hotel. That relationship with Carla had been seamless. Six months later, Xander and she were engaged, and they married within the year. The determined streak had served his son well.

I might just stop here and have an anti-jetlag energising drink, Luke thought to himself, as a coffee shop appeared on the next corner. *I don't have anything on my agenda for a couple of hours. Time for me-time,* he continued, borrowing a much-used phrase from Emily. This New

York visit was a pivotal time in his professional life, acknowledgement by his colleagues of a stimulating career, and on the cusp of a new life phase. But why had such an important time been derailed by this horrible juxtaposition, the simultaneous emergence of Jimmy Smith, and disappearance of Sophie Duval? Despite the calm exterior he presented to others, deep inside, Luke was seriously stressed. But in an attempt to anaesthetise the effects of both, he ordered an americano, settled into a window table with a view of the street, and for a few moments, luxuriated in his afternoon in New York City.

CHAPTER TEN

The London Club
February 2014

Emily, Luke, Felicity, and Alice were having dinner together. Not at anyone's home. And not at a regular eatery. "Let's eat at my club," Felicity had suggested. For several years she'd enjoyed membership at a rather prestigious central London club in Pall Mall, and also for several years she had promised to host her friends there. It just hadn't happened yet. "How about mid-February? Let's do it," she'd continued, relaxing one evening in Emily and Luke's home.

Despite some reluctance from Emily, aware that Lily's baby was due any day, it was agreed that the three of them, and Alice – who at sixteen enjoyed the glamour of dressing up and seeing London society, even despite this entailing eating with adults – would have dinner there on a Friday evening. "It's Lily having the baby, not you!" Luke had reminded his wife. "I'll enjoy eating at the club."

So Emily put on her favourite red dress, added some pearls and black suede shoes, and was ready in good time for their taxi. "Come on, Luke," she called up the stairs. "Taxi's here!"

Felicity and Alice were waiting in the club's foyer, both looking expectant at the prospect of a delightful meal in gracious surroundings, and with good friends. "We'll have a drink first," declared their hostess, sweeping up the grand staircase.

"Wait, not so quick, I want to look at these pictures as we go up." Ever mindful of his retirement role at Lily's gallery, Luke was keen to absorb all the art he could.

"You can buy a book about all the pictures at Reception. Let's do that on our way out," suggested Felicity. "Now, what would you like to drink?"

No one was surprised to see a male majority in the Bar, though thankfully diluted with quite a few women, and a good number of younger members. Varied ethnicities were also represented. "It's good to relax," said Emily. "Alice, have you been here before?"

"Just once, for my birthday. It's very grand. There aren't many people my age here, but it's a good experience. Occasionally." They all smiled with understanding, remembering their own choices, as sixteen-year-olds, for an evening out.

Alice was a friendly and fairly gung-ho teenager who enjoyed socialising, and conversed with ease. As an only child with largely just one parent, she had grown up earlier than some. Just in the process of clinching her 'A' level choices, hers was an exciting phase of life, and she was enthusiastic rather than apprehensive.

"OK, time for our dinner." Felicity led the way into the Dining Room, which was as resplendent as they'd pictured. The four diners were ushered to a table with a panoramic view of the room.

"Well," Emily paused a moment before she continued, "this is truly a great room. It's a combination of its impressive height," At this point she craned her neck as if for emphasis, "Deep wall colour, huge portraits, tall heavily curtained windows...."

"...dramatic ornaments, gilded mirrors, high-altitude mantlepieces, well-spaced tables, silver cutlery and crystal sparkling on white tablecloths; they do combine to make a terrific whole," added Felicity. "It's incredibly traditional, and just what you'd expect in a London club, but that doesn't diminish its dramatic effect when you're actually here, in the room."

"Oh, and the massive chandeliers," added Emily, still looking up. "Two questions: One, how do they clean them? Two, how safe are they? And another question. How often do they need cleaning and polishing? They look as though it was done yesterday."

"Let's look at the menu, love," urged Luke, who was looking forward to his food. Conversation stopped, and each chose a starter and main course.

Apart from enjoying an evening together over a leisurely meal, the friends wanted to discuss the Peacehaven Home situation. Felicity had taken both of her friends into her confidence about Pauline's accusations, and also the general care of residents. The police had interviewed Pauline, and were in the process of tracking down Billy, the latest update being that they were pretty confident they had located him in Lancashire, living with a woman and her son. Apparently they were due to question him the following week, and they had an additional useful lead via Pauline.

"Sounds promising," commented Luke. "Do keep us informed, as you can."

The other issue was one on which they could talk more freely. Felicity's policy over the last few weeks had been to listen, watch, and say nothing. In tandem with that approach, Alice had taken on a volunteer assistant carer position at weekends, working one evening a week for four hours. Following normal vetting procedures, she'd been accepted for the work, and was being vigilant about any worrying care from staff. She'd been working in both the residential and the nursing sections.

"What's your verdict?" asked Emily.

"Lots of the staff are really nice, and do care for the elderly people they're looking after. They are terribly overworked. It's just a really stressful job, and pretty horrible at times too. I would hate to do it full-time," confided Alice. "But I'm also concerned about some of it."

"For example?" asked her mother.

"Well, some things get forgotten. Mostly they're relatively unimportant, like a missed cup of tea, or an item not being brought to a resident. But a message to someone from a relative who's rung up can be lost, and not passed on. That's not good. And the logistics for getting someone to a hospital appointment sometimes get lost in translation. I know because residents have confided in me."

"All a bit familiar," commented Luke, who'd had experience of his father's time in a nursing home, a few years back. He was impressed with Alice's linguistic facility in this report, and her maturity.

"There are other things." Alice warmed to her theme. "I've seen some unkindness, impatience, and even downright rudeness. People not listened to, and failure to keep promises."

"Promises?" Emily was puzzled.

"Oh, you know, staff saying they will do something, and then not doing it. And the person who made the polite request is left waiting for something that doesn't ever happen. I also hate it when they call their clients 'Darling', 'Dear', or 'Love'. When I am eighty-five," Alice looked quite angry, "I do not want to be called by any of those pet names. And I'm not sure I want to be called 'Alice' either. Ms Wheeler, or Mrs X, or Dr X, or whatever my name is then, will do just fine."

"I remember my father being called 'young man'," said Luke sadly. "That was actually cruel. Not funny, as the carer imagined."

Starters arrived, to delighted comments. Wine was *in situ*, water bottles on the table, and candles were lit. "The food's delicious," said Emily.

"From seeing my mother in her home, I can understand how frustrating it must be for residents to wait and wait and not see actions implemented," said Felicity. "Yet the staff are very stretched, and it's a hard job."

"A job which is a job, and which should be done well, and conscientiously," commented Emily. "You mentioned unkindness, Alice. What did you mean?"

Alice hesitated. "I try to imagine how I would feel if I were some of these residents. They have dignity and past lives of service to family, friends, the community, and in many cases, of service to their own clients. They have had clients themselves, and they looked after them, with care. So when I see them being ignored, or spoken to unkindly, it sort of makes my blood boil."

She collected her thoughts.

"For example, a carer told a resident the other evening to 'Hurry up' on her way to the toilet. She also said, 'I can't stand waiting here all night.' This elderly woman speaks very quietly, and several times the carer simply ignored what she said, and didn't try to hear, and didn't ask her to repeat herself."

"Was this carer the one I overheard when I came back for my shopping bag recently? A carer with red curly hair, and glasses?"

"It sounds like her. Shirley I think is her name."

"It all sounds horribly familiar." Luke looked sober. "I met some wonderful staff when my father was in hospital after his stroke, but also several unfeeling and completely insensitive nurses, and other staff who didn't impress me. A physiotherapist told my mother coldly, "There's very little we can do for your husband." Another, his key nurse, strolled off on two weeks' holiday without telling him or my mother. I'm not sure I want to recollect all of it." Emily put her hand on his.

"Alice, this is really useful feedback," said Felicity. "I know you feel a bit like a spy, but we need this evidence before we speak with the matron. Let's see how things go over the next few weeks, and then I'm determined to meet with her, and push for changes."

"It's terrible," said Emily. "Yes, something needs to be done, to be fair to these people. Thanks so much for your report, Alice."

"OK, let's change the subject." Felicity, as host, was keen to move to more upbeat matters.

There was a pause in the conversation, starters now cleared, and new subjects of conversation being pondered. Main courses arrived. The waiters removed each silver cloche with aplomb, revealing individual diners' choices. Out of the corner of his eye, Luke spied the dessert trolley being trundled round the room, and spotted a favourite pudding.

"What will you study for 'A' level?" Emily asked Alice. "I can't decide what I'll do for a career, so I'm covering myself a bit," she replied. "Economics, physics, history, and maths. If I can cope with four."

"What a great selection. How exciting. And might you be a lawyer like your mother?" was Emily's reply.

"Maybe. Or maybe not. But I don't know yet. There are so many options."

"We wish you much success," continued Emily. "Thanks," replied Alice, after her earlier composure, suddenly a bit shy. Felicity looked at her daughter with pride.

"Do you know what I really love about this place?" said Luke suddenly.

"What do you really love about the club?" asked Alice, expecting him to comment on the artwork or the upholstery.

"It's the fact that they didn't start the dinner time conversation with us by asking what we'd like to drink. That's what happens everywhere else." He rolled his eyes, just as his son often did. "Asking us what we'd like to drink before we've even drawn breath is just another ploy to get us to spend more during the evening. We can order our drinks with the food. Pre-dinner drinks are what we have at the bar, not at the table. And secondly," warming to his theme, "they don't interrupt our conversation here every two minutes by asking if we're happy with the food. It's utter bliss not to have to go through that rigmarole. If we aren't happy, they know that we'll simply tell them. Mark of a good dining experience – subtlety, thinking about we'd like, and courtesy."

"A gold star from you for the club," smiled Felicity.

"Make that several gold stars," replied Luke. "The service is superb, as well as the food and drink."

Desserts enjoyed, coffee and tea were taken in the nearby drawing room, an area replete with magazines, journals, and informative publications about the club.

"I wonder how Lily is," said Emily thoughtfully. Luke frowned at her; he'd asked her not to keep dwelling on the imminent birth this evening.

"When is she due exactly?" asked Felicity.

"In three days. It's such an expectant time. But also, especially for Lily, totally awesome as well as terribly nerve-wracking."

"Wow, you will be grandparents," declared Alice, as though this had only just occurred to her, months after the pregnancy had been announced. "You don't look old enough!"

"Keep up the flattery, Alice," purred Luke. "And thanks for a brilliant evening, Felicity. I could stay in this armchair all night, but we should really get home, and be ready for tomorrow's work appointments."

"It was a pleasure. And let's continue talking about the situation at Peacehaven. We'll keep you informed."

No sooner were they home than Luke's phone rang. "Hello Andrew! How are you? Sorry, I see you've been trying to get hold of me. We were out. Yes, of course! Come round tomorrow evening. We're in then (he was checking with Emily by sign language). Is Jessie coming too? Just you? OK, have a drink with us. See you at eight-thirty."

***

Emily was agog. What could Andrew be coming to see them about this evening? She had a bit of an inkling, but it all seemed awfully soon. When had Jessie and he met? Just six months ago. Last night's call from Andrew was definitely sending her maternal brain into overdrive.

He arrived promptly at eight-thirty, looking slightly nervous, but smart in his denim shirt, navy jumper, and grey jeans. "I like this boy," thought Luke. Andrew seemed just a boy to him, although he was Jessie's age, thirty-two. "I like his steady gaze, his warmth, and his good sense of humour. He's a man of the cloth, yet I can relate to him". These two shouldn't have been mutually exclusive, but his daughter's partner being in a profession that he'd never envisaged was slightly out of Luke's comfort zone.

"Lovely to see you, Andrew," said Emily. "Can I get you a drink?"

"A cup of tea would be great, thanks."

They sipped tea together and discussed niceties. "What exactly was the point of this meeting?" Luke was thinking to himself. Then at nine o'clock precisely, as if reading Luke's mind, Andrew said, "Well, I'd better get to the point of my visit." Luke and Emily reined in their emotions, and waited patiently.

"As you know, Jessie and I have been seeing a lot of each other since we met last September. And we've both agreed that we'd like to get married." He smiled nervously.

Luke and Emily smiled back. "Well, that's splendid news!" said Luke.

"And well, I know we're in the twenty-first century, but I just wanted to make sure that you were both happy about this plan?"

"As plans go, I think it's one of the best," said Emily. "We're very fond of you and we'd love you to be our son-in-law. This is a very happy surprise."

"I've just got one key question," continued Luke. "How does Jessie feel about being married to a vicar?" He wasn't really clear how his daughter felt about church and sermons and dog collars and Sunday commitments and so on. He remembered that she'd attended children's camps when growing up, and over the years had had links with various churches, but he wanted to be sure that this couple would be of one mind. Although no expert on marriage apart from his own experience, Luke was wise enough to desire an equal partnership and joint life view for his daughter and any future husband.

Andrew looked more serious. "We've talked about that a lot. She and I share the same faith, and we have the same vision, linked with that faith. We can see how things will work, with my job and her work as a doctor. We're both happy with that vision. We really want to work together in the church and in our life as a couple."

"Then we're both very happy with this great plan, for you to marry each other," was Luke's verdict. "When are you thinking of, for the wedding?"

"July this year, if we can sort out all the details. We don't want a long engagement."

The door had hardly closed after Andrew's departure before Emily was on the phone to Jessie. Luke could hear the squeals from the other end of the house. "Let me speak too," he said, coming into the kitchen, and grabbing Emily's phone.

"I feel exactly like Mr Bennet," he told his daughter, "though in our modern version, Mrs Bennet was there as well. And so, as Mr Bennet said in the great novel, if you love this man, if you are sure that you love him, then you have our complete blessing." Luke had paraphrased Austen's words a little, but they all understood. "I'm thrilled that you like Andrew, and that you're happy about this wedding plan," was

Jessie's overjoyed response.

"Come round together when it suits your work timetable, and let's celebrate with a meal and some champagne," added Emily.

"Let's go to bed," said Luke, when the call had eventually come to an end. "I'm exhausted. In a good way. But definitely dog-tired, and totally ready for a long peaceful sleep as we look forward to the expansion of our family."

CHAPTER ELEVEN

Grand Design
February 2014

Emily had arranged to meet with her clients Tom and Maddy at eleven-thirty. At a quarter to twelve she was still waiting at the site, wrapped up in her warm winter coat and thick scarf, and wondering where on earth they were.

"We are so so sorry," Maddy cried as they parked nearby a few minutes later. "The traffic was terrible." They had both come from work.

"Let's go into the kitchen," said Emily. "We can look at the plans there."

"It's a bit of a mess in here," said Maddy. "We know we've got to move out soon for the work to be done, so we haven't really bothered to make it smart. The rest of the house is much nicer than this area."

The kitchen was no warmer than outside. It was in dire need of an upgrade. The cabinets were old and tired, and the walls needed a good lick of paint.

"Well, here's the plan. I sent it to you with my e-mail last week, too. I haven't changed it since then."

"Sorry, we didn't see the e-mail," said Tom. "Could you just run through all the details now?"

Patiently, and gradually warming to her theme, Emily outlined her vision for their new extended kitchen and adjoining guest room *cum* study, with the small *en suite*, and the couple listened intently. She was skilled in outlining a holistic vision for a project, including lots of creative detail, and enthusing clients, all the while tempered with sensible realism. Maddy and Tom liked what they heard; it gelled with their dream. Since the first consultation, Emily had managed to condense their initial vision so that they could still get excited about the extension even though it wasn't precisely what they had originally requested.

"I envisage it taking six months minimum," Emily advised. She didn't like to be over-optimistic about time spans.

"I like it," said Maddy. "I like the plans for the larger kitchen, and the free-standing items, and the nods to church furniture. And the bedroom-study will work well for our needs."

"Great," said Emily, suddenly noticing to her horror that a series of calls from Lily, just seconds apart, were showing up on her phone, which she'd muted. Strict professional propriety enabled her temporarily to ignore the calls, stressful though it was to see this indication of family drama. "So I'll send you a timeline and final plan, with all costs, by the end of the week. I'll also liaise with the builders and project manager, and discuss a start date with you. How does that sound?"

The meeting was over after another ten minutes and once in her car, Emily called Lily back. "Are you OK, darling?" "Mum, I'm in labour. It started ten minutes ago. Archie's on his way home now. I can't stop. I need to check my hospital bag. Oooh, it really hurts!"

It was twelve-twenty. Emily drove home, her mind on Lily all the time. Luke was at the law firm; she called him with the breaking news, and then busied herself with a mixture of work and tonight's supper, all the while occupied with thoughts of her daughter.

The phone rang. "Lily, is that you?" she said before checking who was calling.

"Emilie, it's Carla's Dad, Giovanni, from New York. I am here for a few days. How are you?"

"Very well," replied Emily politely. "But our daughter Lily is having a baby. Can I call you back?"

"Emilie, I just want to speak with Luke. Great news about Lily. Is Luke there?" As quickly as she could without being rude, Emily passed on Luke's work number.

The day passed very slowly. Emily re-lived her three labours with Lily, Jessie, and Xander. Then she re-lived each of them again. She put the radio on; it was full of news about Russia invading Crimea. Unbearable. She wondered how a grandmother-to-be in Crimea would be coping, her country having been invaded. She called Luke a few times. Eventually he came home. Then, at ten past six the call came. Archie's voice boomed down the line. "Lily has had a little girl," he said in his rich Edinburgh accent. "They are both fine. Six pounds, three ounces. Name to be confirmed."

"Hello Grandpa," he added to his friend, Luke having joined the phone call. "Got to go. Talk later!" he continued, leaving Luke to reflect on his new identity. Emily made a note in her diary: "Baby born to Lily and Archie. Became grandparents." It was Wednesday February 12th.

The freshly minted grandparents were of course overjoyed. Neither could quite believe it. They didn't really feel like grandparents and weren't sure they appreciated the image, with its harbinger of ageing, but meeting the baby, Daisy Jane, provided solid evidence for their new status; they went to Lily and Archie's home the following day to introduce themselves. Emily hugged herself with joy. This unique experience of having a grandchild was an amazing gift, and she swore it would lift her spirits every day from now on. A dainty baby, Daisy thrived from the start, charming everyone with her little face and – in due course – engaging smile. She had red hair like her Aberdonian grandfather. "Nothing to do with me," was Luke's wry comment when he saw her fine strands for the first time.

"It's not red," Emily would correct everyone who mentioned it subsequently, feeling slightly responsible for the colour. "It's auburn." Luke found it difficult to call Daisy "my granddaughter" but obediently did so, as it was the most straightforward role to play. Jimmy Smith was on his mind quite a lot, but he kept his thoughts to himself. He was delighted for Lily, and also for Archie, and determined he would get used to the situation, given time.

Emily was ecstatic, and played her grandmother role to perfection, dancing attention on Lily and Daisy when required but tactfully fading into the background when definitely not needed. She'd moved from full-time work to four days a week, was enjoying the freedom afforded by the extra day, and was available to help if needed.

The events of the last week were almost too much to take in. One daughter engaged, and the other with a new-born. Very Mrs Bennet. Exciting, but quite overwhelming. *Slightly more spaced-apart events would have been welcome*, mused Emily. She felt almost drunk with euphoria at the two developments, moving joyfully from one to the other in her thoughts. Then Jimmy would dive into her psyche, and things clouded over. Her letter of November had prompted an instant reply from him; he'd agreed to meet her in March, and had suggested both a date and a venue. Emily wanted to meet in Edinburgh. She had a phobia of meeting him any nearer to Lily and Luke. So they were due to meet on Thursday March 6th, at the Old Waverley Hotel on Princes Street. Emily would take the train there. After the meeting with Jimmy she'd arranged to see Tina, who was spending a lot of time in Edinburgh at the moment. She hoped it might bring some light relief and some sanity to the day, a day she was dreading.

Several times recently, Emily had seriously thought of cancelling the meeting and just telling Jimmy that it was too traumatic, after all these years. But her conscience nagged at her just as, according to Luke, she nagged him sometimes. Deep inside she knew, as long as Jimmy didn't turn out to be too terrible, that she owed it to Lily to give her the option of meeting her father. That was only fair; Emily had a strong equitable streak which, try as she might, she simply couldn't shake off. And it wasn't Lily's fault that her mother and father had conceived her during a short fling in their student years. Emily felt very responsible. She didn't know if Jimmy did; he clearly hadn't had a conscience for over thirty years. *Stop spoiling your daily life*, she admonished herself. *Don't think about this meeting until just beforehand.* So she did her best to blot Jimmy out of her mind, for the time being.

"Let's go out and celebrate all the family events," said Luke, knowing how tired Emily was, and not as enthusiastic as usual about entertaining at home. "Giovanni can join us." He was pleased to hear that Giovanni's meeting with Luke's New York colleague had proved fruitful. The two had met twice, and James knew of the "shark" (James's descriptor) with whom Carla's father had been dealing. Giovanni seemed happier about the situation, and felt it was in good hands. A business trip had brought him to London, and he'd wanted to update Luke on his personal situation.

"Let me organise," continued Luke. "You're still working full pelt, and I'm down to two days a week."

Dinner was duly booked for the following Saturday for nine adults and a babe in arms. The restaurant happened to be just two streets away from Maddy and Tom's house. "Let me show you my latest project," said Emily before they left home. "We can see the house quite easily from the street; it's on a corner."

"It looks a fairly ordinary house," she explained, as they sat in the car looking at it. "And much of what I've drafted affects the interior, so in the end it won't look terribly different from what we're looking at now. The main exterior difference will be a longer building at the back, but in the same brick, and designed not to look specifically like brand new material." They were looking at the house sideways on, glimpsing the downstairs through an unhealthy-looking hedge that had seen better days. "Inside there'll be much more light, thanks to the bifold doors. Thankfully it's a fairly long garden, so they'll still have room to enjoy their green areas. The kitchen will be quite eclectic, even though I'm designing it from scratch. They wanted a mixture of furniture in there. And the room next to it will major on the study effect, the guest room element being almost hidden."

"How will you do that?"

"The sofa-bed will look exactly like a sofa unless it's being used as a bed. The *en suite* will be hidden behind a floor to ceiling bookcase, part of which will act as a hidden door. And a built-in chest of drawers with overnight storage will be in the same wood and style as the study furniture."

"Sounds impressive. I'm sure it will be splendid." Luke smiled. "It's nearly seven-thirty. Let's find a parking space nearer to the restaurant."

Carla and Xander were already seated when they arrived, celebratory drinks in hand. "Let me get you drinks, grandparents," Xander greeted them. "Congratulations, Emily and Luke!" smiled Carla warmly. "We can't wait to meet Daisy." "And to see Jessie's ring!"

"I think they bought it yesterday," said Emily, who'd been informed by phone that afternoon.

It was a jubilant evening. Daisy excelled herself by arriving wide awake so that she could be admired and cuddled a little, and then duly falling asleep in Lily's arms for the next hour. Jessie and Andrew were radiant in the flush of their hot news. Archie beamed with pride. Giovanni joined in the celebrations enthusiastically. And Carla and Xander were overjoyed for their siblings. Toasts were raised to the newly engaged couple, and to the youngest member of the family.

Just one thing rankled, and disturbed the peace and joy. Only two people were aware of it. And its name was Jimmy Smith.

CHAPTER TWELVE

Old Waverley Hotel
Princes St, Edinburgh
March 2014

Emily got an early train to Edinburgh on Thursday March 6th. Leaving at eight o'clock, she'd be there by twelve-thirty, allowing her ample time to get to where she was staying, and have a drink and sandwich before seeing Jimmy at three. They were due to meet at the Old Waverley Hotel near the station, a place of which Emily had no recollection from her student days. She'd chosen, however, not to stay there, and had booked a room in a boutique hotel near George Street, the wide eighteenth century street beyond Princes Street in the New Town. Nervous that Jimmy might have booked to stay where they were meeting, Emily had no desire to bump into him either in the corridors that evening, or over breakfast.

She debated about what to wear. Not wishing to look as though she was on a date, yet also not wanting to dress uncharacteristically, she decided on dark jeans with a striped shirt, and smart grey blazer. *I'll feel more confident if I look halfway decent*, she thought. As she entered King's Cross Station, pulling her little case along behind her, the loudspeaker blared, "We are sorry to announce that the eight o'clock train for Edinburgh has been delayed by thirty minutes." *Are you really sorry?* Emily looked heavenwards and addressed the loudspeaker, but softly, so that no-one would worry about her sanity.

After this inauspicious start, the rest of the journey passed without incident, and the train rolled into Waverley Station at one o'clock precisely. The approach to the station was always nostalgic. Emily invariably twisted her head from side to side as the train approached the platform, looking to her left at the often flower-laden slopes of Princes Street Gardens, and to her right, head tilted upwards so as to see properly, at the steep cliff of Edinburgh Castle. There was absolutely no doubt about which city they were in.

Emily passed the hotel where they were due to meet, a seven-storey Victorian building on a corner of Princes Street. She hurried, almost ran, to the hotel where she was staying, keen to have some rest and refreshment before meeting Jimmy. This felt like a military operation and like a good soldier, she needed fortification. Luke would be thinking about her a lot, she knew. He would be eager for her call later on. *OK, time to go*, she said to herself, setting off for the Old Waverley with a determined step.

On arrival she walked up the tartan-carpeted stairs, past Reception, into the spacious Abbotsford Bar, then on into the dining room. "There's a table booked for tea in the name of J. Smith," she told the waitress at the door. But there was no need. A tall figure rose up from one of the tables, coming over to greet her. Emily felt a bit strange. *No, be calm and collected,* she reminded herself. Would she have recognised Jimmy in a crowd? Probably not. He'd lost quite a bit of hair, but what remained was still red; he had the same smiling face that had attracted her decades ago; and he was dressed in smart casual gear like her.

"Hello Emily," he said, giving her a peck on the cheek.

"Hi Jimmy. It's good to see you," was her polite reply as they moved to their table.

He'd chosen the one in the far corner. It was in a small alcove, encased by a curved bay window, and suitably private. There was also a great view; they were looking out onto the Scott Monument and to the right, Edinburgh Castle. The room was long, furnished in pastel colours, with crown moulding on the ceiling and pale pillars dotted around its space. White tablecloths and tea-time china created an air of elegance and calm. *Just what I need,* thought Emily. *Especially the calm.* Traditional three o'clock fare arrived – neat crust-less sandwiches; deep scones with cream and Scottish raspberry jam; shortbread and Victoria sponge and a few chocolate items. Earl Grey tea, and milk in small china jugs.

"So how was your journey?"

"The train was a bit late, but fine apart from that. And yours, from Aberdeen?"

"On time actually, and a brilliantly sunny ride here."

They sipped their tea, Emily feeling quite uncomfortable in this unusual situation. Fortunately they had no-one at either table next to them, and the staff were talking together, so for the moment there wouldn't be anyone eavesdropping on what, to the casual listener, might be a riveting catch-up conversation.

"So you qualified as an architect, after Edinburgh? Well done. And that must be fascinating work."

"Yes, I enjoy it. I do four days a week, and that works well, along with family commitments. All three children live in London, so we meet up fairly regularly." She didn't want to give too much away, certainly not immediately. "And your work in publishing? It sounds quite lucrative, producing those coffee-table art books."

"I do a lot of work for exhibitions, and that's always worthwhile. People like a good memento, especially the serious art fans." He smiled. And Emily smiled back politely.

"So, you wrote that you've had relationships, but haven't ever married."

"Yes, I've had two long-term relationships, each now over, and one of those women had her own children. And I've now been with someone for the last six months. Julie is an artist in a village near Aberdeen; we get on very well."

"But no children of my own," he added. There was a pause. They had both stopped eating.

"Emily, I'm sorry if all of this is difficult for you," Jimmy started.

"Of course it's difficult." She wanted to be friendly but firm. In essence this was a business meeting. She had something he wanted and truth be told, they were here to bargain with each other. It wasn't going to be easy. She was conscious of holding a lot of power, probably ninety percent of it, and was reluctant to let it go. What was his ten percent? Simply the paternity, she reflected. Which on paper was a lot, but in reality hadn't amounted to very much at all.

"I wanted to tell you that I'm truly sorry about my behaviour thirty-five years ago, leaving you in the lurch." He looked sorry; were there even tears in his eyes? Though, Emily imagined, remorse would be a good tactic to engage her sympathy. "I was young and callow," he continued. "I didn't want responsibility, but I acknowledge that my behaviour was unforgivable. I know you're happily married now, so of course I'm not looking to resume our relationship."

Of course not. What a cheek, was Emily's thought. Though she did remember why they got together in the first place, and there was still a flicker of attraction between them. Which she firmly rebutted before it had any chance to develop. *I'm angry*, she thought. *Really angry. He just abandoned me. And Lily.*

"So might I hear something about my child?" he ventured. Just the words "my child" made Emily bristle.

"I had a girl. It was very hard having a baby on my own. But my parents were a wonderful support. And then, a year later, I met Luke. He's been truly amazing. He accepted my daughter from the word 'Go', and he's brought her up as his." She looked Jimmy straight in the eye.

He looked down at his scone. "I guess she must be thirty-five now. What's her name?"

"Lily. She's lovely." In her heart of hearts a warm and kind person, Emily decided she had to hand over more key details. "She got married recently, and she has a baby girl."

Jimmy stared at her. "So I'm a grandfather."

"I guess so," replied Emily grudgingly.

"Called?"

Your grandfatherly name or the baby's name? she thought, but decided not to be facetious. "Daisy. She was born last month."

"Lily and Daisy. Very floral," commented the father and grandfather.

"Lily married an old university friend of Luke's. So her husband, Archie, is our generation. With me having had a baby fairly young, the gap isn't as huge as it might have been. He's fifty-four."

"Lily. Lily. Beautiful name. This is wonderful news for me, Emily. But you must surely resent me barging into your life. And Luke won't have been thrilled to hear that I'd been in touch."

"It's not been easy hearing from you out of the blue after all these years. And I'm still angry that you abandoned me, that you completely disappeared. Even though we might not have ended up together, I'd have appreciated some support in bringing up ...." She hesitated before voicing it. ".... our daughter."

He put his hand on hers. She withdrew it hurriedly. "Emily, I'm really sorry. I'd like you to forgive me, but I can't expect that." He emphasised the word "expect", and somehow his accent increased the emphasis. "I'd also very much like to meet Lily. Do you think that will be possible? I regret not having had children. I've made a bit of a mess of my private life. I admire you and Luke for staying together all these years. No, I'll admit it; I'm envious of you for having been married for – I guess it must be over thirty years?"

Emily was silent. She had a sip of tea. Deep in reflection she looked out, beyond Jimmy, across the side street, to the solid façade of Jenner's, the city's 'Harrods of the North'. She had another sip of tea. "I haven't told Lily that you've been in touch. She doesn't even know your name. All these years, we never spoke of you. She thinks of Luke as her father.

He walked her down the aisle last year."

She continued, "But I do admit to feeling guilty that I never spoke to her of you at all. It was the anger at being abandoned that prevented me. Though in a sense, what could I say? All I knew of you was from an eight-week period in my distant youth."

"It's your decision," said Jimmy quietly. "You have all the power here." Strange that his words should echo her thoughts.

"What I plan to do is to tell Lily about you when I get back. But not immediately. She's a totally exhausted young mother at the moment. When I feel the time is right, I'll sit down with my daughter and tell her about our meeting today. And the decision will be hers, not mine. I will hand over the responsibility for her relationship with you, to her."

Jimmy hailed a waiter. "Could we have more tea, please?" He offered Emily some shortbread.

They were both silent for a moment. Then Jimmy continued the conversation.

"You are being totally fair," he said. "And I appreciate that. I'm grateful that you agreed to meet me today. I'm happy to wait to hear from you. I've never been close to tiny babies but I'm not stupid, and I'm sure she must be totally shattered." He paused. "I hope she'll agree to meet me, but I'll be realistic."

"What does she do?" he asked.

"She runs an art gallery, actually. So coincidentally, there's a common thread."

"Maybe she's got some of my books," speculated Lily's father, as the waiter put fresh tea on the table.

Jimmy then asked about Luke, about his work and about their other two children. Reluctantly at first, Emily told him a bit about their life. If she didn't, she reckoned, it wasn't fair to Lily, if she did agree to meet her father, not to have prepared the ground a little. She spoke about Archie too, about his friendship with Luke, and his work. She learned a little more about Jimmy's life, and where he lived. They laughed from time to time, politely, each aware of the delicacy of the occasion.

By now it was half past four. Jimmy had called for the bill, and Emily was due to meet Tina in fifteen minutes, at the far end of Princes Street.

"Jimmy, I have to go," she said. "Thank you for the tea. And thanks for meeting with me. It's been an unusual afternoon. We had a happy few weeks together years ago, with a significant outcome. So let's part as friends. I just don't know if I'll see you again, but I will be in touch. Your next meeting may be with Lily, if she is happy to see you. I can't promise anything, but I will definitely let you know."

They embraced at arm's length, a marginally warmer parting than the greeting. And then Emily walked through the Abbotsford Bar, across the lobby with its tartaned floors, down the stairs, and out of the hotel in a daze. On leaving she noted the splendid floral arrangements dotted around that Carla would have so loved. She saw the sun on Livingstone's statue across the road as the front door opened. But her exit from the hotel was like the exit of someone else, not herself, from the Old Waverley; it was dreamlike. The cold Edinburgh air and brisk wind, instantly attacking with a vengeance, helped to steady her. *Just walk. Walk briskly*, she muttered to herself.

Tina was already waiting in the café. "Emily, how good to see you! How are you?" She looked at her friend, who despite her façade of composure, looked distressed. "What can I get you? A glass of wine?

Brandy?" Though she wasn't certain this genteel Princes Street establishment would have brandy.

"A really strong coffee would be great," answered Emily, smiling warmly. "It's great to see you. I'm so glad our visits to Edinburgh happened at the same time." They sat together at the quiet corner table which Tina had commandeered. Knowing of Emily's meeting with Jimmy, she'd been sure to arrive early. "So how was it?" she asked her friend. In their earlier years they hadn't coincided in Edinburgh, nor at the Lothian Road flat, but Tina and Friedrich had occasionally called in briefly on recent visits to the UK, and then more recently Lily's wedding had given the two women a chance to meet and get to know each other better.

"It was pretty fraught. For me at least. Summing up thirty-five years, which includes telling your ex the gender and name of the child you share, her marital status, details of her husband who happens to be your husband's best friend, her job, and the fact that he's now a grandfather, all over a traditional afternoon tea served with a silver teapot and choice china, isn't an experience I'd like to repeat too often."

Tina laughed, but sympathetically.

"And how was he?"

"It was probably very fraught for him too, though he didn't really show it. He was pleasant, contrite, friendly. I remembered why I fell for him in the 1970s. But that was the 1970s. Now I have Luke, who I love dearly, who I definitely love much more than the feelings I ever had for Jimmy. My relationship with Jimmy, even though it produced Lily, is ancient history." She sighed and looked pensive. "I promised to let him know what Lily's reaction is. Though I told him I would choose the time to tell her, very carefully. She's in a delicate state at the moment."

"So did he apologise for walking out on you?"

"Well, walking out isn't strictly true. We weren't living together. But he did abandon me after I told him I was pregnant. Today we skirted around the fact that he advised an abortion; it would have been way too painful to mention. That will remain for ever a secret between Luke, myself, and Jimmy."

"And now it's your secret too," Emily added. "Yes, he did apologise, and it seemed genuine. I wondered if it was sort of his payment to me, for divulging all the details about Lily and for agreeing to tell her I'd met him, and that he wants to meet her too. But I softened during the tea, and I think …. I think that his remorse is genuine. He seems a reasonably nice person."

"I walked out on Ricky when I was pregnant," said Tina. "And unlike you and Jimmy, yes, we were living together. It was a very mixed-up … *sehr gemischt…* situation. Ricky didn't know I was married to Friedrich, until Friedrich turned up in Edinburgh that evening. I messed up both men. I feel very bad about it. No excuses for me. Apart from the fact that I did eventually honour my marriage, by returning to Friedrich. And Ricky was admirable – *wunderbar* – in the way he handled the situation. He's been a superb father to Fergus. Friedrich has been his "other father" but Ricky has funded the major part of Fergus's growing-up, and saw him every couple of months for years until he was 18. And now he's making possible his professional life, through the art gallery."

"It sounds a very different situation," commented Emily. "Of course, Ricky did have access to money," she smiled wryly.

"Yes, that did help a lot. Ricky's father has been very generous. I'm sorry it has been such a traumatic afternoon, Emily. What are you doing tonight? Would you like to come round?"

Tina was staying with Ricky and his wife Jane for a few days. They had invited Tina to stay when chatting at Lily's wedding. Tina's "messed-up situation" just outlined was ongoing. She had already let Luke and Emily know that she and Friedrich were living apart. "We always had friction," she had told Emily in an e-mail, "even after I went back to him. He's so work-obsessed; day and night he's toiling. And now Marianne is no longer living at home, I found it claustrophobic. I actually think he's better on his own. He can work all hours without feeling he's letting anyone down. I'm in a studio apartment in Hamburg. So we can easily meet if we want to."

"And tell me about Jane. Do you get on well with her? How long have they been married?"

"She's lovely, if just a tad suspicious of me. After all I did have a baby with her husband." Tina smiled conspiratorially. "But yes, they've been married for thirty years, and they have grown-up twin boys who I've met. They're both working in Scotland, one in Edinburgh and one in Glasgow. Jane is also very fond of Fergus, which is a nice bond between us."

"Thanks for the kind offer," replied Emily, thinking it slightly odd that Tina should offer hospitality on behalf of someone else. "But I feel I need a quiet evening before heading off early tomorrow."

"You have had an emotional afternoon," said Tina sympathetically. "Yes, relax tonight, ring Luke, have a long bath. And don't worry about the Jimmy and Lily situation. Once you've told Lily, it will be over to her to manage."

"I do feel so terribly responsible. But what's done is done, and I must do my best to make it as good as possible, for all concerned."

"And please let me know how the situation with Friedrich is, when you're back in Germany," Emily added, very aware that this meet-up had been all about her.

They parted with promises of meeting again in the near future. Emily went straight to her room in the hotel, and rang Luke. Keen to hear how she'd got on, he was glad for her that the meeting was over. They were both conscious of the pending conversation with Lily, but agreed that now was definitely not the time. "See you tomorrow," they said simultaneously.

With dusk due to fall at six o'clock, there was still a bit of daylight left. Emily decided to take an early evening stroll, and wandered down to Princes Street Gardens. It was chilly, but with a coat and scarf she was plenty warm enough as she walked quickly from George Street in the fading light. She knew she wouldn't be disturbed by another Jimmy encounter. He'd been due to catch a five-thirty evening train back to Aberdeen, and would now be on his way home. She sat down on a bench overlooking the gardens and castle, and the panorama of the Royal Mile's historic buildings, floodlights beginning to glow. She gazed at the vast illuminated dome of the Bank of Scotland high on the hill. She immersed herself in the city's atmosphere. *I do love this city*, Emily thought. *It is achingly beautiful.* This was where she and Luke had met, which made it very special. Sadly it was also where she had met Jimmy, a little episode tainting the nostalgia.

What was it about Edinburgh? It was so unique, which of course could be said about many cities. It had character. And there wasn't really just one centre; there were a number of centres, or focal points. Princes Street of course was a key area, and the castle, so dominant from every angle, the distinctive and historic Royal Mile, the New Town where she was staying, Calton Hill with its iconic monuments, Georgian Stockbridge, an architectural gem, Dean Village with its tumbling Water of Leith, the Palace of Holyroodhouse, 800-foot Arthur's Seat in Holyrood Park which she'd looked out on every day from Pollock Halls of residence in her first term at Edinburgh.

There wasn't any uniformity; that was what she loved. The city had character and total individuality, completely unlike the standard pattern of many conurbations. Sitting on that bench, she suddenly missed Luke. She missed a comforting arm around her shoulder. Then eventually, tired of musing about her past and of missing her husband, she headed back to the hotel to spend thirty minutes on her work e-mails.

The next morning, memories of the previous day's meeting foremost in her head, Emily headed for platform two at Waverley. To her surprise the platform was an unexpected scene of morning festivity, as the dark red Royal Scotsman train, which she'd never seen before, offloaded its passengers from a luxury five-day journey. They were feted by an enthusiastic jazz quartet as affectionate hugs were exchanged between a line-up of uniformed staff and grateful passengers.

"It was incredible," enthused an American traveller, still heady with the vacation experience, "We were dancing on the platform last night." Emily wasn't sure if the jolly atmosphere, jazz by now reaching fever pitch, jarred with her heightened emotions, or salved them. Her conclusion was the former, and it was a relief to board the train for London, and reflect; indeed on this one occasion it was actually a relief to leave Edinburgh. Yesterday was still like a bad dream. The train sped along, Emily gazing endlessly at the fluctuating scenery and occasionally reading a few pages of her book. It was an easy journey back to King's

Cross, and then by taxi to Highgate.

"Hi, I'm home!" she called as she opened the front door at three o'clock. Luke, who wasn't working that day, appeared from the kitchen and gave her the hug she'd been looking for on the Princes Street bench the night before. "Welcome home, darling. Cup of tea?"

"Yes, please. Let me just dump my case."

"I'm glad you went to see Jimmy," he said once they were sitting down, tea in hand. "It was important. I just hope that Lily can handle the situation. And Archie. And then it has implications for Daisy, in the future."

"Well, that's the first stage of this saga over." Emily looked thoughtful. "What were those early lines in *Rebecca*? 'We can never go back again, that much is certain.' And I can't. I can't undo those weeks with Jimmy. I can't undo Lily's birth."

"And wouldn't ever wish to," replied Luke sternly. "Come on, love. Let's look to the future, and let's move forward with common sense, and no regrets."

Luke was right, and Emily knew it.

The insistent ringing of his phone during their meal spoke of urgency but they were determined to finish dinner in peace. "I'll ring back after we've eaten," said Luke.

Which he duly did, thirty minutes later. "*Bonsoir Dominique*," Emily heard him say. "*Oui, Luc à l'appareil. Oui je t'entends bien.*" There was silence for a few minutes. Then she heard him gasp, and continue in English. "That's truly terrible. I can't believe it. I'm so so sorry." Emily moved into the hall to see what was happening. There was more talking from Dominique, a long torrent of French which Emily could just hear. "*Les pauvres,*" interspersed Luke. "Yes, yes, you must get off the phone now to make those other calls. I will ring you tomorrow."

He turned to look at his wife, looking deeply sad. "That was Dominique, the French lawyer," he said, unnecessarily as she'd worked that much out. "The news is terrible. Sophie has been killed in a car accident. She was in a taxi, in a town outside Paris. They were hit sideways on at a junction, and she was killed outright. Must have been a crazy speedster."

"I thought she'd disappeared?"

"Yes, she had, and this is the first news we've had since then. She disappeared in October, five months ago. So where she was will remain a big mystery, unless someone comes out of the ether and tells us. Her poor family. The children are distraught, Philippe too though he's angry too that she just disappeared on him, and her sister is over from England now. I wasn't actually aware that she had a sister. My understanding, clearly wrong, was that she didn't have family back in the UK."

"I'm so sorry. She seemed such a lost soul when she came here. I'd have loved to hear that her life had taken off again, not that it had ended."

"Let's go and sit down," he replied.

"And, getting down to practicals, though not wishing to sound heartless, what will happen to your case now?"

"Absolutely dead in the water," replied Luke, wincing slightly at the unfortunate turn of phrase. "Philippe will get the house, he'll get the whole amount, and at some stage I'll get my fee. I know what was in her will. She hadn't got round to changing it following the divorce.

Everything was left to Philippe, nothing for anyone else, small amounts for various charities, and a sizeable amount to the children once they come of age."

"I totally forgot to mention," he continued, changing the subject, "Jessie rang this morning, and asked you to call her back."

"OK, I'll do that before I go to bed. That poor French family. I can't get them out of my head."

CHAPTER THIRTEEN

Jessie's Flat; Pub, London
March 2014

Emily rang the bell at the front door of Jessie's flat. A late lunch had been planned with her, Lily, and Daisy, after Jessie's lie-in, and before the start of her week's night duty. Carla had been invited, but an important client event that evening meant that she had a crazy and overfull day getting ready.

"Hi Mum!" Jessie enveloped her mother in a warm hug. "Come in. I've been up for an hour and I'm just about to heat the soup."

The two-bedroom flat was a six-stop Tube ride from the hospital. With a little help from her parents, Jessie had bought it two years ago, and loved it. In a block built in the late 1990s, it was on the second floor, and boasted a small balcony. She loved sitting there on a warm day. "You can almost see into the bedroom opposite," Luke had pointed out, but Jessie disagreed, countering out that there was an effective blind at the aforementioned bedroom window, and diverting his gaze to the beautiful trees which stood to the right of the nearby block of flats. Jessie

had made the flat her own, choosing idiosyncratic items to her liking –
a deep red long velvet sofa in the living area, thick cream curtains fringed
with the same deep red, vivid art work, all toned down with pale
accessories. Two cream chairs were placed either side of the red sofa. The
table lamps were cream, and the low occasional table was in pale ash
wood. All the cushions, of various shapes and sizes, were turquoise or
red.

The small kitchen had recently been painted. "I wanted something
restful in here," she explained to Emily, who hadn't previously seen the
finished decorating. Pale wood units were set off with dove grey walls,
and a light wood worktop. "Andrew likes it. I'm glad we have the same
tastes."

"What would you like to drink?" she asked her mother. "Water is
fine," replied Emily. "So how are the wedding plans coming along?" she
continued.

"Mum, I'm so happy that all's falling into place. The church is
booked, obviously the church where Andrew's curate. The marquee
company and caterers have confirmed for the reception. We have the
best man and bridesmaids all agreed too. Lily and Carla will be two of
the bridesmaids, plus Lucy and Harriet from school. I'd so love Daisy to
be a flower-girl, but I've decided she's just too young. Flower-baby as a
role doesn't really work, does it? Lily may carry her up the aisle, in a
matching outfit to her mother of course, but if necessary hand her over
to Archie at the last minute if Daisy doesn't cooperate. A transition
which hopefully won't engender loud crying, right at the start of the
service."

"It all sounds wonderful," smiled her mother. "Though I see what
you mean about Daisy. I'm sure Lily and Archie will know what's best

to do on the day. And I'm so looking forward to our trip to the wedding dress shop next week."

"So," looking around the flat, "I guess you and Andrew will be moving in together soon."

"No, we won't," was the swift reply.

"Oh, I guess you'll want to wait until a bit nearer to the wedding."

"Mum, we don't need to do what everyone else is doing. I know some people would call us old-fashioned or "traditional"; but that's an inaccurate description. It's just how we want to approach our wedding," said Jessie warmly but clearly. "We'll move in together when we get married. Simple!"

"This is so odd," she continued. "It feels like role reversal, and there's been such a change in one generation. I bet Grandma had different ideas to you, about you living with Dad before I was born?" She spoke teasingly but made an effective point.

Emily laughed at her daughter's perceptive comment. "OK, point well made. Yes, societal norms have totally changed, agreed. But it's also absolutely right for each couple to make their own decision. Which I think is what you are saying, yes?"

Jessie smiled. "Yes, Mum. Thanks for understanding. Now would you like a nibble with your glass of water? Cheese straw, *vol au vent*, dip?"

Emily heard her daughter loud and clear, didn't pursue the living arrangements conversation, and gratefully nibbled on a tasty cheese straw.

The doorbell rang. "Excellent timing," thought Jessie, who was glad they had concluded the previous conversation without either any ill feeling, or being interrupted. "Hello Lily. And Hello dear little Daisy!"

Daisy was still the perfect baby, but would that continue today? She had slightly more red hair than at birth. Lily wondered if it might change colour, as babies' hair often did once it had fallen out and re-grown. The baby's mother looked pale, but smart, in leggings, new drop earrings, and a deep pink shirt suited to feeding Daisy. Motherhood was suiting Lily well, in spite of the broken nights. Archie was working hard at work and working equally hard at home, doing his best to be a hands-on and committed father.

"Who would like the first cuddle?" she asked, with the air of someone bestowing a great favour. "I think that should be Granny," said Jessie. "She's a delight," pronounced Emily, thrilled to hold her grand-daughter. As if to order, Daisy made tiny cooing sounds. "She's trying to hold her head up a bit," said Lily. "Each new step makes her a bit more of a little person." They held their drinks and ate nibbles, while all gazed entranced at the small human.

"Right, end of baby worship. I'm going to serve up the soup," declared Jessie. "Lily, what would you like to do with Daisy? Put her in the baby chair, or on your lap?"

"Let's start with her on my lap," said Lily. But the plan didn't work. Daisy had decided it was time to cry. And cry. And cry some more. "She doesn't need feeding. I did that before we left," said her mother. "And her nappy is fine."

"Wind?" suggested Emily helpfully. "I'll hold her while you have your soup, Lily."

Emily walked around with Daisy, talking to her, rocking her, and being patient. But Daisy kept crying. "Let's go into the bedroom," she suggested to her grand-daughter, aiming to move the noise away from Lily and Jessie's conversation.

"It's a bit messy in there, Mum," shouted Jessie.

"Not a problem," replied Emily, strolling into the bedroom. She laid Daisy in the middle of the bed, making a well with the bedclothes to keep her safe, and staying a centimetre away next to her on the bed, in case she rolled. Daisy seemed transfixed by the new surroundings, especially the lamp next to the bed with its mosaic-like shade which kept catching the light as the sun came in and out. Gradually Emily saw her eyes fluttering, and eventually, closing.

OK what do I do now? she thought. *I can't leave her, and I can't shout to the others, so I'm trapped in here.* But Lily soon came to see what was happening. "I think if we very gently carry her from here to her baby chair, she might stay asleep." The gargantuan task was completed slowly and steadily by the two of them together, while Jessie warily remained motionless and silent. "Done it!" mouthed Lily triumphantly, soundlessly moving away from the baby chair.

"I have an idea," whispered Jessie, once they were all back at the table. "Why don't the three of us, sorry Daisy, the four of us, plus Carla, do a spa day to celebrate all the good news? We could do it any time, either before the wedding or afterwards, if we can find a date to suit everyone."

"I like it," said Lily. "Let's ask Carla, and then find a date. Daisy can be handed round during the day. It will be her first Girls' Day Out."

The others smiled at the reference to little Daisy's sophisticated social calendar.

"Do you mind if I kip on the sofa?" Lily continued. "I really need some rest."

"Make yourself at home," said Jessie. The bright pink shirt duly lounged on the deep red sofa, and the other two moved around noiselessly, taking what they could to the kitchen but leaving louder objects behind for the moment. They stayed in the kitchen, and quietly closed the door.

"How's that new project coming along, Mum?" asked Jessie.

"Thanks for asking. I'm really excited about it, and the clients seem pleased with the plans. I'm just waiting for their final agreement before allocating the job to the project manager and builders. It's a small project compared with some I've done, but it's quite a low-level challenge, the sort I prefer."

"Why's that?"

"I actually find huge projects that demand total change, and with awkward clients, totally stressful and not enjoyable at all. Some architects would rise to the occasion, the ones who thrive on high-level challenges. But not me!"

It felt intimate and warm, chatting in Jessie's kitchen. Emily noted the chalkboard, with "I heart you!" scribbled on it, presumably from Andrew. She looked at the coffeemaker which Jessie had dithered so much about. "Way too much choice," she'd commented. "So much choice that it's almost depressing." She'd plumped for a mid-range machine that offered just two choices of coffee, which was all she needed.

"Glad it's going well. And are you pleased with the new study?"

"Over the moon. It's transformed the way I work at home. Bizarrely,

I actually smile broadly each time I go into the room. It has a cossetting feel; it's almost like a warm womb where I can retreat within the home, a place that means so much to me."

"Great. I'm so pleased. I must come to see it. I'm just really overflowing with things to do at the moment."

"In a good way, I know. I'm impressed with your organisation, both you and Andrew. Just four months to go! And how's work going at the moment?"

Jessie then spoke at length about her hopes for the future. Now at registrar level, she had her eye on a consultant's post in the long term. She was very committed to her work, dedicated to her patients and staff, and enthusiastic about the efficacy of her specialism. There were so many facets to gastroenterology, and always new developments. Emily was proud of her daughter, just as she was proud of Lily and Xander. She counted her blessings that she and Luke had children who enjoyed their work, and were successful in it.

"And," wondering if it was wise to broach the subject, but venturing there nevertheless, "what will you do with the flat when you're married?" Emily emphasised "when you're married" as clearly as she could without sounding too unnatural.

"I'm trying to get a tenant, but haven't had any luck yet. I know a few friends who are looking, but for various reasons this doesn't suit them. So I'm still searching for the right person, or persons."

A sound of crying came from the living room. It started as a gentle noise, sporadically, and then more persistently, and finally it morphed into full-blown crying. They both left the kitchen. Lily was just waking and stretching. She got up sleepily, and picked Daisy up. "There, there," she comforted her daughter. "Did you have a bad dream? Let's get you home and maybe to some more food." Looking at Jessie, she said, "Thanks for a great time. I must get Daisy home. She's given me the signal.... When she's older I'll decide when to leave parties. But at the moment she gives the orders."

Silence reigned in Jessie's flat after they'd all left. She was glad of the few hours of freedom before starting nights.

***

Luke had had great difficulty in persuading Archie to come out for a drink. "Just for an hour, after you've eaten. To catch up. To have some time out."

"'After we've eaten' is a moveable feast from day to day now. Precise mealtimes are a thing of the past." The new father was sanguine about the change of regime.

"Well, whatever time you're free during the evening, this Thursday. Just give me a call, and I'll come and meet you at the Archway Tavern. Six o'clock, nine o'clock, half past ten, whatever."

"OK, as you're so keen. But forgive me if I have to cancel, for obvious reasons."

Despite his apparent lack of enthusiasm, Archie rang Luke at seven-thirty on Thursday evening. "I'm good to go. At the moment. But let's do it now. Otherwise Daisy might wake up, and I might be needed. See you in a few minutes."

Archie looked terrible. He had thrown on some old clothes that weren't his usual style (laundry not happening as it used to?), hadn't shaved for a couple of days (Daisy demanding his time before he went to work?), and he'd lost some weight (no time for either of them to cook?). He looked at Luke out of bloodshot eyes. "I'll have a pint of the usual, thanks; they have great craft beer here," was his response on what he'd like to drink.

They sat in the corner. It was an old pub, dating back to the early nineteenth century, and amongst other signature features, prided itself on being the site for a Kinks' album cover. Adding to the narrative, "William Hill took his first bet here," claimed the man behind the bar. Archie sat in the corner with his eyes closed, leaning back against the wall. "Really nice to see you, mate," he said, "but can I keep my eyes closed for a few minutes?"

"I remember what it was like when the children were small. You never ever forget that absolute exhaustion, and the feeling of crawling through mud from one day to the next."

"Daisy is really cute." Archie still had his eyes closed, and was leaning back against the hard wall. "But she's ultra-demanding, and it's tiring both of us out. Lily is marvellous, and she loves Daisy so much. As I do," he added. "It just seems to get harder rather than easier. She loves to wake up several times a night. Extremely anti-social."

"My mother put it best," responded Luke, "'His Majesty the Baby'. I think that just sums it up. 'Her Majesty', in this case. It will actually get better, I can assure you."

"Yes, in ten years' time?"

"Tell you what," continued Luke. "You keep your eyes shut. And go to sleep if you like, and I'll talk to you. You can say 'Yes' and 'No' occasionally if you like, but I won't mind if I deliver a monologue. Quite a nice idea really. I rather like the sound of my own voice."

"OK." Archie was already drifting off.

"Let me be your father figure and mentor," was Luke's opening gambit. "I can provide some normality in your baby-filled life. And I'll supply some grandfatherly advice too. The first bit is: 'Get some help.' And the second is the two words: 'labour-saving'. Maybe that's one word. Whatever you can buy or hire to save you work, get it. A second washing machine, frozen meals, food delivery, taxi to work sometimes, babysitters, earplugs."

Archie woke up. "Earplugs? No, that would be cruel. We need to hear Daisy when she cries."

"OK, maybe not earplugs." Luke reviewed his advice.

"Emily told me she saw Daisy this morning. She was enthralled with her. And she thought Lily looked well. I was at work. It was one of my days at work. Just two days a week at the moment, and then, after the end of May, freedom."

Archie didn't comment.

"There's much better news about Giovanni's financial woes." *Did Archie know about this*, Luke wondered?

"Is that the new waiter in the Italian in Highgate?"

"No, it's Carla's father. In New York. Not in Highgate. He's been having a few money challenges, and he confided in me. Sorry; I thought I'd told you, in confidence."

"Anyway," Luke continued, wondering if he'd drunk his craft beer a tad too quickly, "it's all fine now. He may have lost some funds, but nothing very worrying. He seems very relieved."

"Relieved is how I want to feel," mumbled Archie, and headed off for the Gents.

"I think I should go home," he resumed on his return. "Really sorry. I have to be at work tomorrow by eight o'clock, and I'm guessing I may not get much sleep tonight. So if I go home now, maybe I could do a sort of early sleeping shift. I really need it."

"I'm sorry. I do know how it feels. Let me know if you'd ever like to meet again." Luke stressed the word "ever", feeling the evening had been a bit of a disaster. "Give Lily my love. And Daisy!" he shouted after his friend, feeling very sorry for him. Yes, he remembered the sleepless nights, and endless work, but he also remembered that his own experience had been as a twenty-something, and not a generation further on.

CHAPTER FOURTEEN

Parisian Apartment; French Law Firm April 2014

The apartment overlooked the Seine. *Enough said*, thought Xander. *An expensive rental*. But thankfully the law firm was paying. Luke had to make one last journey to Paris to tie up ends with Dominique and Philippe. And he was glad to have Emily and Xander along with him, Emily taking time off from work, and Xander enjoying the last few days of the Easter vacation before he headed home to start his new job in the summer term. Sadly Carla couldn't spare any time from her business, but she'd encouraged her husband to have this necessary and therapeutic break.

It was a two-bedroom eighteenth century apartment on the first floor of the building, boasting those beautiful tall narrow shuttered French windows that characterised Paris. Each room, including the kitchen, was spacious. Many of the walls were panelled, and those that weren't were tastefully filled with displays of artwork. Fireplaces were marble. The floors were in well-waxed parquet. Double French doors opened onto iron balconies. Mirrors were plentiful, with curved tops. The furniture was antique, and of the period. Every room boasted original cornices. "I'm going to enjoy living here for a few days," pronounced Xavier.

Luke was due to spend the first few days at the law firm. He set off the morning after their arrival, sharply dressed as befitted the occasion, and enveloped in a warm overcoat, having chosen to walk rather than take the *Métro*. "It's still only early April," he reminded his wife and son as they stared at the woollen scarf and overcoat-covered apparition about to leave the apartment.

The firm, which Luke had visited for the first time last October, was housed in equally if not more impressive surroundings than their apartment. Luke had the sense of visiting a country house, or grand manor house, a National Trust treasure rather than a law firm. His own company in London was twentieth century and angular, not Frenchly elegant like this one. All the spaces here were expansive, and the ceilings sky-high. The building spoke money. "We have money and we'd like more. To be precise, yours," the building broadcast to its clients. Chandeliers, tall mirrors, Persian rugs, sculptures, sumptuous curtains, decorated pillars and cornices, sweeping staircases, and grand art work characterised the firm's offices. *I'm not sure I could call them offices,* thought Luke. *Palatial spaces might be a more accurate appellation.*

"*Luc, sois le bienvenu!*" exclaimed Dominique as she met him at the top of the stairs. She ushered him into a splendid room, where Philippe was already waiting, along with a junior colleague of Dominique's.

"Well, it's a sad meeting," ventured Luke, not entirely sure, given Philippe's antagonism to his ex-wife, if he should offer condolences.

"*C'est affreux,*" acknowledged her ex-husband. "*Ça m'a vraiment choqué.*"

155

Philippe looked grim. Luke noted with interest that for once, Dominique's client had arrived at a meeting on time.

Yes, it really shocked me too, he echoed mentally.

The meeting continued in French. The business was mainly to handle final details of the sale, the purchase being by a family who'd paid the asking price, and even slightly more. Philippe would get all the proceeds; his teenage children would benefit in the longer term. Luke couldn't help thinking of Sophie's sad face, and her crushed spirit. To his surprise, he missed her. Apparently the funeral had already taken place, and the devastated children were being looked after by relatives of Philippe.

Luke's client not being in the picture any more, he didn't have too much to do in these final stages. Although he'd anticipated being called in the following day, Dominique thought this wasn't necessary. "Au revoir, Monsieur," he said at the end of the afternoon, clasping Philippe's hands in sympathy. "*Je vous souhaite, et votre famille, mes meilleurs vœux pour l'avenir.*" He did sincerely wish them all the best for their future; it was a sad end to his last working law case.

He got back to find Emily and Xander relaxing after a hard day's sightseeing. "We've been to some familiar places, and some new ones," Emily informed him. "We spent the last hour at *La Défense*. We both loved it."

"The range of skyscraper generations there is amazing, four in all I think," added Xander. "And the view from *La Grande Arche* along that perfectly straight line of view, all the way to the *Place de la Concorde*, an incredible six kilometres distant, took our breath away. You can see from that vantage point how well-planned Paris was right from the outset."

Luke sat down on one of the stylish sofas, a warm sense of contentment washing over him, his work done, and the city waiting to be enjoyed.

"So we've just been sitting here ever since, the windows open and the sun having suddenly come out, simply listening to the sounds of Paris. You can hear the occasional moped, and even sometimes if you listen hard, a conversation in French, and we also heard someone in another apartment playing the flute. We wondered if they were practising for a concert. They were certainly playing to a high standard. Then suddenly our peace was shattered when all the car horns started blaring, a real Parisian sound, an *embouteillage,* a French traffic jam!"

They asked Luke how he'd got on. Emily hoped this case was now closed for him, so that he could finally retire, and get on with the next phase of his life. It had felt like a very protracted retirement, a bit like an engagement that had dragged on for too long, she mused; would the projected end-result ever come? She'd enjoyed sitting quietly with Xander this afternoon, hearing about his aspirations for the new job, and admiring his deep commitment to enthusing youngsters about mathematics. They'd talked about her own work a bit; it had encouraged her to share why she loved being an architect. Like her son, she was a visionary, and a bit of a perfectionist. They both had a strong desire to enrich people's lives through their work.

"One of the places that's really inspired me recently is Leighton House in Holland Park," she confided in her son. "Frederick Leighton was involved in every detail of that house, as it evolved over a thirty-year period. And when I visited, I found it enchanting. I could sense his perfectionism, and his creative muse. The Arab Hall was the most engaging room. I just stood there drinking it in; the tiles from Damascus covering each wall, the gilded dome, pillars, the fountain, the absolute peace. And – OK, it all sounds very indulgent, especially as apparently that room cost more than the whole house had cost to build – but Leighton said he had that space created simply as something beautiful to look at once in a while. It was sheer bliss to be there, and enjoy it as he'd planned."

On the subject of architecture Xander reflected on his first meeting with Carla, at the Institute of Education; he well remembered its brutalist architecture. He said that the style of the building had contrasted sharply with the beauty of the woman he'd met that day. Emily knew the edifice; it was a Lasdun creation, tiered, deeply dark, and what people who appreciated it might call *jolie-laide*. She had smiled at her son's warm memory of that first meeting with his wife.

"Let's go out for dinner tonight," suggested Luke. "How about *La Coupole*?"

"Great idea," agreed Xander. "Let me just give Carla a ring. She should be home by now."

"OK, let us know when you're ready, and we can stroll down there together. As long as we're wrapped up, it should be a pleasant walk."

Dinner out in Paris would be a fitting end to Luke's French case. In no way could he call it a celebration, given the death of his client; it would always be a sombre memory for him. But it was a closure, it needed to be marked, and a meal out seemed appropriate.

CHAPTER FIFTEEN

Children's Club, St Joseph's, Reading May 2014

The Maths Club at St Joseph's secondary school, so lauded by Xander to his family, was thriving but would only continue to thrive relative to the dedication afforded it by staff. So Xander, as Head of Department, had chosen to lead it one Thursday in the month. It was held in an English classroom, on strict condition that the room was left in pristine condition afterwards. The intention was to take pupils away from the maths department, so that they were on fresh ground, thus providing a clear division between school classes, and the Club.

It was a normal classroom of the 1970s era, with a view of the playground, and rectangular of course. *Did you ever find a classroom of a different shape?* wondered Xander. Displays around the walls were all English literature-related, some created by teachers, others of course containing pupils' work, and there were various official educational documents on the board near the door, a couple, of necessity, relating to health and safety. Elaine, the teacher who most frequently taught there, had put a potted palm in one corner, which looked fairly well watered. It could have done with a dust; but no-one, neither teachers nor cleaners, had time to add that to their action list. There was an almost empty mug on the front desk, containing the remains of what looked like extremely cold coffee.

The room was west-facing, and it therefore had pleasant warmth and light on this May afternoon. Outside various children were waiting to be collected, some were kicking a football, and a physics teacher was walking to his car, on his way home to catch up with a pile of marking. There was a delightful air of "lessons over" about this time of day. Of course it was indeed after the school day, hence the atmosphere. It was that second act of a teacher's day, reflected Xander, prior to the final act after the evening meal, when most staff would be deep into lesson preparation, or marking, or maybe, for a lucky few, taking time out from work.

And now Luke was arriving; Xander had invited him to the club today to talk about art and maths. His father currently had a full timetable, with finishing up at the law firm, assisting Lily's maternity cover at the gallery, seeing his new grand-daughter from time to time and today, doing a stint at St Joseph's. Xander was thrilled that he'd agreed to help. His father climbed out of a shiny dark grey car, glad to be in the fresh air after his drive from London, and strode across the playground towards the entrance to the main school. "Just eleven here today, Dad." Xander greeted him with a warm hug. Out of a school of nearly a thousand this didn't seem like a great tally, but for a club in pupils' free time, the number was counted a success. "Thanks for coming."

Luke got his laptop out and set it up for a brief slideshow. "Hello everyone! I'm your teacher's Dad. So I'm also ... Mr Wentworth. And today we're going to look at some interesting links between maths and art." Luke wasn't a teacher, but his social skills were first-class. So he began by asking everyone's name, and which class they were in. He made a few jokes as they chatted. Then he showed them the slides. These children were a mix, aged eleven up to fourteen, so aiming at the right level was a challenge. He'd brought a selection of shots of portraits, battle scenes, religious art, modern art, bucolic scenes, still lives. He asked them to count up the people in crowd scenes, and to see if the numbers represented anything (which they often did), he talked about the geometry of painting, he asked them to calculate percentages of women or children in various crowd scenes, he talked about odd and even numbers as they related to flowers in a vase, or to people in a group portrait or dining together, and he talked a little about perspective. Then they discussed geometry and shapes related to their own drawing, and the scale of what they drew, related to real life objects. Luke ended with a quiz, always a popular activity, and handed a prize to the winner, a small puzzle book. The recipient, a Year Nine boy with a broad smile, seemed delighted.

"Thanks so much, Mr Wentworth," said some of the children. "Your talk was cool."

"I enjoyed it as well," smiled Xander, as his father prepared to leave. "What are you up to now?"

"I'm actually meeting Giovanni in a café down the road. He's enjoying staying with you both during his business trip, and wanted to see me to update me on some financial things we've been discussing."

"I know, Dad. Carla's told me a bit about it. She's been so worried."

"So, I'm going to dash off now. Enjoy the rest of the club, and glad things are going well!"

There was a café on a nearby corner where they'd agreed to meet. Giovanni was in the UK for ten days, one week in London for work, and three days to stay with his daughter and son-in-law in Reading.

"Ciao!" they both cried, pleased to see each other. Luke liked Giovanni a lot. He was perceptive and quick-thinking, as befitted his role at the UN, and his friend couldn't quite understand how he'd been hoodwinked by the so-called shark that James had identified. They ordered drinks, tea rather than coffee for both given the time of day, and they caught up on various bits of news. Giovanni was always a rich source of global updates, many of which didn't hit the UK headlines; he invariably had specialist input, which Luke found fascinating. Today his conversation was all about the Eastern Ukraine referendum, the horrific kidnapping of Nigerian schoolgirls, and growing tensions between China and Vietnam.

Then he opened up once more about his financial woes. James had been a source of wisdom, and his intervention had successfully warned off the opportunist who'd taken advantage of Carla's father. But unfortunately it was too late to salvage everything, and although some funds had been recovered, Giovanni had lost several hundreds of thousands of dollars, around £300,000 Luke guessed, reading between the lines. That hurt deeply, and had significantly affected their family finances, but it seemed the main crisis was now over, with Giovanni much the wiser for the future.

"I'm so grateful to you, Luke, for putting me in touch with James. He is a *salvatore*, a saviour for me." Giovanni had absolutely no need to resort to Italian, as his English was perfect, but it added a certain charm to his dialogue, which he wasn't about to relinquish. And Luke enjoyed hearing a bit of Italian, a language he'd hardly used since his degree.

"I'm just glad it has worked out, although I'm terribly sorry about the funds you've lost." Luke grimaced.

They stayed chatting for over an hour, sharing stories about their families, and their joint family as represented by Carla and Xander, the US, Italy, even cricket. Luke was a huge fan and for Giovanni the game was an acquired taste which he was indeed fast acquiring. They agreed to go to Lord's together on a future visit.

While Luke was doing maths, and then tea with what he called his "outlaw", Emily, Jessie, and Lily were on a wedding dress hunt. Both Emily and Jessie had taken the afternoon off, and Archie was having a "hands-on" father and daughter afternoon. Carla once again had been invited but was still up to her eyes at work; she appreciated the invitation, but thought three shoppers were probably sufficient for making a decision. The dress hunters had already been to one shop, and were hopeful that the second would be more successful. "I will absolutely know, when I see the right dress," Jessie had declared. Lily was enjoying the rare few hours off, especially with her mother and sister, though she was still in a fog of exhaustion. The second shop was in a precinct, making parking straightforward. Its window, tastefully dressed to entice customers into the store, looked hopeful.

Emily was feeling tense. She'd been feeling tense ever since the letter had come from Jimmy last October, and the meeting with him had only increased her anxiety. She hadn't yet told Lily about that meeting, still feeling it was too soon after Daisy's arrival, yet aware that she couldn't wait too long before speaking. *There would never be a good time*, she sighed. And when she was with Lily, she felt even worse about the whole situation. She decided that the best place to tell her would be in Lily's home, with Archie present, or at least with him at home so that he could support his wife; she would finalise the best plan, soon.

Jessie selected four dresses, and started to parade in front of her mother and sister. "Definitely no", she said of the first one, before they'd had a chance to comment. "Maybe", she said about the second one; sipping Prosecco in delicate pink glasses, the others agreed. "I rather like this one, though it wasn't my first choice to try on," was her verdict on the next one. Cream, in lace, showing just enough flesh but not jaw-dropping amounts, fitted, and with a swooping skirt, it was definitely a contender. "It's beautiful," was her mother's comment. "Absolutely agree," said Lily. Jessie tried on the fourth dress and, not having shown it to the others, emerged having decided on dress number three. "Thanks so much for coming with me! It's made it a really special outing. And now I'll have my glass of Prosecco too." *Another item ticked off the list,* she thought. *So much to do before July, but all good. Very good.*

While Luke was doing maths and having tea, and while Jessie was wedding dress shopping with her family, Archie was getting to grips with Daisy-care. He had two days' holiday from work, and was glad he would have tomorrow to relax. In effect he was rather good at looking after his little daughter. From his years of hospital work, to this very important new job he brought the mantra: "Alert, alert, alert." From work he knew that you could never ever afford to stop thinking or to cease being vigilant, looking out for everything and anything. So he resisted any temptation to have a quick glance at the paper while Daisy was cooing on her rug, and he was strict with his thoughts, pondering all the time about what to do next to engage her, and making sure he would give her the expressed milk at the right time. He loved having a child; he'd waited a long time, which made the whole experience even more meaningful. Lily was out for three hours. He'd encouraged her to take the time, and to enjoy the temporary freedom. He'd forbidden her from going to the gallery, and after questioning his right to tell her what to do, which she did smilingly, Lily decided it was good advice. Her assistant Lucinda was very capable, and if there were serious problems, she would contact Lily.

Emily drove back home, delighted with the success of the afternoon. The dress was just right for Jessie, and it was a relief to have it chosen. It was only four o'clock, and she'd have time to do some work before the evening. Emily reflected on Tina's visit yesterday. Her friend had been on the way back to Germany via London, where she had some library research to do. "Can I call in before I head off to Heathrow?" she'd asked. She'd spent ninety minutes with them just after lunch and, ever practical, had two items on her agenda.

"Have you told Lily about Jimmy yet?" she asked Emily. "I know Lily is exhausted but, quite frankly, she's going to be exhausted for several years, and you can't wait all that time to tell her. It's only fair to her, to pass on the news."

"You're right," acknowledged her friend. "I've decided I've got to tell her next time I'm at her house. As long," Emily hesitated, "as long as she isn't having a bad Daisy day."

"You never know, she might be quite pleased to hear about Jimmy." Emily gulped. This wasn't the most tactful thing to say in front of Luke.

"Please let me know how it goes. And I have some news for you. I've decided to get back with Friedrich. That is, if he'll have me back." Tina smiled wryly. "I had a lot of time to think on this holiday. And being with Ricky and Jane made me think even more. I do admit to having a passion for Ricky still." She had a rapt audience. "Did I dreamingly but foolishly imagine he might leave Jane and marry me, as we'd planned to marry three decades ago? I'm not sure, but there was certainly an attraction."

"On my part," she continued. "No attraction on Ricky's side. He is committed. What I saw between Ricky and Jane actually moved me. They have a strong marriage, there is great love, and they are each faithful to each other and to their sons. It's a beautiful thing. But I think they work at it. And I've been lazy; I simply walked out on Friedrich because he's a workaholic. No-one's perfect. Not even me."

They all laughed, though in a slightly embarrassed way. This oversharing wasn't terribly British.

"Well that sounds like good news," said Luke. "I'm sure Friedrich will be happy about your decision, and we'll be thinking about you both."

"Thank you," replied Tina. "And thanks for your friendship. We all go back a long way!"

It had been a joyful meet-up, and yet a deeply thoughtful one. Emily was glad for Tina, and trusted all would go well for her and Friedrich. She very much hoped that he would gladly take up the threads of their marriage again.

***

Xander was just finishing his general sweep around of papers, pens, and general detritus in the English classroom before going home. One of the girls, Mabel, hadn't left yet. She seemed to be hesitating about whether or not to speak to him. Xander was very tired, but he sensed that he should stay.

"Did you want to say something?"

Mabel looked worried. Xander hoped she wasn't going to cry. He guessed she was quite scared of talking with the Head of Department, recently arrived at the school. "Is something wrong?"

She nodded. She was in Year Nine, and doing well at maths, so he guessed her worry wasn't an academic one. She opened her mouth, and closed it again.

"You can tell me," he said more gently.

"Miss Jamieson has given me detention, and it wasn't my fault," she said quietly, then continued, speaking very quickly. "Some people next to me were talking and not paying attention, and one of them was quite cheeky, and she thought I was part of the group. She just immediately and crossly handed out detention to us all. I'll get a mark on my month's card. And it wasn't my fault. I was listening in class, and didn't talk at all."

She looked even more worried. Xander noted the repetition of "it wasn't my fault". He sighed inwardly. Something else for him to sort out. He'd have to have a word with Sarah, the teacher mentioned. It sounded as though she'd acted impulsively, and it hadn't ended either well, or justly, for Mabel. "Don't worry," he said. "I'll see what I can do about it tomorrow." She thanked him quietly and left the room.

We all like life to be fair, he told himself. *Whether it's Giovanni or Mabel, we all look for equity. And if only sorting every situation out was as easy as one, two, three, as easy as the maths problems I deal with every day, with their clear answers.* He already had problems of his own at work; two members of his team of five, for unrelated reasons, had handed in their notice, pregnancy and a promotion elsewhere being the drivers. So he had another major item, that of hiring new staff, to add to his action list.

He left the room and made for his car. Was he the last person to leave? The playground was completely empty. No, Bob, the cricket coach was just getting into his car, and Janet, the Principal was having a chat in the foyer with Mike, the caretaker, clearly also on her way home. Xander felt a warm glow inside about this teamwork; he liked his new colleagues, the children were sparky and friendly, and he was just thrilled to have landed such a great job.

CHAPTER SIXTEEN

Luke's Room, Law Firm
May 2014

Luke was at work. Though it neither looked as though he was, nor did he actually feel as though he was at work. In fact, this was his last day at the firm, and to his horror it was over a year since he'd told his wife he planned to retire, a year and more since he'd said, "in six months' time" to her question. Things had dragged on, and not just the Sophie case. But he was completely happy about this timing, a timetable prompted by circumstances. He was especially thrilled that Felicity was moving from her firm to take over from him here as a property law partner. It had been a sensitive time until this was confirmed. He knew she was going to apply, and after the detailed application process and interviews, he and Felicity entered a no-man's land during which time absolutely no information was forthcoming from the firm. *Were they going to appoint her? Did they have their eyes on someone else? Or were they going to re-advertise?*

She called him straight after the firm had made the offer.

"Absolutely brilliant," was his verdict. "Now, can I suggest someone to work with you, actually for rather than with you, a fairly junior lawyer?" This was cheeky, and it might not work, but Luke sincerely hoped that Johanna might get a foothold in his old firm. She was currently working in a very small legal outfit, and he knew it would be an excellent career move if she were to transfer to a larger firm. "I'm just going to mention the name to you, Felicity, and then I'll quietly move into the background." Not quite into the background though. In addition he'd first let Johanna know that there might be an opening, and he'd also encouraged her to apply. For Luke, this would be an amazing Claire synergy, but for now he would withdraw and wait to see what transpired. The outcome would be up to others.

Luke's office was ... corporate. That was the best adjective to describe it. It was a spacious room, with a view from its third floor of other buildings and of some green areas, including trees. Not a bad view. The window spanned the entirety of one wall. His desk was central, with two leather chairs facing. The desk was large, wood-like but not actual wood so that it didn't get spoiled by drinks or sun and for ease of cleaning, and usually it was very tidy. Not today, as he was intent on sorting everything out before he left. There were a couple of pieces of contemporary art on the walls, each carefully selected by Luke from the firm's art store. He definitely didn't want something so modern that people stared slowly at it with puzzled expressions and then asked, "What is it?" The two he'd chosen were each country scenes, both diverging from representational art but still recognisable as interesting landscapes. There was a neat row of wood-like filing cabinets, and drawers. On his desk were family photos, including a recent one of Daisy. And the carpet was beige, Armani beige, and spotless.

On Luke's mind, as well as the fact of this being his last day, was

Emily, who today was visiting Lily and Daisy for morning coffee and, as he knew well, for a significant chat. He hoped fervently that Lily would be understanding and receptive to the conversation. He hoped that so much. She was very dear to him. He was also expecting Felicity during the morning; she was coming for some handover items, and to be welcomed by him informally as she prepared to take on the new role.

There was a pile of papers on the desk. Although the eventual aim and hope of the firm was to be paperless, in practice many legal items needed to be in hard copy and so "paper-lite" was their preferred goal. And although most items were usually meticulously filed on the day, Luke had some recent documents to review before handing over for filing. There was a knock on the door, and Rachel, his PA, looked in. "Felicity Wheeler is here to see you."

Luke got up and went into the waiting area. "Felicity, great to see you. Welcome!"

He ushered her into his office, and moments later Rachel brought them coffee. White china, coffee in an elegant glass thermos jug, a plate of inviting biscuits which looked home-made but most likely weren't, a small jug of milk and just in case anyone needed it, sugar. Plus a couple of silver teaspoons. And two glasses and a jug of chilled water.

He spread his arms wide. "Your room!"

"I'm excited. And honoured. But sad you won't be here any more."

"I've loved this room. I've adored the work. But – and I never thought I would hear myself say this – I am absolutely ready to move on. So I don't feel a bit sad at the thought of leaving. And I forbid anyone else to call it 'sad'. More like transferring to the next phase."

"OK. I get it. I'm glad for you then, as well as glad for myself." Smiling, they helped themselves to coffee.

Luke spent a good hour talking in depth to Felicity about his work, clients, colleagues, the ethos of the firm, and history of some of the cases. She already knew a little of this from the interview process, but she found his personal update on various matters and his insight from years of experience invaluable, as she prepared literally to "take on his mantle". This brief time of intensive mentoring would, Felicity knew, assist her greatly in making an efficient start to her new role.

"And feel free to contact me with any questions, any time you need to," he added.

"Thank you, Luke. I really appreciate all of this. I will aim to be 'Luke Two'."

"Oh no, you will be 'Felicity One'. You'll be your own person, and you'll be superb."

"Do you have another few minutes? I wanted to update you on the murder case that was unearthed at Peacehaven."

"That's a great pun. And yes, please tell me. I'm keen to hear the latest."

Felicity grinned at the pun which she'd inadvertently made, and continued, "So, the police have interviewed Billy a few times, following the account which Pauline gave of his bloodied clothes and evasive manner, and the fact he'd come home very late the night of Timmy Johnson's murder. Unsurprisingly, Billy didn't confess anything." She paused to finish her rapidly cooling coffee.

"However, on their second visit they had much more to go on. Pauline had told them additionally – she seemed just to have occasional recall, or else wanted to keep them dangling for added suspense - that a mate of Billy's, Philip Smith, had informed her, years ago, that he had seen Billy knifing Timmy. This was a brilliant lead, as long as the police could locate Philip. Fortunately he hadn't moved far, and they were able to interview him. Philip is very ill with cancer and failing rapidly but he was able to confirm that he'd seen Billy commit the murder. They got a signed statement from him."

"Amazing story," said Luke, agog to hear the rest.

"So that's it for the moment. Now it's up to the detective leading the case to take this forward. I'm very impressed that they're totally focussed on it."

"Well Felicity, this isn't exactly what you planned when you set up the oral history project, but it's a really positive outcome, so far. I'm looking forward to hearing the next piece of news."

"Yes, it's a curious story. Luke, I must leave you to finish clearing up. What time do you think you'll leave?"

"Emily is coming in, we'll have lunch together, and I aim to be out of here by five at the latest. I wish you all the best for your first day, in a few weeks' time, Felicity."

He had an hour to himself before Emily walked into his office. Rachel had shown her in. She looked pale and appeared tearful. Luke gave her a welcoming hug. "Do you want to go out? Have some lunch?"

"No, I'd rather stay here, in this familiar setting. Oh dear, that's quite a pile of documents you have to deal with."

Luke ordered coffee and sandwiches, and after these had been produced, asked how she'd got on with Lily, and the Jimmy tale.

"It was very very emotional. But she thanked me for telling her. She also didn't blame me, which made me feel a little better. She said she'd had relationships before Archie and who knows, she might have ended up pregnant just like me."

Emily went over the morning bit by bit. She'd arrived just as Daisy had been fed, which was spot-on timing; her granddaughter had been put in her cot where, replete with milk, she had soon fallen fast asleep. Archie was working in his study upstairs. Lily had made her mother some coffee, and they'd chatted a bit. Then Emily gathered her courage and spoke.

"Lily, you know we've never spoken about your father, I mean your actual biological father?"

"Yes, Mum, and I'm not really expecting that to change."

"Well I'm afraid it's just about to change. I'm so sorry to spring this on you, but it's out of my hands."

Lily looked very puzzled, and a bit concerned. "OK, Mum, tell me. I think you're about to tell me who he is."

"Even more than that, darling. He's been in touch with me. I didn't know what to do. He wanted to know about his baby. So in the end I met him."

"His baby. That would be me?"

"Yes. I met him in March, in Edinburgh. I didn't want to tell you immediately, because you have so much on your plate at the moment, with Daisy, and the business too at the back of your mind, and you're newly married." She realised, too late, that she shouldn't have relegated the marriage to last place.

"Please tell me, Mum. I can take it."

Emily looked down at her hands. Then, thinking that she mustn't be feeble, she looked directly at Lily. "He's called Jimmy Smith. He's from Aberdeen. He was studying English when we met. He works in publishing now, and isn't married, and doesn't have any children."

"Does he want to meet me?"

"In a word, Yes." They were silent for a couple of minutes.

"Mum, please don't take this the wrong way, but I have to ask. Was it a one-night stand?"

Emily went bright red. "Absolutely not. We had a warm relationship that lasted for two months, and we liked each other a lot." She added, "But he wasn't ready for a child, and he simply disappeared when he knew I was pregnant. I won't go into the specific mechanics." Her blush deepened. "I'm sorry to tell you that he disappeared, but I must tell you the truth. I tried to find him, but I couldn't. I think he left Edinburgh at that stage, and his studies."

"So he didn't want me," Lily voiced. It sounded terrible, spoken aloud. "Does he have red hair?" she added inconsequentially. "Like Daisy."

"Yes, he does, though he doesn't have much left." Neither smiled; this wasn't an occasion for mirth or light-heartedness.

"How on earth did he make contact? And why, after so long?"

"It was through the University's alumni office. And why? He didn't specify when I saw him but I guess it's because he hasn't had any other children, and he's developed a desire to meet the only one he had."

"So I guess having a child he rejected is marginally better than having no children," commented Lily sarcastically. Emily didn't say anything. It was all too painful.

"Do I look like him, Mum?"

"I can't say that I look at you, and am reminded of him, at all. You and Xander have my eyes, or so I'm told. Your hair is totally your own, not like my fair hair and not like Jimmy's red hair." Emily pondered for a moment. "You have Jimmy's height, but of course Luke is tall too, so that's not really relevant. I guess your smile is one feature that I could identify as common to you both."

"Do you have a photo of him?" Emily was finding all the questions very emotional, but she'd known that they would come.

"No, I don't have a picture of him. I may have had one in the late 1970s, but I didn't keep it. And I certainly didn't take one in March."

"You may think it strange, but what I would really have liked would have been to see a photo of you and him together, so I could picture the relationship which resulted in my birth."

"I'm sorry, I just don't have that."

"I wonder if he does. Sorry, Mum, this is hard for you. Why, why, why did he get in touch now, just when everything in our lives was working out so well? And when Daisy had just joined us."

Emily felt tears pricking in her eyes at the thought of little Daisy, and this new factor which had been brought into her life now, and into her future life. There would be more questions from Lily, she knew.

And on and on they came, as Lily's awareness of her father grew. "What does he know about me? Does he know I'm married? And that I have a child?"

"I told him about Archie and Daisy. I also told him about your work. I thought he should know all of that beforehand, in case you do agree to meet him." "I don't have to see Jimmy again," Emily said to her daughter. "But you can. Only if you'd like to. You mustn't feel you have to. He left you alone for thirty-five years, and therefore you are totally within your rights not to see him. We leave it up to you." The use of the first person plural was the first reference to Luke during the conversation.

Lily looked at her mother, her dark eyes deep with expression. "Luke is my real Dad, and always will be. He's all I've ever known as a father, and I love him so much. Possibly, if I meet him and like him at all, Jimmy might be a sort of occasional father, quite far down the pecking order compared with Dad. Just might be. It depends on so much." Emily could tell that, amongst the anger and puzzlement, there was also inquisitiveness. How could there not be? For Lily this was the closing of an open circle. The answer to a puzzle.

Emily thought of Ricky and Friedrich and their relationships with Fergus, which had always seemed quite like a fifty/fifty arrangement. She fervently hoped that Jimmy wouldn't end up with such a significant proportion of Lily. His emergence on the scene after so many decades felt like an intrusion into their happy family life.

"How can I forgive him for not wanting me? And for abandoning you, my mother, from the get-go? How can I do that? And how can I meet him while I feel this anger and sorrow?"

"It's slightly easier to forgive if the other person is sorry," said Emily. "And I think your father is genuinely sorry, and realises what a fool he's been." It was the first time she'd called Jimmy Lily's father to her face. It hurt, but it was the truth. "Lily darling, I am so very sorry to have put you through this. Please forgive me for the heartache I'm causing."

Lily looked at Emily, and her mother looked into her daughter's beautiful face. "Mum, you have nothing, nothing, to say sorry for. You are the most wonderful mother, and you simply can't," she corrected herself, "actually mustn't apologise for the relationship with Jimmy because that would be like saying sorry for having me." They both smiled, Emily now through real tears. "Mum, this could have been me. I had relationships before Archie, and this could easily have happened to me, just as it did to you. Lots of men run off when they hear a baby is on the way."

Emily had just about enough self-control to stop crying, and to thank her daughter. "I think you should speak with Archie now," she said. "And I'll go to Dad's office to see how he's getting on during his last day. You go and talk to Archie, and see if Daisy's woken up yet."

They embraced warmly, and Emily left.

Emily finished recounting the conversation to Luke. She helped herself to another egg sandwich. Suddenly she felt both exhausted and extremely hungry.

"Well done for doing this," he said across the desk. She felt a bit like a client, a client who needed her lawyer's aid. "If we weren't in this room and if I didn't know that Rachel can see fairly clearly through that glazed door, I would come to the other side of the desk and put my arm round you, and comfort you. This is all so hard." Emily immediately felt less like a client.

"Thank you. I'm relieved I've told her. My gut feeling is that she'll agree to see him, more out of curiosity than out of a desire to welcome him with open arms. But let's see what she says after talking it over with Archie."

"One positive side of this is that I can sort of dodge the father-in-law role. Though I'm not about to relinquish the fatherly one."

Emily decided she would go home, have a rest, and prepare the celebratory meal she'd planned for Luke's retirement. She was glad to have taken the whole day off from work. She took some of his gifts that had come in that morning, the pile of retirement cards, and the family photos. There was no backward glance; like her husband, she knew this phase was over, with a good one on its way.

CHAPTER SEVENTEEN

Test Match, Lord's
Monday 21st July 2014

It was a balmy day at Lord's. Before they left home at ten o'clock, it was already twenty-two degrees, and rising, with just a light wind and by lunchtime it had reached twenty-six degrees, a perfect temperature for sitting in the open air all day. Emily's personal view, which she hadn't hesitated to voice, was that a day of cricket was a strange way for Luke and his three children to celebrate Jessie's forthcoming wedding. However, the memory of years of cricketing talk over meals at home reassured her that all four would view the day as something rather special, something to remember, their last chance to have time together before Jessie's big day. And her aversion to going to Lord's with them meant that she and Archie could share Daisy-care for the day, each taking half a day off work. Xander was celebrating the first day of the summer holidays, and revelling in the freedom.

Their tickets were in the lower section of Mound Stand, the position carefully chosen so that they were in line with the pitch. It was the fifth and last day of the second Test between England and India, the first one having resulted in a draw. It was England's innings. "Yesterday's play didn't look good," announced Xander as they took their seats, "though it would be such great news if they played better today." All four were excited; both Lily and Jessie had played cricket growing up, and Xander still played when he could. Luke had given up actively participating, but delighted in watching the game, whether live or on the box. He adored the atmosphere at Lord's, and its two hundredth anniversary was a special year. He relished all the now frowned-on politically incorrect features of the matches; it brought his total Englishness to the fore.

Unlike in the run-of-the-mill of daily life, in which his Englishness didn't feature, here Luke felt an actual swelling of pride in his nationality, as the team literally fought – sportingly, of course – against other nations, be it Australia, India, or others. It wasn't a condescending pride, merely delight in the country where he'd grown up and which he'd therefore made his home. And he loved the greenness of the pitch, the pristine white kit of the players, quirky vocabulary only understood by those in the know, like nightwatchman (so puzzling to Emily; *was this person like a caretaker at a school?*), the oh-so-traditional summer sound of willow on leather, regular polite clapping from the crowd, the grandeur of this stadium, the largest in the country. The whole setting spoke summer, and summer in London. "Great vibrant atmosphere," he'd once heard someone behind him say. And that spectator had added, "Though I could do without the pompous MCC members." Luke had smiled to himself at the cheeky descriptor. Today, England was making a good start to play; it looked fairly promising.

"Let's go for a coffee," said Lily to her siblings after ninety minutes of play. She'd already established that Luke was intent on staying in his seat as long as possible. They found a watering hole with the minimum of crowds, and settled down, the three siblings, for a relaxing chat, aware of the momentous occasion coming up in six days' time, and of how it would change their family. A new brother-in-law, a new son-in-law for their parents, a new uncle for Daisy, and of course, a husband for Jessie. "It's half-past twelve," pointed out Xander. "Shall we have a bite to eat as well? Give me your orders, and I'll get them." Herself also aware of the big event on Saturday, Lily had nevertheless decided that today would work well for her to share her own momentous news. Emily and she had agreed that it was best for her to be the one to tell them about Jimmy.

So she waited until they were enjoying a light bite and Pimm's. Then she told them about Jimmy, all the details. They knew, of course, that Luke wasn't her father, but they'd never heard anything about her true paternity, and had never liked to ask their parents. They were both enthralled at the whole tale, including the possibility that Lily might meet with Jimmy one day soon.

"So what is he to us?" asked Jessie without really thinking it through. "A kind of stepfather?"

"No, he's nothing to you and Xander," said Lily, almost proprietorially. "He and Mum didn't marry."

"It's a lot to take in," commented Xander. "How has Mum taken it? And Dad?"

Lily thought her mother had now got used to the idea that Jimmy had re-entered their lives. She hadn't really discussed it much with her father yet. There simply hadn't been time, between looking after Daisy, getting ready for the family wedding, and still sorting out their house.

"I'm going to meet him on Monday," she announced, to their

astonishment. "At City Airport. He's flying down from Scotland." She continued, "I just want to see for myself, what he's like. If I don't warm to him, I can decide what to do, then. He's been very fair with me, and has actually said that he'll entirely understand if after one meeting, I don't actually want to see him again."

"It's a bit like a first date," said Jessie, again without thinking.

"Yeah, a first date with your own father." Lily gave a half-smile, and pulled a face. "Really weird."

Xander got up awkwardly. "It's fascinating, and it must be quite emotional for you, Lily. Please let us know how you get on next Monday. We'll be thinking of you then." He hesitated. "I really should get back to Dad. And the cricket. Being as he's paid for it. Sorry to leave you." Jessie and Lily were happy to have a longer chat. There was a lot to cover, a mix of follow-on about Jimmy, final bridesmaid discussions including hair appointments, other wedding details, Daisy, and Jessie's new home. Then they too returned to the cricket.

"It's been an average morning." Luke welcomed them back. "Cook isn't playing at all well. And we need 209 more runs on yesterday's score. Worrying." There was a sudden screech from the crowd. "Sharma has got Ali out to a bouncer," wailed Luke. "And that's it now while they have a break for lunch."

Jessie and Lily understood Luke's dramatic reaction; they had grown up with the sound of shrieking reactions to cricketing disasters. In contrast Carla, hearing these reactions in Luke and Emily's home from time to time, or in her own house when Xander was watching matches, found the cries inexplicable. Cricket hadn't featured in her American-Italian upbringing. Xander now realised that he should have returned to the cricket earlier, but Lily's bombshell conversation hadn't made it easy. In a few minutes Lily would have to leave for an hour to feed Daisy, who was waiting in a nearby café with Emily.

"Come on, I'm going for lunch. Will you join me?" said Luke, oblivious of the fact that they'd eaten already.

"I'll come with you, Dad," offered Jessie, Xander electing to roam around and have a look at cricketing memorabilia in the museum.

"Are you all set for Saturday?" Luke asked his daughter as, fifteen minutes later, he tucked into a juicy steak.

"Yes, it's all organised!" She smiled warmly at him, twisting her fair hair into a high bun.

"I'm looking forward to it," he continued, enjoying the food, and looking forward to more cricket that afternoon. "Are you OK?" he asked suddenly, spotting a few tears glistening in Jessie's eyes.

"I'm all right really. It's just..." Jessie stopped, then resumed her conversation in upper case, and rather quickly. "It's EVERY DAY AND FOR THE REST OF MY LIFE." She looked a bit panicked. "It's so so final," she added.

"It's not at all final. It's the start of something new and exciting. Not final at all. Wrong word, darling."

"When your mother and I got married," he continued as Jessie looked weepy, "we were so young. We just went ahead and did it."

"And you'd lived together before and had a baby. Me! So it wasn't, as you suggest, a random act, to get married."

"Yes, but although this probably sounds stupid, that's all slightly irrelevant, the living together and so on. Because now we were making a commitment – which was totally different from living together. And although having a child had already made a huge difference to our relationship," he smiled at his daughter, "making that marriage commitment was incredibly significant. After all, your mother had already had one man run off on her, when she had a baby. What were the chances of me running off as well?"

"This is a very good thing that you and Andrew are doing on Saturday," he continued as Jessie wiped away her remaining tears. "It's a beautiful thing. And then you take your life day by day and week by week, and before you know it, you've been married thirty-one years." He sounded incredulous. "You can't look at your life as one long sweep when you're thirty-two. You know the commitment's for life, but it's difficult to look right down the road at the whole span of your life, at your age. Just enjoy it, love. I know you'll be very happy together. And I've heard the dress is stunning."

"I do believe it's the way we're meant to live," said Jessie solemnly. "It's just a bit scary, standing here on the threshold."

"Life is all about making commitments," said her father, equally solemnly. "To a spouse, to a child (at which point they each simultaneously thought of Jimmy), to a profession, to a creed if you have a belief, to your country if you're a soldier."

"When we walk down the aisle together on Saturday, Dad, I'll be fine. This is just a tiny blip."

"And you can trust Andrew. He's straight down the line. He's not going to run off with someone else."

"Definitely not, in his profession!" They both laughed.

"When we walk down that aisle, just keep thinking how ridiculous I look in my penguin suit, and you will feel fine."

She nodded, smiling. And then, "Dad, did I see you looking at your watch while you were dispensing your wise words? Is cricket on your mind?"

"Maybe," he admitted slightly shamefacedly. "I think play might be about to restart. And I also think that getting immersed in cricket is great therapy."

Indeed they just got back to their seats in time, Xander hot on their tail. Lily joined them thirty minutes later. It turned out to be a sad cricket day. Within an hour of play restarting, and to Luke's great disgust, England were all out. For India, winning by ninety-five runs, it was a triumph, it being their first overseas Test win for three years. "I wouldn't be surprised if Matt Prior steps down for the rest of the season," Xander commented. "He's definitely injured, and can't carry on that state."

"Come on, let's order afternoon tea, at my expense," said Luke. "If we can't enjoy any more cricket, let's at least enjoy the food and atmosphere here."

"Great idea, Dad," said Xander. "I'll join you after I've got us some scorecards. You know what the queue for those can be like, but hopefully I'll be back within half an hour."

***

Xander got home at five-thirty. Carla wasn't back from work yet. He had a shower, and then pottered around the house. He always felt demob happy at the start of the school summer vacation, but also a bit restless. He wasn't sure what their plans were for supper that evening. He wandered into the garden, and sat on a patio chair.

Five minutes later Carla got home, and came outside to see him. She looked very tired.

"I haven't a clue what we're having for supper tonight," she announced, a glass of water in her hand.

No questions about my day at Lord's, thought Xander.

"I'm sure I can find something in the freezer," he replied.

"OK, I'm going up to change."

At seven o'clock a risotto was on the patio table, and drinks poured. Carla looked less tired now. They ate in silence for a few minutes.

"Aren't you going to ask me how I am?" she volunteered as a conversation opener.

"How are you?" he said, smiling.

"Can't you tell that I'm really down? Why don't you see these things? And I'm utterly exhausted."

Xander was quiet for a moment. Then he said, "I don't know unless you tell me. I am not psychic!!" uttering each word very slowly as he tried to contain his irritation at being penalised for a lack of mind-reading ability.

"Well, I'm telling you now. *Sono molto stanca*!" She glared at him. Like her father, Carla didn't need to revert to Italian. She was only a quarter Italian after all. But in moments of drama, some Italian appeared. It partly irritated Xander and partly charmed him. At this precise moment, irritation was the stronger emotion.

"I'm sorry that you're very tired. You need a rest."

"*Ovviamente*! Of course!" Carla had finished her food, and she got up and went into the house.

Xander sighed. He'd loved to have stayed at the table, sipping his wine and enjoying the unusually warm evening air. But he knew he'd have to follow her, unless he wanted things to get much much worse.

Carla was in the living room sitting quietly and looking close to tears.

"Tell me what's wrong," he said gently, sitting next to her.

She moved away and spoke in a torrent of sadness. "I'm so disappointed that the business hasn't really picked up since my US trip. I've done my best to implement the ideas that Fleur shared with me, but there isn't the spark that I saw in her work; I just can't re-create it. And that trip cost a lot, my travel, the New York accommodation, paying Annabel to cover for me. I'm flaked out getting ready for the wedding on Saturday. Though really pleased to be involved, of course. Dad can't give us the funds he'd promised, because of his financial disaster. And we haven't had a holiday together for ages. First we have a break with your family in France, then I go to New York on my own, and then you go to France again on your own, or actually with your family. And now you have a lovely long holiday from work, just started, and I have a summer filled with wedding flowers. Absolutely no break in sight. That's what's wrong!" There was a moment of silence. "That's all," commented Carla finally in a depressed tone, sarcasm lending extra power to her outpouring.

Xander stayed where he was on the sofa, aware that moving closer to his wife at the moment wouldn't be a wise move. He tried very hard to control his irritation, and to understand and empathise. He'd heard the references to "with your family, "on my own", and "on your own", all verbally bolded and underlined. He also heard the professional disappointment over her US visit, and the contrast between his current work life and hers; she hadn't referred to his promotion, but that too was a fillip for him, and now his long vacation, although peppered as he knew it would be with some significant chunks of work, stood in stark contrast to her wedding-filled summer.

"How good is Annabel?" he asked gently.

"Xander, is there a point here? I've just unburdened myself and you ask about Annabel!" She moved further away, though there wasn't much further to go along their three-seater.

"Give me a break, love. I'm thinking about how to help. If Annabel is a good and competent florist, is there any way you could take a week off, or even just maybe four days this summer so that we could go away together?" He emphasised the word "together". He bolded and underlined it.

"And on the money side," he added, "I know it's a huge disappointment that the funds Giovanni and Anna had promised won't be coming our way, but at least we have a little more money now that I'm head of department. It's good that you have a stream of business this summer, too. And I'm sure that the skills you saw in New York will definitely come in useful, even if you're not seeing change right at the moment."

"A break together would be heavenly," Carla replied. "In reply to your question, Annabel is a very good florist. In fact, though I don't really like admitting it, I think she's better than me. She has a real eye for the right arrangement for each occasion. And she managed the business very well when I was away."

She was silent, thinking.

"I guess we could go away on a Sunday, and come back late on

Thursday. Then I would just be taking the four days off, but we'd have five days away."

"Let's plan on that. You let me know which dates suit, and I'll book something for us in August. And now go and sit in the garden and read a good book."

With the beginnings of a smile, she acquiesced, leaving Xander alone in the living room to have a good think about what he could do to improve life for his wife.

***

Luke and Emily had finished their evening meal. Emily was tired after a full day, half of it at work and half of it at other work, work that was a sheer delight, looking after Daisy. She lolled on one of the cream sofas, looking sleepy. Luke wanted to watch the highlights of the cricket, dismal though the result had been for England. "OK, as long as you turn the volume down," said Emily. He was happy to watch it initially almost on mute, revelling in the visuals. But eager to hear the commentary as well, he soon switched on sub-titles.

However, despite a disappointing cricketing result, he'd thoroughly enjoyed the day out with the three children. The three children, his three children? Over the years he'd got so used to saying "my children" which always included Lily, but right at the moment he wasn't sure how he felt about including Lily in that description, not totally at ease now about saying "my daughter". He'd heard from Emily that Lily was going to meet Jimmy, but she hadn't mentioned it to him face-to-face. He knew how overflowing her timetable was, but he did rather hope that before Lily met with her real rather, she would make time to talk to him.

CHAPTER EIGHTEEN

Peacehaven Home
Friday 25th July 2014

The home was extremely quiet when Felicity arrived. This period after lunch, she guessed, would be when most residents might have a nap. Her month-long break between jobs afforded her an excellent opportunity to carry out some of the oral history interviews in Peacehaven. She had a quick chat with Meriel, who was often on duty in Reception, signed in, and strode down the corridor to see Christopher, who was expecting her this afternoon. To her delight, he was ready to receive his visitor, notepad and various documents including what looked like photographs, in hand. He stood up gingerly, and shook her hand firmly.

"Mrs Wheeler? Lovely to meet you," he said, a Yorkshire accent faintly traceable.

"Please call me Felicity. And you are Mr Moorfield?"

"I am indeed. Well then, if you're Felicity, please call me

Christopher. I'm very interested in your clever project. What a splendid idea, to capture moments from people's lives, and bring us all here to life." He chuckled. "It's just what we need, something stimulating, to give us a bit of direction."

"Well, what inspired me was the conviction that everyone here has had an interesting life. No-one is simply their room number, or just a place at the dinner table. You are all individuals, with fascinating life stories which I wanted somehow to open up."

"I'm just going to call for a cup of tea for us both. They know you're coming this afternoon." He rang a bell next to his chair. "So what did you want to ask me this afternoon, Felicity?"

They chatted warmly for nearly an hour, Christopher recounting some of his early life in Yorkshire, then as a student in Leeds, and afterwards as a chemistry teacher in a boys' school in Hampshire before retiring to London to be nearer to his two children. Tea was duly produced, along with a biscuit. Felicity travelled back with Christopher across the years, in her mind picturing the school very clearly, with its finicky headmaster, spacious playing fields, and academic rigour. At the same time she took in his room and its contents – photos of his family, landscape art on the walls, bed overlaid with a tartan throw, rust-coloured carpet, vase of flowers on the window-sill. The room looked out on the garden, which was beautifully kept.

"Thanks very much for your time, and the wonderful insight into a very small part of your life. Might I or someone else return another time to find out some more? And after that we'll write up what you've told us and ask for your approval to include it in the publication. Along with a photo, of course." Felicity smiled.

"Absolutely. It's been a pleasure to meet you, and I look forward to the next time."

Before leaving, Felicity called in to see Pauline. She'd not let her know, and Pauline already had a visitor, a friend from another room. But she was pleased to see Felicity and shooed her friend away pretty smartly before offering Felicity a seat.

"I just wanted to say 'hello'", said Felicity. "And to thank you for all your help with the Billy case."

"Pleased to help. And I hope they nail the scoundrel. What's the latest?"

"I don't have much more news at the moment." Felicity was circumspect, though she felt a tad dishonest at the same time. "But I know the police are actively working on the case, and they'll let us know when there's an update."

"I gave them some more information," smiled Pauline. "And they were very interested. Very interested indeed." She looked satisfied with the latest snippet she'd passed on to the powers-that-be.

"Really?" said Felicity, doing her best to feign surprise, and smiling approvingly. "That's extremely good of you."

They exchanged a few more pleasantries, and Felicity left, letting the abandoned friend know, as she passed her room, that she had finished her conversation with Pauline.

As Felicity walked back along the corridor, there were snatched glimpses into other rooms, glimpses of people reading, dozing, staring, drinking tea, on the phone, watching afternoon television. She was due to visit her mother's home afterwards, where she knew there would be more of the same. Her mother was fascinated by Felicity's project at Peacehaven, and would be looking forward to her daughter's latest update. Felicity greeted Rob, the maintenance manager, on her way out, and had a quick dash to the toilet, a room which of necessity included a bar on the wall to aid mobility. She noted the beautiful fresh flower arrangement in the foyer. And she had a look at the noticeboard, publicising a concert the following day, and a quiz on Friday.

"How was your afternoon?" asked Alice that evening over supper.

"I popped in to see Pauline while I was at Peacehaven. She was keen to hear the latest on the Billy case, so I had to be very careful in what I said."

"That was good of you to call in to see her, Mum. I can't wait to hear how the police are getting on with the investigation."

"I'll let you know when I hear the latest. And before that I had a wonderful conversation with Christopher Moorfield, a retired chemistry teacher who grew up in Yorkshire," replied her mother. "We had a cup of tea together, and a trip down memory lane."

"He sounds a perfect candidate for the oral history project," said Alice, adding, "I hope the tea was warm enough. Some of the residents I see in the evenings say it's always just tepid when it reaches their rooms."

"I think it was prepared specially for us. I guess it's more challenging to keep it warm when they take tea round for everyone."

"Still, at home you would have your cup of tea hot. This is called a home. So the same standards should apply," was Alice's righteous reply.

"You're absolutely right. When is your next shift there?"

"Next Thursday. And then just two more weeks before I go on holiday. Can't wait!"

Alice looked excited. Then her expression changed. "Mind you, I'm pretty disturbed by some of the things I've heard and seen. A lovely old lady told me last week that she'd been on her own in her room for four hours during the afternoon, with absolutely no-one looking in even to say 'hello'. Sometimes the home runs activities, but not every day, and so if people don't have visitors, they can sometimes just be static in their prisons."

"Not prisons. Alice!"

"The people who run these homes shouldn't just think of material needs. I know it's time-consuming and exhausting just doing all of that – food, washing, nursing, bathing, toileting, cleaning rooms, gardening, and then the same all over again. But these people are still alive. They need stimulation. They need visitors and social lives. And the material needs should be fulfilled really well. Care means care, not just an action list to get through."

"What would you recommend, if you were in charge, Alice?"

Alice looked thoughtful. "I've had a good think about that. Well, if I was the matron here, I would make sure that every inmate, sorry resident, had a visit each week either from her or from the deputy matron. There are forty people here. So that shouldn't be too difficult to arrange. Just for a brief chat, a sit-down chat, not a quick 'Hello' from the doorway. And I would expect there to be regular feedback from the clients. They are clients, not simply residents. They're paying a lot of money. They should be able to tell it as it is, and not be criticised for complaining."

"Those are good ideas."

"You know, some of the residents are very gentle, and have been kind all their lives, and although there are some brilliant carers and nurses here, there are definitely some who are sharp in what they say, who don't carry out what they've said they'll do, and who use inappropriate bodily language and are sometimes downright condescending. Like they sound really surprised if someone they're looking after remembers their name, or remembers something about their previous day's conversation. And they give them almost a congratulatory pat on the arm for being so clever. It makes me mad."

Felicity had no idea her daughter could take up a cause with such passion.

"Here are my suggestions for what a good home should do." Alice disappeared for a moment and returned with a notebook. "Here, I've written it all down!"

"Teach staff the real meaning of empathy. Give them a short chat about this when they arrive. Remind them that these old people will be them, in a few years' time. Don't be impatient if they share their woes and illnesses with you. Some of these people are really suffering."

Felicity sank into a welcoming armchair to listen further.

"Some of this is for the nursing floor people. Understand people's illnesses. If they have Parkinson's, remember that stress and pressure slow everything down, so the individual needs gentle encouragement with walking, and not a telling-off, or any physical pressure."

Felicity was shocked to hear what Alice was saying now.

"Ask the resident what they would like when moving around, and listen, really listen to their replies. Ask them if they want to walk to the dining room, or use the wheelchair. Give them the choice. They have this right. Don't just use the wheelchair because it makes your work easier and quicker."

Alice was looking very stressed herself as she read all of this out.

"Listen to, and implement, any requests made, for example, to be woken in time to get ready for a hospital appointment, because otherwise residents get very anxious. Don't forget this kind of request. It's important to the person involved. Understand the significance of her room to her as a home. Realise how stressful constant references to changing this, are. Don't keep referring to rearranging her room, to make your caring work easier." Alice had written the next sentence in upper case for emphasis. "That room is the only place she has left."

"My mother, thankfully, isn't in the nursing section of her home, and she seems to be well looked after," commented Felicity in a low voice.

"I've nearly finished, Mum."

"Show real care and compassion. Spend some sympathetic time with her if she is very concerned, or make sure someone sympathetic is sent to be with her – just for five minutes.

"Be polite. Don't use words like 'bum', and don't tell her off. Be patient with her."

"Did that all happen on one evening?" asked Felicity

"No, this is a compilation." It sounded like a music album. "Of all the sad things I've seen and heard. Amidst wonderful dedicated caring work from the majority, which I don't overlook."

"Sweetheart. This is all very emotional. I'm sorry you've been exposed to all this sadness, at your age."

"Well, Mum, to be frank, I'm actually very glad I've seen some of this. Because before I worked at the home, I naïvely imagined that all the carers and nurses would be kind and gentle. A lot of them are, and I really admire them, because theirs is a hard job and sometimes quite disgusting (Alice would never make a nurse or a carer, her mother knew). But there are some who no way should be in those jobs, and who regularly get away with inappropriate behaviour simply because no-one is watching them. Apart from me, in recent weeks." She added. "You probably guessed that some of my comments come directly from observing the treatment of one particular lady."

"And you still don't want to be a lawyer?" smiled Felicity. "No, Mum, I have other career aspirations I think. But thanks for the thumbs-up on what I've said."

"I want you to know that I won't let this rest," continued her mother. "I do want to meet with the matron. And I think Emily might come with me. Would it be OK if we mention some of what you've told me?"

"I would be furious if you didn't."

Alice went up to her room, leaving Felicity to reflect. She sat there for a long time, taking in what she'd heard. Next week, with the wedding over, she'd confide in Emily, and then they would decide how to proceed.

She went into her study. It was a little room just off their living room, perfect for her needs. Three of the walls were filled with floor-to-ceiling bookcases, all full. In the middle of one wall, facing the door, was an opening amongst the shelves for Felicity's oak desk. Her collection of books continued above the doorway, a shelf of tomes sitting proudly above the entrance to the room. Almost half of the fourth wall featured central French doors, each with fifteen window lights, opening out onto the garden, and flanked on either side by Felicity's certificates and other small framed items. Looking out, her view was an area of garden adjacent to one side of the little walled garden separating Felicity and Alice's garden from grounds allocated to the weekend café. Photos of Alice were dominant on the desk, along with other beloved people.

There weren't any pictures of Matt, her ex-husband. They had parted when Alice was three. Felicity had been suspicious for over a year, but Matt's unfaithfulness was confirmed when she inadvertently found texts on his phone from Sylvia, a colleague in the law firm; all the content indicated that she was having a relationship with Felicity's husband. So there being no chance of a reconciliation, Felicity and Matt parted. He was dead set on marrying Sylvia. Happily for Felicity, Matt was not only in receipt of considerable inherited wealth, but he was also doing particularly well in the firm. So her divorce settlement was very comfortable, and her own salary was good too. She counted herself very fortunate not to have any financial worries, and could bring Alice up with all possible advantages. As so often happened when men married for a second time, she wondered if Matt and Sylvia might have children, but that hadn't happened. Matt saw Alice from time to time, but not as often as Felicity thought he should. Felicity had had a few relationships since the divorce, but apart from one which didn't work out and which almost broke her heart, she didn't have anyone in her life at the moment, and had a full diary working, looking after Alice, keeping up with her own mother, and enjoying a buzzing social life.

She got down to work. The prospect of taking on the partnership at Luke's old firm excited her and, as well as rest and vacation, Felicity wanted to use this month to catch up on important background legal reading. She'd of necessity absorbed the changes to property taxation introduced in April the previous year for non-UK residents, and relaxation of some planning rules later that year. On its way later this year would be changes in rates of stamp duty and, before then, an Intellectual Property Act due to be passed in October. It was bliss to have time to absorb all the detail. Felicity had also made notes from her meeting with Luke, and she was keen to study those before she started at the firm. Plus there were always the dreaded legal journals; she liked to keep up with those, and usually that was an impossible task.

She had been impressed with Alice's passion for the unfairness she'd witnessed in the home. Her command of vocabulary and what almost amounted almost to oratory, were both very good; there was something even instinctive about her facility with language. Felicity was hugely proud of her daughter, and was navigating the teenage years as well as she could. Sometimes Alice simply needed to be on her own, at other times she needed to be with her peers, and occasionally she was happy to spend time with her mother. That was all right and proper, as she prepared to fly the nest in a couple of years' time. Felicity didn't much like to think about that empty nest phase. For the moment, living in the present would do very well.

Alice had retreated upstairs to finish some homework, and to ring a friend for a chat. It was tempting to call her friend first, but Alice really enjoyed maths and wanted to produce a good piece of work, so she knuckled down to some daunting algebra for forty-five minutes, and then rewarded herself with the phone call. It was always nice to chat to her mother over a meal, but then, as if called by some hidden force, she usually disappeared to her bedroom for most of the evening. She loved her Mum, but they were from different generations, and she actually feasted on her friends' chat, gossip, friendship and, yes, love. It was a kind of sisterhood. Along with love for her mother, which in her heart of hearts, she admitted to being a constant in her life. She was looking forward to Saturday, when she and her friends would luxuriate in a day together, getting ready for the gig that evening, and enjoying a day totally free from school work. Felicity would be at Jessie and Andrew's wedding, and Alice would have the house to herself.

CHAPTER NINETEEN

Jessie and Andrew's Wedding
Saturday 26th July 2014

It was a beautiful church. In terms of architecture, Andrew was convinced that he wouldn't ever work at such an historic gem in the future. The interior was stunning, an awesome example of Romanesque with its characteristic round arches, sturdy pillars, and symmetry. Emily drank in the grandeur of the building; momentous in style, it seemed a fitting preparation for a momentous and joyous day in the life of their family.

"Just look at the thickness of those walls," Luke commented to her after the service. "And the arches, well they really rise up to heaven, you might say." Lily was intrigued by the church's art, all unsurprisingly depicting biblical scenes, along with sculpture along similar lines. She was struck by so much colour and gilding. Sitting with the other bridesmaids, Daisy on her lap, she simultaneously gazed at the building and listened to the service.

Jessie had completely overcome the blip she'd shared with Luke at

Lord's, and the run-up to the wedding had been seamless on all fronts. Andrew was the perfect groom, looking handsome and calm and as a Scot, he was kilted up. Jessie looked magnificent in her lace gown. The bridesmaids carried out their roles to perfection and even Daisy performed as directed, being carried up the aisle by Lily without even the tiniest cry. *This is the changing of the guard,* thought Luke, as he metaphorically eyeballed Andrew at the altar. He sounded to himself fearfully politically incorrect, and was glad that no-one could read his dangerous thoughts. Though of course he didn't mean what he'd just uttered mentally; neither he nor Andrew had any trace of ownership of Jessie. He was merely pondering the closing of one family unit, and the heralding of a new one. Seated back in the pew next to Emily, he found himself to be quite moved during the service.

Maybe it's due to a surfeit of Wentworth weddings, he told himself, *or possibly it's the thought of Jimmy's ghostly* (*or do I mean "ghastly?",* he thought ruefully) *intrusion into our family.* He noted, "And they begin a new life together in the community." *Wow, yes they do,* thought Luke. *It's pivotal, this new unit they're entering into. These are powerful, and incredibly exciting words, uttered weekly in countless churches all over the country, and possibly more or less unnoticed by many who hear them, especially as most couples nowadays have already begun that new life.*

But in effect this wedding service is, in its own way, quite revolutionary, he reflected further. And when the vows were exchanged, for the first time ever, Luke was struck by the phrase "according to God's holy law", spoken clearly by both bride and groom. *This means something to them, to each of them,* he thought. *That's quite a beautiful and dramatic group of words, sealing this union.* In his mind he was briefly transported back to his 1978 essay, and Pascal's wager.

The bride and groom had chosen to have several pictures taken inside the church before going out into the garden for more. Such a wonderful backdrop couldn't be ignored. And Jessie had thought carefully about how the bridal party would look in front of that backdrop. So apart from some Scottish colour on the part of the groom and best man, and in the rust-coloured flowers in bouquets, the bridesmaids were all dressed in beige silk, trimmed with rust and cream. Carla's flowers were accordingly in rust, cream, and pale yellow. She had toiled long and hard that week, and hadn't slept well the night before the wedding. But her professional commitment had paid off. The displays in the church, the romantic bouquets, and the flowers at the reception were all superb.

"You have done Jessie and Andrew proud," said Xander, holding her close after the service. The sculpted shapes of her displays in the church echoed its architectural style, and complemented it. Carla had been careful not to dominate this richly decorated building with her floral arrangements, but to employ them as a tasteful accessory.

"Thank you," she said to Xander. His compliments meant more to her than the praise of anyone else.

During a photographer-induced break between shots, Andrew daringly broke away from the wedding group for a moment. Carla kissed him and offered congratulations, and Xander did the same, though minus the kiss, slapping his new brother-in-law on the back. "Carla, the flowers are just right. I'm thrilled with them, and so is my wife." Andrew smiled with delight at Jessie's new status. "Thanks so much for all your work. You have a great flair with flowers; it's a real gift." Thrilled and quite pink with pleasure, Carla thanked him.

"Andrew, come back. We need you!" called Jessie. "Just coming." He ran back, his Buckingham kilt swinging, a blur of green and orange.

The reception was held in a marquee in Emily and Luke's garden, its openings flung open to reflect the day's high temperatures. "Splendid marquee," said Felicity to Jessie. The bride laughed. "Yes, they were a bit floored when we requested a Romanesque marquee. Twenty-first century creation masquerading as a medieval building. But they've done a good job."

To carry out Jessie and Andrew's wishes, the marquee designers had created fake pillars, draped in gold, in its four corners, and had arranged overhead lighting in continuous rounded shapes to echo the church's arches, at the top of all four sides. They had creatively hung on the inner face of the marquee, replicas of some of the church's religious artwork, skilfully photographed and blown up, and framed in ornate gilt. And Carla and her colleagues had arranged each table with a central Romanesque-shaped arch of flowers, under which there was a twirling gold J and A symbol.

Jessie was proud of her father's speech, and of Andrew's. "Just as I was nearly both best man and father-of-the-bride at Lily's wedding, so Andrew could easily today have been both groom and clergy; he could have married Jessie in both senses. Though I think it would have been a bit of a feat, extremely comic, and one never before attempted," said Luke in his clear voice. "Unless I've missed something, we're now all weddinged-out in our family, until it's Daisy's turn." There were smiles from the guests, and an anguished look from Lily, who at this precise moment in time never wanted that day to come. In his groom's speech Andrew recalled the first happy meeting with Jessie at Lily and Archie's wedding, recommending these celebratory occasions as excellent dating opportunities to anyone present looking for a life partner. He described their marriage as a perfect pairing. "She'll look after my medical needs, and I will keep a weather eye on her spiritual health." The floral arrangements were highly praised, and received their own warm round of applause.

"Dad, can I have a word?" Lily had asked her father quietly just before the wedding breakfast. They'd therefore now retreated to a private corner of the garden, the garden in which she'd spent so many happy summers in her youth. "I think you know that I'm meeting Jimmy on Monday?" She didn't want to call him 'my father'.

"Yes, Mum told me. I hope it's a helpful meeting for both of you."

"Well, I've no idea what I'll think of him. But whether I like him or not, I wanted to let you know that you will always always be my real father." She hesitated. "Whatever Jimmy ends up as being to me, it definitely won't be a father. If I have any relationship with him at all, he might I suppose be a sort of a surrogate figure." She avoided the word 'father'.

"That's very sweet of you, love."

"I'm quite nervous about meeting him. I get quite jittery when I think about it. And I'm training myself not to be angry with him."

Luke said, "Well, I've never met him. Your mother has, of course. And now you are going to meet him. To me he's a slightly mythical historical figure. Yet without him, I wouldn't have this treasure that's you. So he's not all bad." They both smiled.

"Go with an open mind on Monday, and try to forgive him," urged Luke. "He'll be feeling nervous as well."

"Thanks, Dad. I'll let you and Mum know how I get on."

They re-joined the festivities. Luke was relieved and pleased that Lily had talked with him and he was quite moved by what she'd said about his fatherly role in her life. Yet he admitted also to feeling very strange about her forthcoming meeting with her biological father. He felt oddly like someone whose partner was about to be unfaithful to them, and was totally overt about it. He and Emily had talked at length about Lily's meeting with Jimmy, and they both had the same sense of almost betrayal. It was totally irrational, they knew. All down the decades, they had never dreamed that Lily's father would come back into their lives, but now they had to face this reality, and despite his reappearance having unsettled them considerably, they were of one mind that it was absolutely right for Lily to meet him.

The following morning heralded a post-wedding breakfast for the residue of the wedding party. It made sense to make use of the marquee again, and Emily, who wanted to enjoy this continuation of the festivities rather than cater for it, had arranged for an outside company to prepare an appropriate feast for breaking of the overnight fast. It was already twenty-two degrees, with temperatures forecast to climb. So tables which yesterday had held a sumptuous wedding breakfast now creaked with every possible fruit, artisan cereal, fresh juice, tempting smoothies, cooked food of all varieties, cheeses and charcuterie, and bread and rolls from the local bakery. There was a *crêpes* station, and omelettes were on offer too. Coffee was brewing, and champagne was still flowing. Bridesmaids, best man, ushers, extended family members, Andrew's parents from Perthshire, his aunt and uncle and two cousins, were present, along with all the Wentworths and various close friends. Andrew's father and one of his cousins still sported their kilts.

No-one was sure where Jessie and Andrew had overnighted, and there was lively debate over where they were due to be honeymooning, the majority conclusion being that they were jetting off somewhere warm for the week. Hamish, Andrew's cousin, wasn't looking too healthy this morning. Emily had noticed his great enjoyment of champagne at the wedding, and this morning he definitely seemed to be suffering the after-effects.

"Would you like a coffee, Hamish?" she said, seeing his pale face. "And some fresh orange juice?"

"Thank you," he said gratefully, sinking into the nearest chair next to a group of his relatives. "It was a wonderful day yesterday, but I confess I over-indulged."

"It was a wedding. Just the right time to indulge," she replied with a conspiratorial smile.

Archie, also still sporting a kilt, was sitting at a table with Xander, Carla, and Luke. Carla got up every so often to busy herself with some of the floral arrangements, dispatching any which were threatening to droop. Lily was chatting animatedly at another table with Lucy, a fellow-bridesmaid, while Daisy, snuggled up to her mother, was almost asleep. Xander moved to the next table to have a chat with Hamish and his brother. "I'm a bit concerned about Lily's meeting with Jimmy tomorrow," confided Archie to Luke, in a subdued tone. "I did offer to go with her, but she was adamant she wanted to meet him on her own. It feels like an unwelcome shift in our life that I'm not happy with right at this time." By "this time", he meant so soon after Daisy's birth.

"I completely understand," replied Luke. "It's shaken us all up, in different ways. Even Jessie and Xander, with whom there's no real link, are a bit unsettled and like you, concerned for Lily. I hope that Jimmy will be content with just the occasional contact, in future. I don't think I could cope with regular intrusion into our lives."

"Lily seems keen to make it a reasonably short meeting," added Archie. "My mother is going to look after Daisy, and we don't anticipate her needing to be around all day for that. I won't be home until late tomorrow."

As they chatted, Lily came over with a now fully awake Daisy, and handed her to Archie so that she could circulate more easily. Carrying Daisy as if a trophy, he moved over to the table where Andrew's parents were sitting, and engaged in conversation with his mother, a fellow doctor. Lily glided around happily, a dark red dress setting off her post-baby impressively svelte figure to perfection. She spoke with some family members, then chatted with one of the ushers, discovering to her delight that he was an artist. Lily was fascinated to discover that he regularly exhibited in art galleries, and ended their discourse by exchanging business cards. Xander was reconnecting with Harriet, one of Jessie's bridesmaids, an old schoolfriend of his sister's. He remembered her coming round to their house in her teenage years. He also recalled finding her very attractive, and regularly being too shy actually to speak to her. Now, at their exalted age, they had a perfectly civilised conversation, catching up over the years. Harriet and Jessie had both been violinists in the school orchestra, and Harriet having taken her musical gifts to a higher level than Jessie, was now a professional violinist in a regional orchestra. Xander, who'd played the clarinet at school but not since, was fascinated. "So what's the life of a professional musician like?" he asked.

"It's not as glamorous as people think," Harriet smiled. "A lot of hard work, rehearsing over and over again, working with colleagues who can be quite temperamental, and occasionally playing music which doesn't inspire you. And the performances obviously take place in fairly anti-social hours. But on the plus side," her face lit up, "it's also a joy to be part of a team that's doing something creative and life-enhancing, not only for audiences, but also for ourselves." She reflected for a moment. "There's really nothing to beat the surging feeling of playing a beautiful piece of music with others, experiencing that great sense of teamwork, and fulfilling what you feel the composer had in mind when writing the piece."

"That's a fascinating insight," replied Xander. "Yes, from the outside your job does appear glamorous, but I guess that's because audiences only see the final product after endless hours of hard work. We see the end result, when you are all dressed up and showcasing the final performance. And I know exactly what you mean about teamwork. I'm not sure that every job provides that richness, but I experience it in teaching, and it's part of what makes my work so enjoyable. It's good to know there are high moments in your work, amid the everyday."

It was nearly twelve o'clock, and the crowd was gradually thinning out. The caterers were preparing to leave. One by one, guests queued up to voice thanks to their hosts. Hugs were exchanged, and promises made to meet again. As in succession they went on their way, and the noise died down, it felt to Emily as if the closing notes of the quiet movement of a symphony were gently sounding. Soon just the seven members of the Wentworth family were left. They had a final leisurely coffee together, exchanging enjoyable feedback on the last twenty-four hours. Then just Emily and Luke remained, the final notes, the coda of the movement. They collapsed happily into easy chairs, the business of any remaining clearing-up a very distant event in their timetable. Guests had disappeared to various Sunday afternoon occupations, a nap on the sofa, a stroll in the park, for some the inevitable work catch-up, a quick dash to the corner shop, a visit to family or friends. Then Monday morning and its humdrum would call, the events of Jessie and Andrew's wedding now a moment in history, yet assuredly to be recaptured time and time again in much-loved pictures.

CHAPTER TWENTY

Restaurant near London City Airport
Monday 28th July 2014

Lily woke up early. Or rather, she was awoken early, as per usual since Daisy's birth. As soon as she jumped out of bed to attend to Daisy, she remembered with a jolt, what she was going to do today. It had been uppermost in her mind before going to sleep, sleep which hadn't come until the early hours. And now it came back to her in a rush. She was going to meet her father for the first time, thirty-five years after her birth. *About time, too,* she thought to herself.

Daisy's feed finished, they both went downstairs. Archie was still asleep. It was only six o'clock, and he wouldn't rise until nearer seven. Lily put Daisy securely into her bouncing chair, and looked up the weather forecast on her phone. Last time she'd looked, it hadn't been promising, and the skies looked very full of water at the moment. Yes, extremely heavy rain was being forecast for mid-morning. She hoped that it wouldn't delay, or even prevent Jimmy's flight. Apparently he'd spent the night in Edinburgh, where he had business meetings the previous day, and was due to fly into City Airport at ten-twenty.

"You're going to play with Granny today, darling," she told Daisy, who was completely oblivious to what her mother was saying as, fascinated, she watched a row of dancing animals on the mobile hanging from the low ceiling above her. "Granny Fiona. You can learn a Scottish accent from her." Daisy smiled obligingly at her mother's humour, though in reality it was a low-hanging dancing sheep that had triggered the smile. Lily had what she called a scared feeling in her tummy. It was a sensation brought on usually by exams, a visit to the dentist, or an interview. Or, remembering Jessie's facile comment when they'd talked at Lord's, before going on a date; since meeting Archie, that was an historic feeling, but not actually so terribly historic. None of those scenarios would take place today, but her feelings were exactly the same as if they might be about to happen. Or perhaps this would indeed be a kind of interview, she thought, Lily interviewing her father, and he interviewing his daughter.

Archie kissed her 'Goodbye' at eight o'clock as he left the house. "Remember, be positive, and don't commit yourself to anything. Don't forget that he abandoned you, but also remember that he's penitent." Musing on the strangely archaic word, Lily kissed him and took Daisy upstairs to get them both dressed. As it wasn't a date she was going on, she didn't dither about what to wear, but chose a simple top and new jeans, and decided to take her long trench coat and umbrella.

Jimmy too woke up early. His flight was due to take off at eight-fifty, so he was up and ready to leave for Turnhouse Airport, a short taxi ride away, by seven o'clock. Once at the airport he realised he'd arrived way too early, so he had another coffee and tried to read the paper. But he simply couldn't concentrate. This, what he was going to do today, was what he'd desired for so many years. He thought about so many of his contemporaries and their children, the activities they'd shared together, the holidays they'd enjoyed, the school pick-ups, the relationships they'd built over the years. While he had waited for children, and none had come. Not with Maggie, his first partner, who already had two of her own and didn't want any more, and certainly didn't want Jimmy to keep in touch with them after he and Maggie split. Not with Mary, his partner of twenty years; they had tried to conceive but it hadn't worked. And with Julie, at the moment, it was definitely too late. She was fifty-six. And all the time, lurking at the back of his mind, there had been the thought of this baby that Emily had carried. Had she indeed given birth? Was the baby healthy? Where were they? He had had a gnawing feeling deep inside, and a deep longing actually to know, to find out what had happened. Did he in fact have a child? He desperately wanted to know the answer, and then, one way or the other, he would at last find peace.

Like Emily before her at their meeting in Edinburgh, Lily would hold all the power in this encounter. Jimmy was aware that he hadn't invested any love or commitment into the situation. Not for thirty-five years. Not until now. He was just beginning, tentatively, and with a tiny spark of hope. He'd been nervous before meeting with Emily, but that was different. He had known what she was like, slightly. And in the end, he'd quite enjoyed their tea together. He remembered clearly why he'd fallen for her years ago, even though she had now ditched the short dress and sleek white boots. And he was grateful that she had graciously opened the door to this meeting with Lily. But Lily was a total unknown. He was a bit scared. What if she simply didn't warm to him, and never wanted to see him again? The very thought sickened him, and he quickly dismissed it.

Having left Daisy safely in Fiona's care, Lily walked briskly to the Archway tube station, and took the Northern Line to Bank, then switched to the DLR, and got off at Blackwall. It was a nine-minute walk to the restaurant, and fortunately it hadn't started raining yet. They'd agreed to meet in a quiet restaurant rather than amid all the busyness of the airport, initially for coffee, but most likely followed by an early lunch. The towers of Canary Wharf rose up nearby. She loved this area; it was full of hope and enterprise. It felt more American than British, with its gleaming skyscrapers. Jimmy and she were due to meet at eleven o'clock and it was now ten-thirty, so she had oodles of time, and she stopped occasionally to absorb the view. Walking along to the appointment felt like a few more minutes of freedom; entering the restaurant would be another matter. A plane came in to land at City. *He'll be on one of those, and soon,* she thought. She found their meeting place; it overlooked the Thames and the O2. "You have a table booked for two," she said to the greeter, "in the name of Jimmy Smith."

Jimmy's flight was exactly on time. He'd not read much during the ninety minutes on board, remaining deep in thought about the next few hours. He walked out of arrivals, visited the Gents, and joined the queue for taxis. To his surprise, he reached the top of the queue quickly, and was promptly on the ten-minute ride to the restaurant. *I mustn't arrive early,* he panicked to himself. "Can you let me out by this tube station?" he instructed the driver who, surprised at the sudden stop, nevertheless let him out at Canning Town underground station. Jimmy strolled the rest of the route, arriving a few minutes after Lily. He took a deep breath before entering, and then spoke to the greeter.

The restaurant was nearly empty. He spotted her immediately, sitting at a window table, framed by a background of the O2 and vast expanse of river. She stood up to greet him. "Lily!" he said warmly, feeling totally choked up inside. *I'm in a public place. I must control myself,* he thought. "Hello Jimmy," said Lily quietly but with a courteous smile. They sat down in tandem, without any physical touch. No handshake. Definitely no hug or kiss. He took in the vision that was his daughter, tall, with long dark hair, her pretty face very like Emily's, dressed in smart casual clothes, and with style. She took him in, her biological father, tall, receding red hair, metrosexual dress, nice smile, crinkly eyes.

"How long have you been waiting?" he asked.

"I just arrived a few minutes ago. How was your flight?"

"Great. It was right on time, and then I had an easy onward journey to here."

The rain had started, that rain forecast for precisely now. It made the whole outlook appear grey and slightly sad, though it was also a dramatic vista, given the in-your-face size and architectural style of the O2 building, combined with the wide flowing river.

"Let me get you a coffee," he said. "What would you like?"

"A cappuccino, thanks," replied Lily.

"May we have two cappuccinos, please?" he said to the waiter who'd just appeared at their table.

There was a pause.

"Thanks so much for meeting with me," Jimmy said. "It must be very odd for you. I gather you didn't know much about me until very recently."

A plane was descending towards the airport.

"Yes, it's very strange. Though I had always wondered who you were. Mum and I didn't ever talk about it. And we were all busy, growing up. Mum and Dad (Jimmy inwardly winced at Luke's nomenclature) busy working, the three of us at school and our other activities and seeing our friends."

"A busy social life?" he ventured. He was listening to her voice, her accent, very English and of course with not a trace of any Scottish influence.

"Yes, Jessie and Xander, my sister and brother, are both quite musical, and I've always been arty. So they went to orchestra, and I was always being creative in a studio or at a kiln. Or visiting an art gallery." She was aware that she was starting to open up to this stranger, this stranger who in another reality could have been part of her growing-up, if he'd so chosen.

"Tell me about your art. Do you still paint, or do anything creative, outside work?"

"I don't really have time now, with Daisy, and looking after the gallery. But I used to do watercolours, mainly of some of the London parks, often incorporating passers-by."

"Tell me about Daisy". He was a good listener. Was this what her mother had fallen for? And he had a pleasant clipped Aberdonian accent.

"Daisy is my world. Along with Archie of course. But while I'm on maternity leave Daisy and I are simply enjoying getting to know each other. Every day she does something new. She's so alert, and smiles, and is really happy. She's nearly six months, and a real character."

"Do you have a picture of her?"

A failsafe question to a new mother, thought Lily.

The rain was getting heavier, and the wind was swirling round the big window next to them. In spite of effective double glazing, they could hear the rain and wind quite clearly.

Lily got out her phone, and showed Jimmy a couple of pictures of her daughter. She didn't want to go wild by scrolling through twenty or more as she was always tempted to do.

"She's beautiful. I can see why she's your world. Might I guess that she's got my hair?" he commented daringly.

"Yes, she's a darling. And yes, it is your hair colour. Neither of my parents has any red hair in their ancestry." Jimmy winced at the reference to 'my parents'.

He had never been close to a small child, not even when he was growing up, birth order having dictated that he, the younger of two siblings, was the baby of the family. So he was slightly in awe of the photos of Daisy, his flesh and blood.

They were both quiet, sipping their coffee. The section of the restaurant where they were sitting was a beautiful one storey extension, and the rain was now drumming on its roof. Another plane was descending, and Lily wondered if it might be the last for the time being. The weather didn't look at all favourable for flying.

"This is difficult for me to say without getting emotional," said her father. "But I wanted to tell you, as soon as possible, that I am very very sorry for having left your mother in the lurch when she was pregnant with you." *Were those actual tears in his eyes?* wondered Lily. *Real tears, or manufactured ones?*

"I was mean and callous and thoughtless and totally unfair to her. I should never have left her, expecting a baby, and alone. And I apologise totally. I know that doesn't change the situation, and doesn't make up for her hurt and abandonment. Nor for your lack of a father in your early years."

She looked down at her coffee.

"But if possible I would like," he hesitated "and only if you agree, to have some kind of relationship with you now. I don't expect anything major. But if I could see you occasionally, that would be so appreciated." His last line sounded rather like a business proposal.

"This is moving too fast," replied Lily, now feeling as though their coffee together was indeed very similar to a date. In her work she had learned to make her feelings clear rather than beat about the bush, and here she was careful to adopt the same approach.

"OK. OK! Point taken." He put up his hands as if to indicate that he was retreating. "Again, sorry." He smiled, and he was relieved to see the ghost of a smile on Lily's face. "Shall we order some lunch?"

The menu was eclectic, but fun. Lily ordered a salad, and Jimmy a curry. They chatted about less controversial issues, what it was like to live in Aberdeen, a city Lily had never visited, her new home in Archway, a little about Archie and a little about Jimmy's partner Julie, and where they had each travelled over the years. Then she asked about his work. In the time since Emily had told her about Jimmy, Lily had looked him up, and realised she'd seen some of his work at a couple of exhibitions. He was pleased she was interested in his publications, and was secretly delighted that they had a professional link. They ordered more coffee after their meal.

"I'm sorry we can't sit outside to drink our coffee," he smiled. Outside there were sad-looking patio tables and chairs next to the river, which on a warm day would have been perfect for enjoying the view. "The O2 is amazing," he continued. "It reminds me of Dynamic Earth."

"What's that?" asked Lily.

"It's a place in Edinburgh, next to the Scottish Parliament. It's a science centre and planetarium. It was opened in 1999; it's smaller than O2 but some of the design is similar. It's meant to look like a giant white armadillo." He pulled a face. "The outside is white fabric with steel masts sticking out of it, very like the ones atop the O2."

The rain on the roof was relentless, and sounded louder and more determined by the minute. "It almost sounds as though it's raining in here," commented Jimmy with a quizzical expression.

Jimmy liked Lily. He liked her open face, her business-like manner, and her style. He was enjoying her conversation. Lily wasn't sure what to make of Jimmy. He seemed pretty nice, and was being very friendly. But then why wouldn't he work hard to make a good impression on his newly minted daughter? She was cautious, yet also aware she mustn't close the door on the relationship, certainly not at the moment.

"Thanks for your apology," she said, returning to their previous conversation. "Of course it's hard for me to forgive you for leaving Mum. But I appreciate that you've got in touch at last. If you hadn't, I might never ever had known who my father was. I will have to think hard about the future. I've only recently married, and have just had a baby, I'm trying to keep an eye on the gallery, and my sister's just got married too. So I'm a bit up and down about lots of things. And I'm very tired." As if to illustrate, she yawned. "Sorry. My sleep is interrupted every night, and I can't rest during the day."

"It must be exhausting, even though your daughter looks so adorable."

"Is that water I hear dripping behind me?" said Lily suddenly. Just as she spoke a waiter appeared with an old black bucket that clashed horrendously with the muted grey and pale wood décor. "Apologies," he said with a smile. "The rain has invaded our flat roof. I've never seen such torrential rain. We'll have to catch the continuous drip-drip in this bucket." They both smiled back indicating non-verbally that they didn't mind the bucket.

"I have an odd question," continued Lily. "Do you by any chance have a photo of you and Mum together?"

Jimmy thought for a moment. "I'm not sure. It's very unlikely, after all these years. But I can have a look in my collection of old university pictures, and I'll let you know if I find one. Why?"

"I thought it might be nice for me to have a photo of the two of you together, the couple who are my reason for being here." As she spoke Lily also couldn't help finding it a bit gross to think of the two-month long relationship between her mother and Jimmy that had led to her existence.

"I hope your flight back isn't delayed by the weather. It's so unusual for it to be so vehemently rainy and windy."

Jimmy rather liked how his daughter attributed human characteristics to the elements. He smiled. "I'm sure I'll get back tonight, even if the flight is slightly late. I'm flying back from Luton, to get a direct flight to Aberdeen. I'm scheduled to leave at six-thirty, and the rain is forecast to stop well before then."

After a pause, she added, "I should really get back soon. My mother-in-law is looking after Daisy and I don't want to leave her too long. I said I'd be home by mid-afternoon, and it will take me nearly an hour to get back." They chatted for another few minutes.

"It's been just perfect meeting you," he said. "Promise me you'll think about seeing me in the future. Just from time to time." He was speaking slowly, and looking straight at her. "I'm aware that I've just barged into your life, into Emily and Luke's life, and I have no wish to be annoying or intrusive. I have no right to suddenly be a huge part of your life, but to feature just a little—" He stopped, and Lily glimpsed moisture in his eyes again.

"I promise I'll think about it, and I promise to get back to you letting you know my thoughts. Thank you for coming all this way to meet me." She stood up and put her coat on with the collar tight around her neck and hair. She picked up her umbrella.

"Let me call a taxi for you."

"No, it's fine. I'll just walk quickly and this massive golf umbrella is excellent protection, thanks. I think the rain is at last getting lighter."

They parted with a quick but rather formal hug, Jimmy paying for the meal, and remaining at the table for another coffee and substantial reflection, as Lily left, her characteristic brisk walk taking her out of the restaurant and along the path back to the underground station. Out of the restaurant but not, Jimmy fervently hoped, out of his life again.

CHAPTER TWENTY-ONE

Four Kitchens
July & August 2014

Lily and Archie's kitchen July 28th

Lily did get a bit wet on her walk to Blackwall tube station, but she needed the exercise after the meeting with Jimmy. It had been a stressful and strange experience, and a good walk afterwards helped. She was hungry to see Daisy again. Being apart from her baby daughter was always painful, and she was excited about their reunion. The journey home seemed long, the underground connections not as fast as she'd expected. She was struck by the vast range of people on the trains. It was a kind of global and multi-age salad; that was Lily's best attempt at summing it up. And in one carriage every single person opposite her was wearing blue jeans – a man nudging seventy, a teenager, a young mother with her toddler, a tourist and his wife. She gazed at the ten legs facing her, all clothed in denim and all different lengths and shapes. *Like society in general I guess,* she mused. *A mix of personalities, but we all have the great unifier, our human needs in common. And denim in common too.*

Jimmy lingered a bit in the restaurant, then headed off on the Tube and continued via the Thameslink to Luton airport. His flight was delayed by thirty minutes, so he sat in one of the inevitable airport coffee shops, thinking, and occasionally reading his book. He called Julie, and had a brief chat. He had decided that he liked his daughter a lot. She definitely looked like Emily, and she didn't have his colouring. But in his favour, she was into art, just like him, and that seemed to present a bonding opportunity. And she had smiled at him a bit. There was so much he wanted to know, but how to catch up on thirty-five years? It would be utterly impossible. He would have to content himself with a gradual knowledge, if permitted, a gradual friendship, and maybe if he was very fortunate, a feeling of love between them. He felt deeply ashamed and even, to use a fairly strong word quite unfamiliar to him, actually convicted of his behaviour before Lily's birth, but he forced himself to be realistic, knowing that he couldn't change the past. He fervently hoped she would agree to see him again. So he and Lily both made their journeys home lost in thought about their respective daughters. As was life and as nature had planned, the love from older generation to younger invariably being stronger than the reverse.

Fiona and Daisy were in the kitchen at Lily and Archie's home. The newly married couple were planning to refurbish this room in the long run, but for the moment it was a work in progress, spacious but with tired units, and with a large pine table at the dining end. "Daisy!" cried Lily, holding her daughter close as Fiona released her. She absorbed the delightful familiar baby scent as they cuddled, and her warmth, as she kissed the little girl's round face. "How has she been?"

"The perfect baby," Fiona assured her. "We've had great fun together, and I've attended to all her needs."

Lily and Archie hadn't wanted to tell Fiona about Jimmy. Not yet anyway. So according to Fiona, Lily had been to a work appointment today in connection with the gallery. "How was your appointment?" her mother-in-law asked with interest.

"An excellent meeting," lied Lily. "It was very useful for my work, and I hope it will help the gallery." She felt a touch guilty at not being truthful, but also perfectly justified, as she didn't want to divulge such sensitive personal news. Maybe in the future, depending on what happened with her and Jimmy.

"Will you stay and have supper with us, Fiona? You were so kind to bring the delicious food." Fiona had arrived that morning armed with a delicious-looking home-made meal and dessert, purchased from a rather superior delicatessen on her way to their house.

"That's kind, but Ailsa is expecting me back to eat together. And you and Archie will both be tired."

Fiona had stayed with a friend last night, and would do the same tonight before catching the train back to Edinburgh the next day. She had been thrilled to spend time with her grand-daughter. "Let me know if you'd like me to look after Daisy again," she said as she left. "She's a delight."

Lily settled on the kitchen sofa with Daisy and fed her. She pondered her lunch with Jimmy. *What to do?* She would discuss the situation with Archie, and with Emily, before deciding how to proceed. And not forgetting Luke, too. She strapped Daisy into her high chair with a favourite soft toy to occupy her, and put the casserole in the oven. Her mobile rang.

"Archie. Thanks for ringing. It was … interesting. Difficult, but not as bad as I'd imagined. When will you be home?" He would be home in an hour, just enough time for her to combine a quick tidy-up of the kitchen and bedroom before he was back. "Come on Daisy, let's go upstairs," she said, scooping up her daughter.

Archie was as good as his word, arriving home within the hour. He was tired, but keen to hear about Lily's day. "You must have got soaked. They said on the news that we've had more than half of the average monthly rainfall today. In just one hour, would you believe?"

"We were inside for all that time, so it was fine. He was nervous I think, Archie, just like me. And very apologetic. I think it was genuine. I did quite like him, but I don't want to hurt Dad. I'm in a bit of a quandary. Can we talk about it, please?"

Emily and Luke's kitchen July 28th

Luke was carefully preparing a new recipe for their supper. He wasn't a natural, but he could produce a good meal if he was extremely careful. Each step had to be checked, and then checked again. He'd made mistakes before, and the results hadn't been pleasant. Meat not properly cooked through, a horrible surfeit of Cajun powder, and chewy pasta were some of his nastier memories. Emily was due back soon. He'd just spoken with Archie on his way home on the tube. Luke was very on edge today, aware that Lily would be meeting her biological father, the "potential usurper", as he'd been calling him in private.

"I'm sure Lily will tell Emily about her meeting, when she's ready," he said to his friend. "Please give her our love. Did I mention that Emily and I have booked a long weekend in Edinburgh, in October? Old times' sake. We haven't been there for years."

"October? Which dates? I have to be there for a conference around that time."

After some diary consultation they worked out that their visits would coincide. "Let's meet for a meal. I'm sure we can find an excellent restaurant in Edinburgh."

Emily waltzed into the kitchen, earlier than anticipated. "You look happy," said her husband.

"My project is all set and sealed. Maddy and Tom have agreed to the figures and terms, and the builder has committed to start next week. What a huge relief."

"Fantastic. A lot of work to do still, but the finished project will be great, I know." He was focussing hard on his cooking.

"What's for supper?" She looked suspiciously at the selection of pans adorning the hob.

"Salmon risotto. Just give me a few more minutes of concentration, and then I can serve it up."

Five minutes later, they were sitting down to a nigh perfect risotto.

"I've got some good news too," he ventured. "Dominique was in touch, a courtesy call which I appreciated, just to let me know that the house sale has gone through, and the money's been transferred to Philippe. She's sending the final paperwork to Felicity. So that's now a closed case. Sad, but closed. At least they got a good amount for the property. I enjoyed working with Dominique. She's super-efficient."

"I'm glad it's all gone through," said Emily soberly.

She cast her mind back to Sophie with her depressed face and downbeat demeanour, thought of the tragic crash, and was silent.

"I heard from Tina this morning," she said after her moment of reflection.

"Oh yes. How is she? Are things all good now?"

"Not totally. It seems Friedrich wasn't as keen as she was simply to get together and make up instantly. I can understand why. Tina has left him twice, once in the 1970s, and then again recently. So he's agreed that she can move in for three days a week, to see how things go."

"She'll be on a sort of trial run, a test of her good behaviour." Luke had to smile.

"And I imagine that she will be the perfect wife during that time. She's desperate to make things work again."

They then talked about what was uppermost on both of their minds. *How had Lily got on today, meeting her father for the first time? What had they each thought of the other? How long did they spend together? And what were Lily's thoughts about the future?* Emily was due to see her daughter on Friday, her day off; she was going round to Lily and Archie's home for an early evening drink, after Daisy's bedtime. She and Luke both hoped that the verbal post mortem would signal some future contentment for all.

Jimmy's kitchen July 28th

It was nine-thirty in the evening, and Jimmy was hungry. He knew he wouldn't sleep if he didn't eat something. Knowing of his long and stressful day, Julie had thoughtfully come round with ready-prepared food. Her house was just a twenty-minute drive from Aberdeen. She was a total contrast to Emily. Where Emily was tall, Julie was of medium height, where Emily was fair, Julie was dark with sallow skin, and where Emily was slim and now, Jimmy had noticed, more slim-ish than slim, Julie was even slimmer than Emily had been in her student days, with a whippet-like figure toned by physical training and a strict diet that perfectly defined the adjective.

Jimmy's kitchen was welcoming and comfortable. At one end there was a browsing area, bookcases either side of a low teal-coloured sofa almost covered with cushions, bookcases that included all of his purchased art publications as well as the illustrated coffee table books he'd produced, the name 'Jimmy Smith' prominently displayed on each cover and spine. And his personal collection of a huge variety of books, some even as far back as his English Literature student days in Edinburgh, shelved in random order. The kitchen end was carefully thought through. Its end wall housed a galley kitchen painted deep blue, the central dining table in front doubling up as a workspace as well as his daily eating area. And he had one work of art in his kitchen. Painted by Julie, and displayed centrally at the opposite end to the kitchen, was her vivid depiction of Maggie's Centre in Aberdeen. The painting was special to Jimmy; the centre had been a refuge for his late mother, and its receipt of the Small Project of the Year Building Award in April had given the piece of art extra significance.

"Well," she said hesitantly after Jimmy had eaten half of his tuna salad, and looked less drawn, "what's your daughter like?" She knew how much it meant to him to have the word 'daughter' included in his personal vocabulary.

"She's lovely," he smiled. "Not quite what I'd expected. Much better than I'd expected, actually."

"And how about your grand-daughter?" Another new word in Jimmy's personal lexicon. In the brief call from Luton he'd told Julie about Daisy, and she'd immediately sensed his great excitement.

"From the pictures I was granted access to, she's lovely as well." He sighed. "I don't know what to think, Julie."

"You both have to take it in, and reflect. You can't form an opinion that quickly. Nor can she. Do you think she liked you?"

"Like is a very strong word for someone who was abandoned before her birth." He grimaced. "But I think there was a slither of warmth, towards the end of our conversation."

Julie listened, and saw his concern, and shared it. She really loved this man. For many years she hadn't had a serious relationship, and meeting Jimmy had been a radical change, a good change, and she so wanted their liaison to last. Yes, she ardently wanted that continuation.

"You must sleep now," she counselled. "And let's hope and pray that you get a positive message from Lily, when she's ready. She'll have a lot to do when she gets home, and she'll want to talk to her husband. And Emily and her husband." She wisely avoided calling them Lily's parents.

With a grunt, which was all he could manage, Jimmy acquiesced. He was flaked out. He left the kitchen, and dragged himself upstairs.

Jessie and Andrew's kitchen August 16th

Jessie and Andrew had been back from their honeymoon for one week precisely, and they were hosting four people and a baby to an evening meal. "It will be an extremely simple and cosy kitchen supper," Jessie warned her siblings. She'd invited Emily and Luke too, but they had a diary clash, so they'd now been scheduled for the following week. Jessie had the Saturday off, and Andrew was all set for his Sunday work. So they did the food preparation together, a large traybake ready to pop into the oven, and a huge apple pie to follow.

Their kitchen in the curate's house was small, but contained everything they needed. It boasted a table next to the wall, with a bench and cushions one side, and chairs the other. Next door was a larger dining table, waiting to be assembled. That exercise would be the after-supper entertainment, Archie and Xander having agreed to join Andrew in its construction.

"Apologies for a bit of a mess here, but we wanted to have you all round for a meal soon-ish. And as we're family, we know you'll understand," said Jessie confidently as she served up the traybake.

"When do you start applying for your vicar-ing job?" Archie asked Andrew.

"In six months' time. So we've got a while yet to go here. And I've still got lots to learn."

"And how was Milan?" asked Lily.

"Absolutely wonderful," smiled Jessie. She knew people thought it odd that they'd gone to a northern Italian city, rather than Venice or Florence or Rome, but she and Andrew loved art galleries and old churches, and wisely they had avoided the tourist hotspots, knowing that in high summer those would be fairly unbearable. The combination of intolerable heat and heaving crowds definitely wouldn't have been the basis for a happy honeymoon.

"Milan Cathedral is absolutely breath-taking," she continued, an almost beatific smile on her face. "Our first sight of it was in the early evening as we came out of the metro, and it was simply covered in evening light. The Gothic façade towered up before us as we climbed up the steps into daylight, a golden vision. I was totally in awe."

The others were silent, taking in her description. Daisy cooed. "I've been there with my family," said Carla. "I know exactly what you mean. It's incredible."

"When do we see the wedding photographs?" asked Xander. "Not for a good few weeks," grimaced Andrew. "They take an age. You'd think we were celebs, or vying for a slot in *Hello* magazine."

The meal over, Xander and Andrew got to work on the dining table. "Archie, do you mind if I ask some professional advice?" ventured Jessie.

"Absolutely, especially if it gets me out of table-building," replied Archie with his characteristic smile.

"Let's go into the living room," said Jessie. They left the others drinking coffee and Daisy-worshipping, and sank into sofas next door. "It's just a problem that's been growing over the last few months, and now I've had a complaint from a patient."

"Oh oh," commented Archie. "Tell me about it."

So Jessie unburdened herself. The issue was about appointments in the outpatient clinic running very late in her department, a situation which had built up gradually, and Archie could soon see what had caused it. Jessie was hugely hampered by staff not fulfilling her requests on time, in particular a couple of staff who were temporary hires. So she couldn't complete what was needed for her patients, appointments ran over time too often, and people had to wait inordinate lengths of time. Having been in similar situations, he listened sympathetically.

"Is it just you who's running late, or the other registrars too?" he asked.

"I honestly think it's me more than the others," she replied. "I tend to run over a bit anyway, probably because I'm too sympathetic, and give patients too much time to unburden themselves. But it is a problem for all of us. I personally have had a complaint because one patient had several appointments with me over an eight-week period, and each time he had to wait … two hours … for his appointment," she said rather shamefacedly. "That wasn't actually just my fault; it was a combination, but I was still to blame in a major way. And now the whole thing means committees, and bureaucracy, and me trying to justify myself to lots of people."

Jessie looked a bit outraged, but controlled herself in the interests of remaining calm at a family gathering.

"I think you need to delegate a bit more," was Archie's advice. "Don't take everything on, yourself. And you need to hurry people up when you're in a consultation. If necessary, and politely of course, cut them short if they ramble on and on and are repeating themselves."

He continued. "Don't worry about the complaint. These do happen, and as long as you're careful in how you respond, you'll be OK. Would you like to talk it over again, maybe when you have more information, I mean more documents and forms and so forth?"

Jessie was a bit resistant to Archie's advice about delegation. She'd so often asked junior doctors she was line managing, or nurses or admin staff, to do something for her, and had been let down or disappointed with the outcomes. But she could see the sense of what he was saying, and she was keen to keep to better time with her appointments. So she bit her tongue. "Thanks, Archie. I'm sure you're right about delegation. And I'd really appreciate another chat once I've heard more details about how this is being taken forward."

CHAPTER TWENTY-TWO

Matron's Office
August 2014

"'Justice will not be served until those who are unaffected are as outraged as those who are.' I'm quoting Benjamin Franklin, Emily. When we meet with Matron, we need to see that she can empathise with those residents who haven't been treated well. How would she feel if she wasn't listened to, if her requests weren't carried out, or if someone was rude to her? She needs to be outraged, like us. And like her residents. Otherwise, nothing will change."

Felicity was drinking coffee in Emily's lounge-cum-dining area-cum-kitchen, where they were discussing their action plan for a meeting with Peacehaven's matron, later that week.

"I totally agree, Felicity. So we need to be clear about what's been witnessed, and let her know that these aren't isolated cases."

"I'll also update her on the oral history project, and on the murder enquiry, of course just saying the minimum on the latter."

Luke came into the room to have his mid-morning coffee. "How is your battle plan?" he asked.

"Luke, come and join us for a minute. We'd really value your insights," said Felicity.

"My main insight is that this conversation has to happen," Luke said as he poured his drink. "I saw this kind of behaviour with my father when he was ill, and now you are seeing exactly the same. It's got to stop, and it's got to be monitored more effectively." He thought for a moment and then continued. "I think it would be good initially to let the matron know about the good care you've seen. I remember one nurse who looked after my father. I called her a "Real Nurse". Not to her face, of course. She was loving and compassionate. She was busy, but when she was with us, she gave us her attention."

"I've seen staff like that at Peacehaven," said Felicity quietly.

He walked over to where they were sitting. "I'm trying to remember what it was about Helen that stood out. She understood what we were going through. She put flesh on the skeleton of merely performing her duty. She smiled from inside. Her smile reached us, and was fuelled by concern, and made us feel secure in her care."

Luke was still standing up, and his impassioned words were taking on the form of a campaigning speech.

He paused for breath, and continued, "Other staff smiled; their smiles performed the same physiological function, but, translated, they really meant: 'I'm your nurse, but I haven't even got time to do all you need, let alone put emotion into the job.' In effect, a Real Nurse simply tries to understand how she would feel if she were in the patient's position."

They were all silent for a minute, pondering his heartfelt oratory.

"That's the sort of care the home should be aiming at," commented Emily. "I know they're frantically busy, but I wonder if they ever have training sessions."

"I could give one," smiled Luke. "Now I keep remembering things from when my father was in hospital. They told him in the first hospital that he would be put into a specialist stroke unit in the next one, and my mother and I were looking forward to that specialist care. But when he got to the hospital, he was told that the unit was just for under-sixty-fives. Why didn't the doctor who misinformed us know his facts? Sadly I can recall one bit of misinformation after another during that period."

"It must be distressing to remember it," said Felicity.

Luke nodded. "Distressing, but it also brings back my righteous anger," he smiled. "Broken promises also used to upset us. My father was suffering greatly, so we wanted to do all we could to uplift him. Once I asked the staff to put on a favourite TV programme for him that evening. He couldn't even operate the remote control himself. But when I got to the hospital the next day it hadn't happened, because the staff were too busy. When I expressed my disappointment, I was reprimanded and told in no uncertain terms that there were many other patients with needs. So my expectations of patient care had been too high!"

He sighed atypically. "And I could go on, and on, and on. But I'll shut up now. I really hope you have a useful meeting with the matron." Luke picked up his coffee, wished them well, and disappeared upstairs.

"That's all truly terrible," said Felicity thoughtfully. "And this is why we must stand up for the residents at Peacehaven, Emily. So that they get the best possible care, emotionally and socially, as well as physically."

"It really upset Luke," said Emily. "His mother wasn't well, and yet she had to deal with the situation. He was a great support to her. He got so frustrated that he eventually wrote a long piece about his experiences. I think he was hoping it might be published. It never was. But he did pass it on to a local lecturer in nursing, who regularly read extracts to her students, and apparently they were very affected by what Luke had written. So his account did serve a purpose."

"From what Luke has just told us, and from what we've witnessed, I could sum it up fairly simply. Staff need to listen well, to deliver promptly, to action what they've promised, to give accurate information, to apologise if things get messed up, and try to understand their client's perspective. And to be polite," was Felicity's verdict. "And I meant it when I said 'client.' As Alice said, these people are paying good money for their care."

The two friends spent another fifteen minutes finalising what Luke had called their battle plan, before each had to leave for work commitments.

***

Matron's office overlooked the garden. The room was bright and spacious, enabling her to host meetings. Her desk was mostly clear, housing the usual administrative items and also, surprisingly, a pair of blue rubber gloves, prominently displayed. Emily wasn't sure if their presence was deliberate, to show literally how 'hands-on' she was, or an oversight. On the walls were a certificate (presumably hers), a couple of inspiring pictures, and smaller framed items that looked like health regulations. The room was clean and polished, with bright curtains, and a blind to deal with glare.

Emily and Felicity sat opposite her, with cups of tea in front of them, and a plate of assorted biscuits.

"Thanks for coming to see me, Ms Wheeler," said Matron. "And you, Mrs Wentworth. I'm so grateful for the work you've done in encouraging our residents to talk about their lives. It's a fascinating project."

"We now have ten accounts," said Felicity, her face lighting up with enthusiasm. "They read very well. Everyone was happy to supply a picture, and they've all approved the drafts. I'd like ideally to have twenty accounts, which would make for a splendid publication."

"I'm so pleased," replied Matron. "And I hope it might be a model for other homes."

"Yes, that's our hope too. Thank you for making it possible."

There was a slight pause. Matron smiled at them both.

"There are two other items we wanted to discuss," ventured Felicity. "The first was simply to let you know that the police are continuing their enquiries about the case Pauline told us about. They are being scrupulous in their work, and I'm confident that they'll let us know when their search can be made more public. I'm sorry I can't tell you much more, other than to say that you will be informed."

"What a terrible case," said Matron, who knew that a murder had been reported, but nothing more. She was the only staff member who'd been told. "It must be hard for Pauline. I've been to see her, to check that she's OK."

"She seems fine," replied Felicity, thinking to herself that Pauline actually seemed to be thriving on the whole story and its exposure.

"The other item is a concern we have," she continued. She could see Matron's expression changing. Inside Felicity felt terrible. She knew that her comments would be upsetting, and might even provoke anger, hidden anger, but anger nevertheless. What she was about to say was a criticism of the home. Emily felt apprehensive too, yet totally justified in what was about to be reported.

"I think you know that Alice, my daughter, has been working here some evenings, during her school holidays. She's really enjoyed getting to know the staff and some of the residents." Felicity deliberately mentioned the staff ahead of residents. "She's been very impressed with the care she's seen."

"We have some outstanding staff here," said Matron.

"But I have to tell you that she's also seen some worrying behaviour. And during my brief visits, I'm afraid to say that I have, too." That was it. She'd spoken the damning words.

"Oh," said Matron, now without any trace of a smile. "What was that?"

"Both Alice and I have heard staff being rude to residents, ordering them around, using inappropriate, even crude, bodily language, and being impatient. They also sometimes use pet names."

"Our staff have very high standards," commented Matron calmly but firmly. "I am surprised to hear what you say."

"I am telling you what I've heard and seen. And Alice too. I was surprised myself when Alice told me some of what she'd seen. She was very concerned, so concerned that she's made a few notes." Felicity took Alice's notebook out of her bag. She had already copied all of the content, before bringing it in to hand to Matron. "Alice is on holiday at the moment. Otherwise I know she would have been happy to come and talk to you."

Matron took the book and flicked through it casually, alighting on the odd sentence as she did so. "I can't read all of this during our meeting," she said. "I will look at it tonight."

There was a knock at the door. "Come in!" said Matron. A staff member put her head round the door.

"Oh sorry, I didn't realise you were in a meeting."

"Is it urgent, Margaret?" asked Matron.

"No, no, it can wait." Margaret hastily retreated, and Matron returned to their conversation.

"Our point is," said Emily, speaking for the first time, "that we are both extremely concerned about the fact that some staff here don't treat their clients as they should. The people who live here," she continued in a clear voice, "are frail and vulnerable. Many of them can't speak for themselves. They trust the home to look after them. They are paying for this care. And they deserve to be treated fairly."

"Have you personally seen any of the poor care which Ms Wheeler has just outlined?" asked Matron, her tone a degree sharper.

"No, but I totally believe her, and her daughter. And my husband is a lawyer, just like Ms Wheeler. We would like to see justice done."

Felicity wondered if Emily had gone a bit too far. She was hoping to introduce the lawyer card, if necessary, at a later stage. They didn't want to sound threatening. "I think that when you read these notes, Mrs Walker, you'll not only be surprised, but shocked. I'm sorry to come to you with this distressing news, but we couldn't keep silent. For the sake of the people involved."

Matron was momentarily silent. Then she said, "I appreciate that you've brought your concerns to me. I've heard what you say, and I will read the notebook. I'd also like to have names of staff and residents involved in these cases. Do you think you could send that information to me?"

"Yes, of course. I can do that tonight," said Felicity.

"Thank you." Matron smiled tepidly. "Was there anything else you wanted to mention?"

"Only that we've appreciated your time today, and that we look forward to talking further. Thanks too for the tea," said Felicity.

"Yes, I'll be back in touch. Good to see you both." With that, Matron shook their hands politely, as they closed the conversation.

Felicity and Emily signed out, headed for Emily's car, and drove back to Felicity's house to regroup.

***

"I'm sorry I made the legal threat," volunteered Emily as they drove away.

"It doesn't matter. It was probably good that you did. She needed to be convinced that we were serious about the situation."

"I see there's a missed call on my phone," continued Felicity. "It's the police. I'd better take it when I get home."

"Shall we discuss all of this at a later date?"

"Yes, let's arrange a time when we can both focus on it, and if I hear from Matron before then, I'll be sure to let you know."

Felicity rang the police as soon as she got into the house. She appreciated how conscientious they had been in keeping her updated. But this time they had all the news needed, to complete the saga. She was riveted.

To the utter amazement of the police working on the case, some of the murder victim's clothing had been retained from his death ten years previously. *You see that happening on a crime series on the screen, but I didn't realise it actually happened in reality,* thought Felicity. DNA tests had now been carried out on the clothing and the investigators weren't particularly surprised to find that the residue matched Billy's DNA. So Billy had since been charged, and was in custody awaiting trial. As well as DNA evidence, they had the signed statement from his friend Philip, and Pauline's account.

"So justice has been done," she commented. "But how ghastly for Timmy's family."

"Yes," said the detective leading the case. "Obviously this has brought all the trauma back to them. Not that it had ever totally left them. But this has revived the deep pain. They are very grateful to you for your help in making this possible. And grateful to Pauline, though less so to her, because they blame her for not speaking earlier. And for allowing Billy to roam free when he should have been locked up for murdering their son."

"It's really terrible," said Felicity, suddenly feeling that right at the moment, her whole life was surrounded by horrendous incidents.

"Sadly Timmy's mother has died. But his father and two brothers would very much like to meet you. And your daughter, if you would be happy to do that. They'd like to thank you."

"We would be honoured to do that. Please do arrange a meeting. And thank you for all your work on this, too. I guess this news is now public?'

The detective confirmed what Felicity thought, and agreed that Pauline and other relevant people might be informed. *Something to put us back in Matron's favour,* she thought.

***

Emily and Lily were sitting in Lily's beautiful drawing room, enjoying the light August evening. It wasn't quite warm enough to sit outside. They were drinking white wine. "Soft drinks not appropriate. It needs to be this strong, to reflect the situation," said Lily.

How to sum up to her mother, the encounter from the beginning of the week? Lily still wasn't sure how she felt about the meeting with Jimmy. And it was awkward, this new triangle comprising her mother, Jimmy, and herself. It almost felt like a new family. She was only just getting used to her new family with Archie and Daisy. Her family up until now had always been Emily, Luke, Jessie, Xander, and herself. She didn't like the way this new situation ignored Luke. It almost deleted him. He was left outside the circle, irrelevant.

"I'm glad I met him, Mum," she began. "A puzzle has been solved, and that's given me some peace."

A faint smile appeared on both faces. A smile of understanding from Emily, and of relief from Lily.

"I quite liked him."

"Quite?"

"Well to be honest I went to that meeting expecting not to like him at all. Because of Dad. I don't want to be unfair to Dad. But taken as a short meeting, it was fine. He's courteous, intelligent, has a warm smile, and is into art. He's also sorry for the past. It takes a huge 'sorry' to make up for it, but he seemed genuinely remorseful."

"I agree," said Emily gently. "He was full of apologies when I met him. He was quite emotional."

"So I've told him I need to think about it for a while. And to talk to you and Archie. And to Dad."

"That seems very sensible."

"So that's it, really. He told me a bit about himself, about his work, about Julie, his partner. And I told him about the gallery, Archie and Daisy. And Dad and Jessie and Xander."

"I'm glad you've met, darling." Emily felt very emotional. This was a horribly unsettled chapter in all of their lives, and she wanted it to calm down. Soon.

"One thing I wanted to tell you," she continued, looking at her daughter's lovely face, "He has been in touch with me to request a phone call. Not a meeting. So I've agreed to that. I'll let you know what he says."

"Hopefully to congratulate you on a great daughter!" For the first time in a while, Lily laughed.

"That should definitely be why he wants to speak to me!" Emily laughed too. They chatted for another thirty minutes before Emily wended her way home.

***

Matron was weary. It had been a full day, starting at eight o'clock when she'd arrived at work to discover the plumber was hard at work in one of the *en-suite* bathrooms where a toilet was leaking. Lunchtime hadn't happened thanks to various meetings with staff, an appointment with a local councillor, followed by interviews for a vacant staff post, and general administration for the home. Then there had been the difficult meeting with Ms Wheeler and Mrs Wentworth.

It was six o'clock, and thankfully Reception was now closed. On her desk was a tray with a teapot, cup and saucer, jug of milk, and an inviting plate of sandwiches garnished with crisps and bits of salad. It was wonderfully quiet. The gardener had finished his work for the day. The kitchen staff had almost completed their clearing-up after the residents' tea. If she wished, she could go home. But she didn't plan to do that just yet. Alice's notebook glared at her from the desk. Of course she wasn't happy to hear what Felicity had reported. And she suspected she knew who the culprits were. Some difficult conversations beckoned, she was sure.

The phone on Matron's desk rang. She ignored it. She opened Alice's notebook and began reading.

CHAPTER TWENTY-THREE

Local Sports Club
Late August 2014

It was Friday. Lily was enjoying her walk to the sports club. Due to meet Emily and Luke for a hot drink after her ten o'clock swim, she had time on her hands, and was having a leisurely stroll through Waterlow Park, pushing Daisy. She loved that this park had been given by nineteenth century Lord Mayor Sir Sidney Waterlow as a "garden for the gardenless." *There are so many people in that category,* she thought, *now that apartments and high rises proliferate. What a beautiful gift.* It was a clear sunny day, not cold but the air was fresh, and there was a very un-British deep blue sky. *Carla would call this an Italian sky,* she mused.

Lily stopped by the lake. She admired the deep green willows diving down, nearly touching the water. She gazed at the rounded shrubs at the edge of the lake. There were a few ducks bobbing on the surface, and a curious object that looked rather like a wooden door, floating along. She sat down for a moment on a long bench. Unusually, there wasn't anyone else around. Daisy was enjoying a deep sleep, and the sun was still shining. Lily relaxed, and had a sensation of deep peace as she absorbed the scene. It was health-giving and profoundly therapeutic. For a brief interlude, this was a picture, frozen in time; at this precise moment it was hers alone, a gift, just as the park had been to Londoners years before. She breathed in deeply, and savoured it. And utterly exhausted from broken nights, Lily almost fell asleep, Daisy-like.

But after a few minutes she roused herself, and went on her way in the direction of what was the main sports club in Archway. Fourteen minutes later, she had arrived, and was heading for the crèche. The interlude in the park had passed but almost magically, it had filled her soul. "Hello Daisy!" said the crèche manager, noting that the little girl was just waking up. Lily knew Cheryl well, and was confident that Daisy would be in excellent hands for thirty minutes or so while she did her regular lengths. Sometimes they came to the club for Daisy swimming, which meant that Lily couldn't swim at all, but there were days like today when she had a brief period on her own, indulging in some welcome exercise.

Emily and Luke arrived at half past ten, and made straight for the coffee area. Lily joined them fifteen minutes later, looking refreshed, with almost-dry hair. "I'm going to pick Daisy up after our coffee," she announced. "I wanted to talk to you both alone. About Jimmy."

The café looked out on the pool, where a group of parents and small children were gathering for a lesson. The two Wentworths and one ex-Wentworth sat on primary-coloured chairs, in front of a round white table, and sipped their individual drinks, each one subtly different, Emily's an americano, Luke drinking a cappuccino, while Lily cradled a latte. There weren't many customers in the café; Emily imagined that it would fill up after the swimming class. And school holidays were very hit-and-miss. Sometimes the centre was extremely busy, and at other times it felt almost peaceful.

"So what did you want to say?" asked Luke pleasantly, albeit inwardly semi-dreading what Lily was going to tell them.

"Just a minute," she said, looking around the room, and standing up. "Could you two have a conversation for a minute, not a terribly loud one, and I'm just going to saunter to the end of the room to see how audible it is." Feeling slightly foolish, Luke and Emily duly obliged.

There was only one other person in the café, a middle-aged man in a jacket staring into space, four tables away from them. Lily came back looking relieved. "It's OK," she said. "I could only hear mumbling from you, and nothing I could really understand. Thanks!"

Her parents smiled at her. "Hopefully no-one will come and sit right beside us," commented Emily, thinking that Lily hadn't chosen the best of venues for a private conversation.

"OK, so I've had a good think about my meeting with Jimmy," continued Lily, pushing her hair behind her ears. "And I've talked with Archie, and both of you. I've talked to Daisy too." Further smiles from her parents. "She's relevant, you know. Daisy is part of this. She can't ask questions now, but I suspect she'll be a major interrogator when she's older." Emily frowned, feeling this was all her fault for imposing this quandary upon her grand-daughter, and on other potential future grand-children, as well as on her daughter.

"My heart is with you, both of you. You have been my life, all I've known, until now. Apart from Archie and Daisy of course, but they are fairly recent. You are my mother and father, and there's no changing that."

Luke was quite moved, but was determined not to show it.

"But Jimmy has come into our life now, and that affects us all. I did quite like him when we met. We had a few things in common, professional things. But I wasn't sure if my impression was genuine, or if he was on his best behaviour especially for our meeting."

Emily and Luke listened intently. The man in the jacket continued to stare into space, giving no indication that he'd even noticed the trio sitting four tables away.

"So I've made a few enquiries in the art world. You'd be amazed how incestuous it is. It's a huge buddy network. Most people are only two connections away. So I spoke with a couple of people in art publications, who know Jimmy, and who have worked with him."

Luke held his breath, praying that Jimmy wouldn't emerge as a paragon, a wonderful person with multiple good qualities. Emily was sort of hoping the same, though because she and Jimmy had had a relationship, she didn't want him to turn out to be an utter rogue either.

"I know you think of him as the usurper, Dad," she teased. Luke jumped, almost physically. How could Lily so accurately have guessed his thoughts? He gave a half-smile.

"It turns out he's fairly well respected by colleagues. I didn't get any negative vibes. And they didn't have a clue why I was asking. So that's all on the plus side."

Her parents didn't say anything. They were waiting for the crunch point.

"What I think is that I must be fair to Jimmy, as well as fair to you. There's no denying that I am his biological daughter. And I know he wants to get to know me." She sighed gently. "What I'm thinking of proposing to him is that we meet up twice a year, no more, just to have a chat, possibly to spend a day together. I'm not sure about longer than that at the moment; when you spend more than a day with someone, that gets a bit deeper into a relationship." She paused. "I'm also not sure about Daisy, and whether or when to introduce her into the equation. I simply can't make that decision at the moment."

"That all sounds very fair," said Emily.

"And I will call him 'Jimmy', and I will call you 'Dad'," she said to Luke. "You have acted as a father, all my life."

"Thank you," he said. It was as much as he could say without losing it.

"And in order to suggest this way forward for the future, I need first to forgive Jimmy, really forgive him, for what he did when he abandoned you, Mum." Lily now had tears in her eyes. The man in the jacket got up and left the room. An unrelated action, thought Luke, trying a spot of dry humour to keep himself in check.

"That won't be a two-minute thing. I will have to make myself forgive him each time I see him."

"We'll have to do it together," said Emily, her eyes also moist.

"What do you think, Dad?" asked Lily.

"I think," began Luke, speaking carefully and quite slowly, "that you are a very mature and wise young woman, and I admire you for what you've just said. I hope I don't sound presumptuous or intrusive, but I'd like simply to say that you have my blessing to go ahead as you suggest."

"And mine," Emily quickly added. She continued, "You know that Jimmy wanted to speak to me on the phone? Well, he rang a couple of days ago."

"What did he say, Mum? That I was a beautiful and impressive daughter?!"

"Well you're almost right. He did say how much he was totally blown away by you. And yes, all the rest which you've just complimented yourself on. But the other reason for his call was simply to say 'Thank you' to Dad and me for bringing you up so impressively – his exact wording. I was quite touched. He said that he knew he had no right to call you his daughter, but he did hope that he might maybe have five percent of you."

Then Lily cried. She wept little tears of relief, of love, and of the beginnings of forgiveness.

***

Lily had some shopping to do after the intense conversation with her parents, and Emily and Luke were delighted to be tasked with collecting Daisy from the crèche, and amusing her for three-quarters of an hour before her next feed. They'd brought some baby toys and books with them. They contented themselves with baby talk, not wishing to discuss the forward plan for Jimmy for the moment. Daisy was just starting to ask for food, when thankfully Lily appeared; she had begun making little noises in baby language which made Emily and Luke particularly eager to see her mother. With Lily back, her parents each made use of the club, Emily in the gym before a quick swim, and Luke deploying the gym more seriously, using virtually the full range of equipment, and pushing himself as far as was sensible. He wanted to move up a few kilos with the weights, and spend longer on the cross-trainer, and as usual he was competitive on the rowing machine, vying with others to achieve the fastest stretch and pull.

Bodies refreshed yet minds in overdrive, the couple set off in their car in the early afternoon.

"What do you make of Lily's speech to us?" asked Emily.

"I'm still taking it in," said Luke, as he navigated the London traffic, "But my main sense is quiet relief. She's made her peace with us all, with you, Jimmy, and me. She's talked to Archie." He smiled, "And Daisy."

He slowed down for a cyclist who was unnervingly veering in and out of a cycle lane. "And she's also worked out a way forward. Very sensible. How do you feel about it, love?"

"Like you, relieved, but also a bit tentative. How will this work in practice? Will Jimmy be an annoying extra in our lives forever? And will he start to encroach more and more?"

"I think," said Luke, turning down the heating as they waited at a red light, "I think that he will certainly be a presence, but not an obtrusive one. We mustn't worry about him. In some ways he may fill the gap on Archie's side where there is only Fiona, and no grandfather. We must leave it up to Lily and him, and not worry." He almost emphasised the words 'not worry' but aware of Emily's deeper involvement, decided not to be too prescriptive.

Emily reflected inwardly on how the future might be; this was literally her baby and the issue was never far from her mind. Sitting next to her, by contrast Luke was experiencing the most wonderful physical sensation of refreshment, akin to stepping out of a long soak in a warm bath, cleansed and free, joyful with the sheer relief that his fatherly role in Lily's life was secure. They continued the journey in companionable silence.

Back home, Emily's mind turned to her other daughter. Invigorated by her exercise and swim, Emily recalled Jessie's plan to have a girls' spa day. *I must remind her,* she thought. *It would be a great bonding time for us all.*

The memory spurred her on to ring Jessie that evening. "How are you?" she opened the conversation. "And are you free to speak at the moment?"

"Yes, it's fine. I'm just sitting down with a book, and Andrew's in the study. How are you, Mum?"

They chatted for a few minutes, and Emily revived the spa idea. "It had totally slipped my mind. Sorry! Yes, I'll contact Lily and Carla, and try to find a date that works for us all," said Jessie.

"I've actually had a lot on my mind with work," her daughter continued. "I've talked to Archie about it a bit, and he was helpful. I had a complaint from a patient."

"But I don't really want to talk in depth about it," she added, forestalling questions from her mother.

"I'm so sorry," said Emily. "And just after your wedding."

"Actually all around my wedding, a few weeks before and several weeks afterwards," said Jessie philosophically. "But I think it will be OK. I just need to be careful what I say and what I write, to conclude matters."

"It's really useful having another doctor, a more senior doctor, in the family," she admitted.

"I won't mention it to Dad. And try not to worry about it. Thank goodness for Archie. He's very sensible."

With promises to be in touch, they finished the call. Emily was restless. The conversation with Lily, her call with Jessie, and various work issues, all collided in her mind, and wouldn't leave her. Fortunately, her phone rang, and it came as a welcome distraction. It was Nicola, Ben's wife, who she hadn't heard from since their last dinner together.

"Emily, would you like to meet over a coffee? I thought of the sports club in Archway; I go there a lot for a swim. Are you free next week? I think you have Fridays off. And I'm off all next week. How about a week today, mid-morning? We could meet after my swim."

***

This was becoming a habit, thought Emily as she crossed the threshold of the sports club, though a pleasant habit. She decided to have a swim after the meeting with Nicola, and not before. She knew her uncooperative hair, with its challenging chin-length bob, would be a terrible sight after a few lengths in the pool, and she preferred to look vaguely groomed when meeting up with her new friend. Because, despite the slight awkwardness she'd felt at the last meal with Ben and Nicola, she did count her as a friend, or rather, as a potential friend.

Nicola appeared at the table in the café, her dark pixie cut just about dry, wearing a smart tracksuit and trainers. "Hello, Emily!" They exchanged a quick hug, and Nicola, having insisted, went to buy drinks and an indulgent cookie. The café was much busier than before, a mix of retirees, young mothers, and others. Emily slotted herself into the latter category.

"It's great to see you," said Nicola, returning with two coffees and two huge chocolate cookies. "I'm rewarding myself with this indulgence after fifty lengths, and I'm rewarding you before your long session in the gym."

Emily acknowledged the rewards with a chuckle. "Thanks; very kind of you. And how are you, Nicola? And how's work?"

"Well, I actually have some big news. I've been appointed Pro-Vice-Chancellor for Research and Enterprise at the University. It's a huge honour and also a huge challenge, but I'm really excited."

"Congratulations! What wonderful news. I had actually half heard that this might be on the cards. When do you start?"

"Not until the spring term, early January. So I have time to prepare myself, and catch my breath."

"What will it involve? It sounds a fascinating opportunity."

"It's quite a mix of areas, but it'll let me use skills I've built up over the years, covering research and business within academia. And I'll probably also be monitoring issues like inclusions and regulatory compliance. It will be hard work, but I think I'm up for it." Nicola looked excited, and confidently so.

"I'm really pleased for you."

They chatted about this and that, and Emily asked how Johanna was.

"Working hard, but also rather hoping that there might be an opening for her at Luke's old firm. Did you know about that?" said Nicola.

"Well again, I had heard a whisper. How likely is it?"

"I'm not absolutely sure. She's had a couple of interviews there, and she's met Felicity, who she really admires. But if it doesn't work out, she'll be quite happy to stay where she is. She's got a good associate position."

"Please let us know how it goes. Fingers crossed."

Nicola hesitated. She looked thoughtful. "I hope you don't mind me asking, but after our evening together, I mean with Ben and Luke, I wondered if we'd upset you in any way?" she said tentatively.

"Why did you think that?" Emily spoke cautiously.

"I'm not sure. It was just a feeling I had. Sorry to be so vague, and I have no desire to pry. I just wanted to say that I'd love to know if we, or if I, have done something to upset you both."

Emily thought for a moment. "I don't mind you asking. I really don't. I think you're right, that there was something amiss, but it's definitely not something which either of you did. Please don't think that." She paused. "To be honest, I have a weird sense that it's Claire who's affecting the vibes between the four of us. I don't mean a ghost. I don't believe in people reappearing after they've died. It's just, like you, I had a vague feeling which was unsettling. A sort of shadow over us."

"I guess that Luke is very shocked to have heard of Claire's death," said Nicola. "And I suspect that seeing Ben brings it all back to him. I know that Luke and Claire's relationship was over. But there's still shock, suddenly to hear that someone you were close to, has died, and that any relationship you had with that person is now totally terminated."

"Forever," she added slowly, looking very solemn.

Emily was reminded of something her mother used to speak of, something she'd read, and which had made a profound impression. It was the concept of the educated heart, a quality not possessed by all. Emily didn't know if it was innate, or could be acquired or learned. Nicola seemed to have that attribute, an ability to understand, and to connect.

"Yes, it upset him a lot," replied Emily.

"I don't talk about it very much, but I lost a boyfriend twenty years ago, in a car accident, and I sort of understand how Luke feels. Not completely of course. No two losses are ever the same. But I will never forget remember the horrible shock. For Ben of course it's hugely painful, but it's pain that was at its most acute ten, nine, eight years ago. For Luke I guess the pain is quite raw."

A raucous group laugh sounded from the other side of the room. Emily was silent for a while. Why were her past relationships, and Luke's past relationships, all being resuscitated at the moment?

"I'm so sorry to hear about your loss in the past, Nicola. It must have been terrible. I actually think the shock about Claire is waning a bit now. And it's more the shock of someone having died, rather than the loss of a relationship; that had already happened. The additional sensitivity for me is that when we first met, I reminded Luke a lot of Claire. And so that's a strange factor in all of this."

"Well, one thing you and I have in common is that we never met Claire," commented Nicola wisely. "I think it would be good if you and I met separately from the men, for the time being. I actually think—and this sounds horribly cruel—but I think that both Ben and Luke should consign Claire to history." Nicola looked pensive, and frowned. "That sounds heartless. But Claire, who sounds to have been a lovely person, definitely wouldn't have wanted her memory to have clouded several people's lives. She should be a treasured memory, and for Johanna too, an inspiration, but not a shadow. Definitely not a shadow."

"I absolutely agree, Nicola. You never spoke a wiser word. Let's hope the men do what you suggest. And actually to be honest, we've had a different crisis to deal with these last few weeks, and Luke's been very stressed with that. I'm afraid it's not something I can share. It's just a bit delicate."

Nicola looked at her friend; her gaze was direct, but warm. "Emily, I'm so sorry to hear that you've had something else to deal with. And I understand that you can't tell me about it. Why do things happen all at the same time? Please don't bother mentioning what I said, to Luke, unless you feel it would be useful."

"Thanks. I appreciate your sensitivity."

"Shall we meet again, and do something relaxing to try to alleviate some of this stress?"

"That sounds a good idea."

"Do you like art galleries?"

"Nicola, that would be great. Yes, let's do an art gallery and lunch together. It would be fun to look forward to." Emily's initial feelings that she liked Nicola were reinforced. She enjoyed her company, and was grateful that she had tried to be helpful.

"And Luke would love to see Ben again. Maybe they could go to the cricket."

They parted, and Emily lost herself in gym work. For a moment she wondered why she'd had two very deep conversations at a sports club. A venue with leisure and relaxation as its aim didn't really fit with stress and sad memories. Then she focussed on her workout. She used the treadmill energetically, then the rowing machine, cross-trainer, exercise bike, and finished off with weights. An hour's intensive work did the trick. By the time Emily had finished, and had a shower, she felt much less stressed, and definitively more philosophical about everything.

CHAPTER TWENTY-FOUR

Visitors' Room, Luke's Old Law Firm
Early September 2014

Luke had spent most of the morning at Lily's gallery, relieving the maternity-leave staff member who wasn't due to start work today until midday. Thursday was their late opening day. Lucinda would be on duty until eight o'clock, and from six o'clock onwards there would be drinks and canapés to introduce the new exhibition. Luke hoped to pop along for an hour to the reception, together with Lily, who was gradually easing herself back into work. He was enjoying using his self-confessed paltry knowledge of art to help customers, while also adding to what little expertise he had. It had been a fairly quiet morning, though one eager customer had been delighted to find the doors open at nine o'clock.

"Most shops don't open until ten," he commented. "Some customers like to be out and about earlier than that." The man, who Luke guessed was in his mid-fifties, showed some interest in a watercolour landscape, and indicated he might return to buy it once he'd mulled it over a little more.

At eleven-thirty, Luke's phone rang. Surprised, he noticed it was Rachel, his PA from the law firm. "Hello Rachel, how are you?" he said into his phone, having first checked that the gallery was empty.

"Luke, we've got a bit of a problem here, and without beating about the bush, you're the only one who can help. Are you able to come in today? Even quite soon? I'm really sorry to bother you."

Luke had a quick think. Apart from personal plans like exercise and e-mailing, he didn't have any appointments until the exhibition in the evening. "Yes, I could be with you within the hour. I'm in charge at Lily's gallery until twelve, but I can grab a taxi then."

It felt strange walking into the firm again, four months on, but Luke was confirmed in his decision to retire. It felt absolutely right, and he had no regrets. He was enjoying the temporary rest from all responsibilities, and planned to take up a couple of advisory roles into the autumn.

Rachel came down to meet him. "I've booked a meeting room for you, the small visitors' room on the sixth floor," she said. "It's so good to see you. I didn't know what to do, so I'm really glad you could come in today. I've arranged a tea tray," she said. "Have you had any lunch? Would you like sandwiches?"

"I'm fine, thanks," said Luke. "I don't expect to be here long, and I'll grab lunch at home."

She showed him into the visitors' room. Basically, it was a fully glazed cube, with dizzying views down to the ground floor and entrance, and dazzling views up to the twenty-fifth floor of the building. But it was a very glitzy and impressive glazed cube, with its square marble desk, four leather chairs, deep beige carpet, coffee and tea-making facilities, and smart lighting. Luke didn't sit down immediately; instead he stood gazing down and then up, watching the escalators, and the mix of people, mostly in business attire, and some with laptop cases or briefcases.

The door opened and someone he didn't recognise, a young girl with long wavy hair and glasses, came in with a tea tray.

"Hello," he said, "I don't think we've met."

"I'm Rupika," she smiled. "I started work here two months ago."

"I'm a retired partner, Luke Wentworth. Nice to meet you."

"Yes, I've heard of you," she said warmly. "I'll bring your visitor in shortly."

Luke waited, bemused. So he had a visitor? Who wanted to see him, and so urgently?

He didn't have to wait long. Rupika was back promptly, ushering in a woman who looked vaguely familiar. "I'll leave you alone," Rupika said, closing the door.

Luke looked at the woman again, and immediately felt very peculiar indeed. He felt the way he'd done when he'd heard of his mother's sudden death, and of how he'd felt when he heard that Claire was dead, a bit too like the shock of hearing that Jimmy had resurfaced in their life. He wondered for a moment if he was actually in a real situation. He sat down, and so did the woman, unbidden. "Is it....are you...?" he said in a low voice.

"I had to see you, Mr Wentworth and not your successor," said Sophie. For Sophie it was, Sophie who had been buried in Paris in

March, Sophie who had disappeared in October of last year. She was here, now, sitting in this room. Completely alive.

"Madame Duval, this must sound very odd, but the truth is, I thought you had ... died," he managed to get out, speaking slowly, still feeling very odd, and also feeling slightly rude, or as if making an accusation.

She looked at him quite calmly but in a puzzled way. "I don't understand," she said. "I am alive. I am here. Why did you think I was dead?"

He rang for Rupika, or Rachel, or anyone who could bring some strong coffee. He was suddenly feeling unusually cold, and needed warmth, as well as caffeine.

You must collect yourself, Luke, he told himself, gripping his chair as hard as he could. *There must be a perfectly rational explanation. You are a lawyer, a professional. Deal with this.*

"You disappeared eleven months ago," he began, his thoughts shooting out in all directions. "In March this year a body was found, someone who'd been killed in a road accident, near Paris. That body was identified as you."

"By whom?" asked Sophie grammatically.

"By Philippe, and by your sister."

"I don't have a sister," said Sophie, frowning.

Luke felt peculiar again. The situation was getting more problematic by the moment. And it still felt awfully dreamlike.

"Before we go any further," he said. "Please can you tell me where you have been for the last eleven months? In detail," he added.

Unlike Luke, Sophie, despite having just been told that she was dead, looked perfectly composed. Luke remembered that he'd never seen her express any emotion. She recounted her story. After the meeting with him in his holiday home in October, she had been perfectly all right for twenty-four hours, but then she had had a recurrence of the deep depression which often dogged her. She was desperate, not knowing who to contact, or what to do. Luke suspected that Sophie didn't have many friends and from what little she'd told him of her children, she sadly didn't seem close to them.

In the end she hastily packed a bag, and called a taxi, which took her to a convent in a village outside the city. She had had a vague contact there, and was taken in and looked after very well for a month. But the nuns were worried about her, and they transferred her to a hospital. Luke suspected it was a psychiatric hospital, but Sophie didn't give it a name.

"I was in that hospital for ten months," she said in a matter-of-fact way. "I forbade them to contact any of my family or friends. I said that if they did, I would leave. I simply didn't want to see anyone. I had a terrible time, fighting the horrible depression, and wondering if I would ever recover. And then after a long time they said that I was better. I felt better too. They said I could go home. But I didn't want to go back to Paris. I didn't want to stay in France. I wanted to be back in England. And I wanted to know what had happened about our house in Paris. So I came straight here."

"Why haven't you been in touch with your children, Madame Duval?"

Sophie was silent for a moment, staring at Luke with a very confident expression on her face. "They aren't the most important people in my life, Mr Wentworth. I have finished with my life in France. I am in England now, and intend to stay here. I am staying with a friend from years back, who agreed to host me for a few weeks. I have no relatives over here, just a few old friends."

She added, "But I can't access my bank account, and my phone had stopped working. So the nuns, who kept in touch with me, lent me some money, and gave me a phone. Otherwise I would have been lost. I flew to London yesterday."

Luke did a rapid, non-medical assessment of his former client. She seemed quite calm, and in control. She actually seemed a little brighter than when he'd last seen her. The dramatic news about her fictional demise hadn't fazed her.

The coffee arrived, and Luke was extremely glad to see it. "Do you think I could have some sandwiches?" he asked Rupika. "Sorry to ask another favour, but I'll be staying here longer than anticipated. Sandwiches for two, please." He added, "Is Felicity free for a quick call?"

"Of course. I'll get back to you," said Rupika.

"Madame Duval," he continued. "I'm sorry to inform you that the house has now been sold, and the proceeds transferred to your ex-husband, Philippe. It was all completed at the end of July." He continued, "It seems that a gross miscarriage of justice has been done, and a great deal, a huge amount needs to be sorted out." He wanted Sophie to be in no doubt about the serious nature of the situation.

"A miscarriage of justice indeed," said Sophie clearly. "I suspect the involvement of my ex-husband. I am perplexed at how it has all happened."

Felicity had a packed diary of appointments that afternoon, but instantly understood the gravity of the situation. She instructed a paralegal colleague to offer to her next clients, either a meeting with him as an initial note-taking process, or else to meet with her the following week. She handed another appointment to a junior colleague who had a cancellation. Then she met with Luke and Sophie in her room, all drinking strong coffee.

"I'm glad you came to see us, Madame Duval," she said. "This is very serious, and we need to find out exactly what has happened, and who is responsible. I'm going to ring Dominique, the French lawyer, now."

Luke and Sophie sat in the room, Luke still feeling everything was quite unreal. For one thing it felt quite odd to sit on the opposite side of what he still thought of as his desk. And the series of events seemed nothing short of a fantasy tale. Felicity, whose French wasn't good, was conducting the whole conversation with Dominique in English. Although they were the other side of the desk, Luke and Sophie could hear Dominique's screeches fairly clearly. Felicity held the phone away from her ear when the astonished sounds, and what sounded to Luke's ears like expletives, reached crescendo pitch. Every so often Felicity consulted with the other two to clarify facts. After fifteen minutes she finished the call.

"Dominique is going to get in touch with the police," said Felicity. "She'll update us very soon. She doesn't understand what has happened, though she suspects some foul play on Philippe's part. Who, for example, was the woman who claimed to be your sister? And, even more mysterious and also worrying, who was the dead woman who was buried as you?" she said, looking at Sophie. "I'm sorry it's so distressing. I'd like you to sign a statement containing all that you've told us this afternoon. And Luke, if you don't mind, please could you do the same?"

Luke nodded his assent.

"I am fine," said Sophie. "I haven't been dead before. It's ever so slightly amusing." The others looked surprised at her composed demeanour. "But I would like my money. As soon as possible."

"Can we call you a taxi?" suggested Luke to his ex-client. "Felicity will update you as soon as she can. In the meantime I suggest you stay with your friend, and keep all of this completely confidential. For the moment."

"Thank you. Yes, a taxi would be very welcome. And I look forward to seeing you again, Mr Wentworth. Thank you for your help this afternoon. It's been very informative."

"You won't be seeing me," Luke informed her. "Felicity will be handling your case now. But she will let me know what happens. I wish you all the very best."

Sophie looked a bit resistant, but Luke was firm. Felicity could handle this fallout. He would, however, be fascinated to hear the onward story.

***

Emily was still at work, for once ensconced in her office in town. So Luke arrived home to a silent house to absorb, over a welcome beer, all that had happened since his art gallery shift. A client resurrected; that certainly was a new one on him. And such a strange client. He had rarely met anyone so composed, and so emotionless. Yet also clearly capable of deep depression. He hoped that Sophie's money could be recovered, and the sale re-run. But he foresaw huge difficulties, and significant legal barriers, plus associated costs. Luke was heartily relieved that this was no longer his case.

Two hours later, Emily was home. "Don't ask," said Luke, as she started to enquire about his day. "But actually you can ask, only later this evening, and not now. Let's go out for dinner after the art exhibition. Somewhere quiet and peaceful."

Sadly the exhibition was a bit run-of-the mill. Lucinda had assembled a group of works, in tandem with the artist, that neither Lily nor Luke thought were his best pieces. Luke could tell that Lily was disappointed, and starting to get itchy feet about getting back to work soon. "It's fine to delegate," she sighed, "but not when the result is mediocre." A good number of people had turned up, which made the disappointment even greater. A couple of items were sold, and interest shown in a handful of others. "The trouble is that we put a lot of effort and money into these exhibition openings," confided Lily to her parents, "and we need to see returns."

Luke and Emily found their quiet restaurant, a few streets away from the gallery. In a weird way, he was looking forward to relating the Sophie tale to his wife. The place wasn't anything fancy, just a local *brasserie*. The room they were shown into in was relatively small. There were two medium tables, two larger ones, arranged in an L-shape, and several more on the terrace outside overlooking a landscaped garden. Although the September evening was relatively balmy, it felt too cold to sit out; a few diners were eating in the open air, but Luke and Emily weren't brave enough to face the evening temperatures, and they agreed to a medium-sized table inside. The waiter whisked away an extra four settings, and they settled down to their peaceful dinner, Luke relishing the tale he was about to recount.

While they were eating their starter, Emily noticed two women being shown to the table behind her. They seemed to be on their own.

But two minutes later, to her horror, she suddenly heard a joyous female cry of "Hi everyone!" behind her, uttered to the entire room. Did this mean a group gathering, she wondered? It did. Luke grimaced at her. That "Hi, everyone!" sounded ominously like, "Hi, everyone, here we are to enjoy our huge gathering, the one we've been planning for such a long time. It's happening now!"

"Close-table syndrome," groaned Luke, a scenario they always dreaded when eating out. "But even worse; all of a sudden it looks like we're going to be part of some kind of celebration, all up close and personal to our dinner chat."

Others piled in, around fifteen in all. They stood talking for a while, one standing right behind Emily, almost touching her, towering over her, a rucksack momentarily pushing against her back. The newcomers seemed not to have noticed the couple already dining.

Eventually the group all sat down, cosily surrounding Luke and Emily in the L-shape, and in the end, they mercifully weren't too noisy. But cries of "Happy Birthday, Grandma!" were soon relayed across the table multiple times to someone behind Emily, but who Luke could see from his vantage point, the birthday Grandma. These were cries which almost persuaded them to join in, so much had they inadvertently been absorbed into this family fold. "Happy Birthday, Grandma!" they whispered to each other with a smile. Too much bother to move to another room. They stayed, co-opted addenda to Grandma's Big Day, while the stress of the afternoon's revelations melted away as Luke unfolded the utterly absorbing and mystifying story. And Emily listened, open-mouthed and incredulous, as they ate their dinner.

CHAPTER TWENTY-FIVE

Two Concerts
Mid-September 2014

Jessie was utterly exhausted. A combination of work, and rehearsals for the concert at the weekend had demanded all her strength, both mental and physical. Hospital commitments had meant she couldn't attend the full tally of orchestral preparations over the last few weeks; that had piled on the stress, as she furiously tried to catch up and ensure she was as perfect as possible as a violinist in Sibelius's second symphony. The orchestra was local, but of a high standard, with committed musicians, and a fairly fierce conductor. Jessie dreaded seeing another e-mail from Anthony. It usually heralded a request, either announcing an unexpected extra rehearsal, or reminding them to practise daily at home (which she already did), or suggesting they circulate publicity for the concert to their friends and colleagues.

The concert was due to take place in a nearby church, though for various reasons not at the one where Andrew was curate. Emily, Luke, and sundry friends of Jessie's and Andrew's would be attending. Carla was working at a wedding which had been in her diary for months, but Xander was planning to take the train up from Reading. Archie and Lily had excused themselves, an ultra-busy week behind them.

The day before hadn't been a good one for Jessie. Her full day's shift had ended late, and she had to travel straight from work to the final rehearsal, which lasted a full three hours. Feeling almost sick, she'd headed home just after ten, sincerely wishing that she hadn't agreed to play in the concert.

"I'm going to do some practice first thing tomorrow, and then let's go for a long walk before I have an hour's rest," she had said to Andrew when she got back. "No big meal, please" having been her request to her husband, Jessie silently and gratefully ate the snack he'd prepared, and headed straight to bed.

Yet by six o'clock on the Saturday she was in a totally different frame of mind; dressed in black, her hair in a smart ponytail, she was eagerly looking forward to the performance as they drove to the church, Andrew at the wheel. Since early childhood Jessie had always had an affinity with classical music, and she loved being a violinist.

"Are you and the other strings the backbone of the orchestra, or the heart?" Xander had once asked her.

She had thought for a moment. "In a sense, both," she had then replied "but maybe I'd put it another way and call us violinists the life-blood. That's what appeals to me, that sense of being vital and indispensable. It totally empowers me." Her passion was infectious and Xander, from his own experience of orchestras, understood.

Andrew watched his wife as the orchestra took their places at the front of the church. She looked determined, though slightly apprehensive. He was inordinately proud of her skill as a musician. Someone had thought very carefully about lighting and atmosphere in the auditorium. The orchestra naturally had all the full light they needed, the audience was in semi-darkness, and to either side, at the front of the church, were two traditional standard lamps boasting large fringed shades, highlighting dimmer areas to the side of the performers. A huge floral arrangement in yellow and cream adorned the front of the dais, and each musician sported a delicate yellow corsage. Visually appealingly programmes had obligingly been created by a graphic design professional, partner of one of the cellists. Anthony came onto his platform. The audience applauded. Silence reigned. And then Sibelius took over.

Emily knew this symphony very well. She'd often listened to it at home, and had seen it performed at several concerts. It was one of her favourite classical pieces, a haunting symphony, and she settled down to enjoy the evening. She focussed on the music, and put stress-inducing thoughts of Lily, Jimmy, Sophie, Billy, Matron, Tina, and Claire to the back of her mind. The opening movements took her mentally to Finnish forests and their blackness; yet amidst the darkness she knew it was all going to change. At the start of the third movement there was some fierce string-work, and Jessie had a look of intense concentration on her face. Then into the third movement came the first intimation of the beautiful melody which was going to recur five more times, and to be gently echoed twice more, once in the final minutes of the piece; in that last crescendo they would hear a quiet reflection of it before the end.

Emily absorbed the melody physically, receiving it in her body as well as in her spirit. It was a resounding refrain of hope; some said that it represented Finland's hope, after years of national oppression. But whether one was acquainted with Finnish history or not, this melody, without any question, signalled solid hope. She said to Jessie afterwards of the symphony, especially of its third and fourth movements, that, "it unlocked my heart." Emily had once heard a famous conductor eulogising about this piece of music, and had never forgotten what he said: "It is utterly entrancing." He had paused, not actually for dramatic effect, but because he was thinking of its perfection, and he had then added, "I wouldn't change a note." When tonight's performance came to an end, Emily had a deep sense of what she could only call satisfaction

"You were brilliant, brilliant," said Andrew, embracing his wife warmly. "Thanks. I'm so so tired," Jessie replied, leaning her head on his shoulder. He knew what these performances took out of her. Anticipation, hard grind demanding body and soul, exhilaration, and then complete exhaustion. "Let's say goodbye to the family, have a quick celebratory drink with your colleagues, and go home," he said.

***

It was Thursday evening. Felicity had come round to see Emily and Luke for a detailed debrief. On Peacehaven, not on Sophie, the latter still at present being ongoing, and classified. "I hope to have more information on the Sophie case before you leave for Edinburgh, Luke," said Felicity. "I am totally happy that you're dealing with it," he replied wryly.

"But there is a substantial update from Peacehaven," she added. "You'd heard about Billy's imminent trial of course, and the plan for Alice and I to visit Timmy's father and two brothers. And the police have also informed Matron, and naturally, Pauline, about the whole situation."

"A sad tale, but good to be near to a conviction after all this time," said Emily.

"Well, we visited Timmy's relatives, and although it was indeed terribly sad, it was also very gratifying and moving to see how thankful they were that justice had been done for him. His father must be in his mid-fifties, and the two brothers are early thirties; they were slightly older than Timmy. His mother only died last year, so they are still grieving for her, and now they're grieving that she never knew that the murder was solved, and the killer caught."

"We had a cup of tea and cake with them, and they talked a lot about Timmy, and about what he'd hoped to do later on," added Felicity.

"And all discovered because of your inspired idea to do some oral history in old people's homes," commented Luke.

"Yes, and I'm pleased that that project's ongoing, despite the complaint we've brought before Matron," said Felicity. "Alice and I, and one other student friend of hers, have only four more people to interview before we can publish something."

"And how about that big complaint?" asked Emily, pouring drinks for all three.

"Yes, that's the other interesting news. Matron called me in to discuss further, after thinking over what we'd said, and having read Alice's notebook."

"She didn't ask me to accompany you this time," smiled Emily. "She didn't want any more legal threats."

"Admittedly she did ask just me to visit again, but I'm sure there was no offence intended. She actually asked me to pass on her greetings to you."

"So what's the outcome?" asked Luke, keen to know Matron's reaction to what had been substantial complaints.

"I was pleased with her reaction. She's taken the situation very seriously. To the extent, first of all, that the main culprit, Shirley, has been fired for gross misconduct. Summarily dismissed, accompanied by substantive evidence. Apparently there had been complaints about her before. So that's really good."

"What a relief!" commented Emily. "And it should be a message to others."

"I think Matron was quite impressed with Alice's notebook. She made several comments. One was that from now on every single resident is to be asked how they'd like to be addressed, and that has to be noted, and to be adhered to by every nurse and carer. She pointed out that some residents either don't mind, or even welcome being called "Darling," "My dear", or by their first names. Which I completely understand. But now everyone will have the choice, which is excellent." Felicity paused to have a sip of her elderflower *pressé*.

"Regular feedback will be requested from residents, confidential feedback. And she's going to stress to carers that they shouldn't impose anything on their clients simply to make life easier for themselves and their work. So there should an informed decision, made jointly by carer and client, about whether to walk somewhere or use a wheelchair, about whether to use a hoist or not. That joint decision will then be one in which the resident has been involved."

"That's good," commented Luke. "I well remember the request from my father's hospital ward for us to buy him tracksuit bottoms and a sweatshirt. The reason? To make life easier for staff. My father would never have dressed like that. We refused. His life had been altered quite enough by the stroke."

Emily and Felicity were silent, each feeling Luke's reawakened pain.

"She noted the broken promises, and while I agreed with her that staff are very stressed and time-poor, it's terrible that messages don't get passed on. So Matron is going to have a stern word with all staff about that. She was intrigued by Alice's interesting suggestion about having CCTV in each resident's room, but felt it was a step too far, requiring too much regulation and liaising with each client on an individual basis. I can see her point, although I predict that some kind of CCTV may be introduced in the future, just for those who don't mind attention to their personal needs being filmed. It would certainly ensure consistently good care."

"That all sounds very encouraging," said Emily.

"And she's also going to emphasise—something which staff did know already—that no crude language is to be used about people's bodies. Respect is to be the order of the day."

Felicity added, "I suggested to Matron that staff might be reminded of the importance of empathy. They should aim to put themselves in their clients' situation. She agreed. And she's taken note of the point, allied with respect, about dignity, about not being condescending, and showing understanding when people are in pain. It was a lot to take in, but I think she definitely does plan to change things. She said, without me reminding her, that it's vital for carers really to listen to their clients, and to remember what they have said! I said I was of one mind with her on that. And told her that I come from a caring society in Northern Ireland, a province where there's a lot of natural kindness, and it's important to me to see that care everywhere."

Emily and Luke were listening intently, extremely satisfied to hear that things were happening in response to their concerns.

Felicity continued, "I was also able to say something more positive about care in the home, which I thought was important. I really didn't want Matron to think I was just an annoying complainer," she said, pulling a face. "Alice had related to me the tale of Sue, who lives in a corner room near the garden. Apparently one day when she was feeling very low, a carer stayed for an amazing thirty minutes after her shift had ended, listening to her woes, and quite movingly, Sue had commented to Alice, "And then I felt, that day, that this really was my home." Matron seemed gratified that I'd told her that story, and she plans to praise the staff member involved."

"Felicity, well done for all of this work. You're doing this for some important people."

"Well, the nurses and carers are really important too. We're looking for mutual respect. What was quite lovely was that, at the end, Matron thanked me for bringing all of this to her notice. She seemed much gentler than when we met with her previously. I can see that she's very firm, and she needs to be firm in her role, but she has listened to us." She thought for a moment. "I told her what a vital role her staff play, and also said, as tactfully as I could, that I thought they should be paid more than they are. Not that I can do anything about it."

"I wonder if Alice will be given holiday work at Peacehaven again." commented Luke, with a slight smile.

"Who knows?" said Felicity. "Though I imagine that her holiday work next summer, if she gets what she'd like, may well be at some crime or police force facility. Her current ambition, and given that she's had now such impressive pre-career success, is to be a detective. Not an armchair detective, one of those amateurs who seem to people social media, but a real detective, with a degree and proper training behind her."

"Well," said Luke, "Emily has told me about your apposite Benjamin Franklin quotation. It does sound as though Matron might be approaching your level of outrage about all of this, if not entirely there yet. In summary I'd say we're looking for more integrity. I salute all your work on this, Felicity, and Alice."

"Integrity isn't a word we often hear," commented Emily, looking pensive. "It's a high benchmark for us all, and often impossible."

***

After Felicity left, Emily had some items to attend to before her work-free Friday; she spent an hour in her newly inspirational study, finalising various documents and replying to e-mails. One e-mail was from Tina, which she clocked, but decided to look at after her work. She relaxed on a sofa downstairs, looking out at their autumnal garden lit up by the occasional solar lantern, and pondering Tina's message. Two pots of Michaelmas daisies brightened up the terrace, but even in the half-light, it was obvious that some containers needed attention, their summer glory long past. They would have to wait on Emily's timetable.

She read Tina's e-mail.

"Friedrich and I are spending three days together each week, which is working in a sort of way. But I really miss him when I'm in my apartment. And I have a slight suspicion that there might be someone else in his life. Marianne met a woman once in our home, who was having coffee with Friedrich. She was introduced as a colleague, but might she also be a 'friend?' However, I'm not worried. You know me, Emily ☺. I'm doing my level best to woo him back to me, and we've actually planned a holiday together in the Lake District in October."

It sounds a bit hopeful, thought Emily. *Not totally hopeful, but maybe getting there.* Tina was always so positive, and it stood her in good stead. Emily replied to her friend, suggesting that she and Friedrich visit her and Luke in Highgate after their holiday. And Emily would keep her fingers crossed that the marital relationship would soon be fully restored.

Yet another concert beckoned the following day. Two concerts in less than a week was certainly not par for the course for Emily and Luke, and it was a real treat. Xander had invited the whole family to a special evening at St Joseph's. A fairly well-known professional singer, an alumna of the school, had agreed to star in a fundraising concert on Friday evening. And, thanks to a seismic effort from all concerned as they juggled their busy schedules, virtually the whole family was free to attend. Lily was the only no-show. She was actually relishing the thought of an early night with Daisy, exhaustion regularly continuing to dictate her timetable. "But in a good way," she always added. "And it will pass."

The playground was almost full when they arrived, but Luke managed to locate a space in its lower area. As they went into the building, the school entrance and corridors were spilling over with supportive parents and siblings. A few mothers and fathers were chatting with their excited offspring who, having escaped unobserved from backstage, were just moments away from performing. The air was full of lively chatter: "This is where I'll be standing. Look out for me!" "See my name in the programme?" "Got to go, Mum. See you later!" The programme was eclectic, a mix of classical and light music, of orchestral, choir, and brass band, plus solos, both piano and vocal. Nearly everyone was in place, apart from a few late stragglers attempting unostentatiously to find their places. Jessie, hotfoot from work, joined them in the scramble to sit down and relax. The school principal was now on stage, ready to speak. A small child cried, and was quickly exited.

The first piece began, the Radetzky March, played by the senior orchestra, tentatively at first, then with growing confidence, and as a first offering, was applauded loudly and encouragingly. The march was followed by a group of pieces with an ongoing Austrian theme, excerpts from 'The Sound of Music', a guaranteed favourite. Charlotte, the alumna soloist, made her first appearance with 'My Favourite Things,' surrounded by a bashful group of seven assorted children, sitting very still, their eyes focussed on her. There were offerings from the brass band, loud and triumphant, and the choir sang two Gilbert and Sullivan pieces. Performances were impressive; the school clearly had both talent and excellent musical direction. This wasn't a professional offering, but for a senior school event, the standard was high.

Xander wasn't on duty this evening. Despite his musical interest as a former clarinet player, there were already enough staff members to lead tonight's groups. He'd been told that he would be roped in for an event later in the year. And having recently started the new job, he was content to remain a spectator at the event today. So the Wentworths sat in a row: mother, son, father, daughter, three children-in-law; architect, maths teacher, lawyer, gastroenterologist, curate, florist, haematologist. Emily was lost in the music, Xander partly so, though also aware of the individual performers he knew, Luke appreciated the pieces with which he was familiar, and Jessie was thoroughly enjoying the act of watching violinists as opposed to being one. Andrew was glad that he and Jessie would have tomorrow delightfully free, a day together before the busyness of Sunday, Carla was also luxuriating in the prospect of a welcome day off, totally free from floristry this Saturday, and Archie relaxed knowing that Lily and Daisy were drinking in beautiful sleep, or so he hoped.

In the second half of the concert, the family reverted to couple mode, each sitting together, and Archie next to Luke. For this second part of the evening the musical director had opted initially for a section focussing on Handel, followed by four Beethoven pieces of varying lengths and later on, a Beatles medley to finish. Xander, hand-in-hand with Carla, watched the clarinets with interest during Handel's Music for the Royal Fireworks. He smiled at her every so often, and she smiled back, secure in their relationship, the weekend ahead of them, and a holiday planned for the October half-term break. Then the soloist came on again, with two arias from 'The Messiah'. Her voice was pure, and her stance eloquent. She sang with power, but not might, a curious and skilled combination. And even the small children were mercifully silent as she began, "I know that my Redeemer liveth". Jessie leaned forward, and Xander watched her as she followed the piece. Her face was a study, simultaneously rapt and enraptured. *She's really listening to these words. And they do mean something to her,* thought her brother. Loud applause greeted Charlotte as she ended the aria. The Beatles medley, the Fab Four's hits in effect a musical genre accepted as a new classic, made a clever end to the evening. Everyone joined in as encouraged to do, in a chorus of "Hey Jude", and afterwards they unashamedly gave in to group soppiness, lustily singing, "All you need is love."

The crowd wended its way home, relief palpable at the absence of school on the morrow. There were Wentworth farewells and hugs. Five of them set off for London. And all the time before he fell asleep that night, in his head Xander kept hearing "I know, I know" its second note a long minim, a high E, along with Jessie's rapt face, and the beautiful voice of the professional soprano.

CHAPTER TWENTY-SIX

Edinburgh
October 2014

Luke and Emily were on the train to Edinburgh for their four-night break. "Just like our first journey here in the 1970s, I guess," he said to her. "Yes, I got the train up from Birmingham for my first term," she said dreamily, the rhythm of the journey having its usual drowsy effect. Their carriage wasn't terribly busy, the week immediately preceding any half-term breaks being free from holidaying families; there were empty seats and for the moment they had a table, seats opposite each other, and no travelling companions. "I actually drove up with my father, and then he drove back to Cheltenham," Luke reflected, unnecessarily detailing the return journey. "But after that I got the train up many times."

They reached York within two hours, glimpsing the city walls and Minster ahead of the magnificent Victorian station. "These nineteenth century stations are overwhelming," said Emily. "They literally take my breath away, and their grandeur is astounding." Her nose almost touched the window as she took in the view. Another hour for Emily of gazing dreamily at the countryside and for Luke, of flitting between his I-Pad, and Matt Prior's recently published autobiography *The Gloves are Off*, and they rolled into Newcastle Central. "Now here's a station that almost got demolished," commented Emily, continuing and unaware of her pun. "In the 1970s. British Rail did their level best to get rid of it, and rebuild, but fortunately it was listed, and escaped."

"Unlike what happened to Penn Station in New York," commented Luke. "It makes me mad how they destroyed it, and then compounded their craziness by building the current concrete monstrosity that's replaced it." He'd made many journeys from Penn, searching for his train track number on the departures board in the claustrophobic concourse, its low roof a dismal contrast to what had preceded it. "I love the Art Nouveau touches here," he said, returning to the present. "Added in the 1890s," Emily informed him, having fairly recently read a book on the UK's railway stations.

After Berwick-upon-Tweed and its Royal Border Bridge with twenty-eight astounding arches, spectacular views of expansive harvested fields and the sea beyond continued their route to the Scottish capital. The train hugged the coast as it approached Edinburgh. Inevitably by this point in the journey, seeing the sea, and almost feeling the northern air even when still inside the carriage, Emily's anticipation of arriving in the city really took hold and heightened. Book and I-Pad abandoned, and each lost in their individual thoughts, they awaited the last section of their journey, in a short time rolling into Waverley station as Emily had done in March, the majestic castle and long stretch of Princes Street Gardens rising up on either side.

"I don't mind where we stay, as long as it's not the Old Waverley Hotel," Emily had specified. "Significantly nicer. I've booked us into the

Balmoral," replied Luke with a grin. It wasn't far from the hotel where she'd met Jimmy, but that didn't matter. She loved the Balmoral, with its Scottish baronial architecture, and spacious reception rooms, and was totally happy with Luke's choice. Their programme for the few days sounded perfect: dinner at Ricky and Jane's home along with Archie, lunch with Archie the following day, a few strolls around the University campus and up to Lothian Road, and exploring new areas of the city. Plus an unexpected booking at the Usher Hall for their last night. "I couldn't resist it; one of your favourite piano concertos, Tchaikovsky's first," Luke had announced to Emily on their journey.

"Look at his Audi soft-top," he drooled as they stood outside Ricky and Jane's front door later that evening.

"Do you think it's his?" asked Emily softly; with no front drives she wasn't sure of the provenance of the cars parked opposite. Appropriate to the wealth he'd inherited and also to be fair, for which he had also worked all through his advertising career, Ricky lived on Carlton Terrace in Edinburgh's New Town, an area dating back to the late eighteenth century. "I feel as though I'm in Bath," she continued. "It's very like Royal Crescent."

The evening with their friends was light-hearted and fun. They'd only met Jane a few times. "But we three all go back a long way!" said Ricky to his two friends, a comment deep with meaning, thought Emily, Tina and Fergus coming to mind. "Come in and have a drink."

He was simply an older version of 1970s Ricky. He still smoked, still had shoulder-length hair, wore slightly bohemian clothes, and owned what Emily called a rather louche manner, tempered for her by the fact that she knew he wasn't at all shady. It was simply his own idiosyncratic style. Emily and Luke drank in the dimensions of the house, its high ceilings, sash and case windows, spacious rooms, and warmly congratulated their friends on its beauty. They stood chatting in the kitchen for a while; its high walls were painted strawberry pink, units were all dark mahogany, there was a vast sash window, and a crystal chandelier. From the kitchen, via a wide door-less opening, they could see into a comfortable sitting room, and on the other side, a narrower arch led through to a snug with more deep windows.

Archie had now arrived, having just had a drink in town with Mike, his best man. "Come upstairs," said Jane. Their sitting room was on the first floor, a totally sensible decision as it looked out on views of Holyrood Palace and the most elevated of Edinburgh's seven hills, Arthur's Seat. "We're fortunate in that we can use Regent Gardens," said Ricky indicating the eleven-acre area nearby. "We just love entertaining, so this house is perfect," he added, "and now that Marcus and Tobias have left home, we have lots of room." The conversation covered a range of subjects, including the gallery where Lily and Archie had held their reception, and Fergus's role in managing it. He'd been in touch with Lily and once her maternity leave was over, they hoped to effect some collaboration. "I enjoyed having Tina here recently," said Jane with genuine pleasure. "She's such a breath of fresh air, if a trifle coquettish." She smiled and Emily mirrored her smile, totally understanding the undertones of Jane's comment.

***

It was a fifteen-minute cycle ride from his mother's house to the Stockbridge restaurant and despite a sprinkling of autumn rain, Archie needed the exercise. He'd enjoyed the conference, was satisfied that his paper had been well received, and had made some useful contacts. He'd spoken to Lily that morning; she was glad to have Jessie staying while he was away, and was about to go to her weekly parent and baby social. Archie was still in awe that he'd found his life partner at last. Lily was undeniably what up to this point he hadn't attained, the 'love of his life', and that was how he was proud to describe her to all he knew.

But he hugely craved more time alone with his wife. Seeing Luke and Emily together on their city break had brought this home to him. He would love to have some couple time like that with Lily. It had been a whirlwind period; he'd only known her for eighteen months, had been married for a year, and Daisy had joined them seven months ago. He and Lily loved each other, yet there was hardly time for love in their relationship; the pattern of their lives consisted mainly of exchanging pleasantries between Daisy nappy changes, Daisy feeding, and playing with Daisy. He did love Daisy and was thrilled to have a daughter, but he yearned to spend more time with his wife. After all, this was the so-called honeymoon period of a marriage. Archie gave way at a roundabout, and mused on how they could connect again, and be a couple, as well as a family of three. He would talk to his best friend, his titular father-in-law, about it.

A table had been booked at a stylish restaurant in Stockbridge. "We'll have time to enjoy a totally luxurious and long lunch," Luke had announced to Archie as they'd all shared a taxi back to their respective accommodation after the dinner with Ricky and Jane. Archie was staying with his mother Fiona in Morningside; he was due back home late the following day, his conference already over. The restaurant was exactly what appealed to Emily. Tables were well spread-out, white tablecloths proliferated, the deep coloured walls, matched in the same colour on the ceiling, displayed colourful modern art, subtle daytime-suitable spotlights lit their table, and the menu was varied and tempting. Out of the twelve tables, just two others were occupied. '*Sophisticated*' *is my summary word for this place,* thought Emily, as she relaxed into her chair. She planned to enjoy this lunch.

After perusing the substantial and tempting menu, all three ordered. "It's a book, not a menu," said Archie, "and the wine list too. How did you find this place, Luke? I come to Edinburgh regularly to visit Mum, and I've never been here. And I actually used to live in the city."

"Careful googling," smiled his friend, "and some personal recommendations." He continued. "So what's your verdict on the result of the referendum last month, Archie? Scotland still part of the UK. A good thing, or not?"

Archie's familiar grin deepened. "You know I never discuss politics with friends. Or family," was his comment. "However," he continued after a suitable pause, "how about going for a drink at Deacon Brodies later today? My flight doesn't leave until seven." Luke smiled at the hidden message.

"So Archie, would you like to hear the Sophie story, on which we virtually now have all the details? We can tell you now, and you can pass the whole tale on to Lily, and we'll let the others know when we see them."

"I'm all ears," said Archie, sipping his sparkling water.

"I'd already told you the saga of Sophie turning up at my firm, seemingly returned from the dead, terrifying me out of my wits, and telling us about her sojourn first of all with the nuns, and then afterwards in a psychiatric institution," his friend began. "Well, now for the fuller version. It's the traditional long story. And in true traditional fashion, there's a villain. Dear Philippe boldly identified the body of someone called Sophie, but it wasn't his ex-wife. And he asked his sister, who speaks excellent English, to claim to be Sophie's sister, and to identify her too. So he's now under arrest, and his sister is being charged as an accessory."

"Why did the police think the body belonged to his ex-wife?"

"Sheer incompetence," snorted Luke. "I can't believe how badly the French police have behaved. They found a body, discovered from the few cards on her body that her first name was Sophie, and thought fairly naïvely that it didn't matter that her surname didn't tally with our Sophie's. "Women have so many surnames," one of the *gendarmes* claimed. "They had Philippe's wife's name on a list of missing persons, this Sophie had similar colouring and was the same height, also approximately the same age, so they just contacted Philippe saying that they'd found his wife, dead."

"It's utterly amazing," said Emily. "I've heard the story from Luke already, but I'm astounded each time I hear it."

"Philippe was acting out of pure greed, to keep all the proceeds from the house sale for himself?" conjectured Archie.

"So it seems. But he was also acting with great stupidity. How did he know that the real Sophie wouldn't turn up eventually, as has now happened? My guess is that he thought she'd died. She'd always suffered from bad episodes of depression and they hadn't heard from her for months. He must have assumed that his theory was a fairly safe bet."

"So who's the person who died in the taxi accident?" asked Archie, still trying to put the pieces of the jigsaw together.

"The police have absolutely no idea. There's no-one on their list of missing persons who matches the description. To their credit, they are still working on finding out who it was. There must be someone who's wondering what happened to their Sophie."

"It's a huge puzzle," said Emily. "I simply don't understand why Sophie didn't contact her children, once she'd left the hospital."

A smiling waiter brought their starters. They'd finished the unexpected pre-starter, a small savoury confection in delicate glasses. Luke was an *aficionado* of these additional treats provided by the best eateries.

"Sophie is a total mystery," said Luke. "She's the most unmaternal woman with children, that I've ever encountered. My sense, from having talked to her recently, is that her priority, once recovered, was to return to England, and to ensure her share of the house proceeds. Property first and the money from it, and then maybe, possibly, contact her children after that. Totally bizarre. She's currently staying with an old friend, and now has access to her old bank account, so she's got just about enough to live on, and seems content to live a life of limbo until this whole farce is settled." He added, "She has actually been in touch with her children now. She waited until after Philippe had been arrested."

"It's a terrible story," commented Archie.

"At least I wasn't at the fake funeral," said Luke. "That would have made all of this even more surreal."

"So what happens now? And how about Sophie's share of the house sale?"

"That's for Dominique and Felicity to sort out. I imagine it will take a very long time. First up will be the sentencing of Philippe and his sister, and once that's concluded, the case of the house sale will need to be re-opened. I would hope that in the long run, Sophie might be entitled to the whole amount, but it's a very complicated set-up, and I'm sure that a skilled lawyer will argue for Philippe to have a share, despite his misdeeds."

"I'm glad Luke doesn't have to deal with this," commented Emily drily. "But it will be interesting eventually to hear the outcome, after what promises to be a long procedure."

The empty starter plates were removed. At the same time another table was being occupied, far enough away not to overhear each other's mealtime discourse. It had all the hallmarks of a business lunch; sharp suits, super-polite chat, courteous laughter.

"How is Lily?" asked Emily. "And Daisy?"

"Really enjoying Jessie's stay with them," replied Archie. "Although she's only there in the evening, she's been very hands-on with Daisy and with other things needing to be done."

He continued, "I'm glad the Jimmy situation seems to be sorted now?" It was more of a question than a statement.

"Yes, we really appreciated Lily letting us know how this will be taken forward," said Emily.

"She seems quite satisfied that the arrangement will work. I think she's planning to see Jimmy in late November," said Archie. "On her own," he added, clarifying that Daisy wouldn't be involved.

"I'm glad too," volunteered Luke. "The last thing Lily needs at the moment is stress of any kind. I'd like to do all I can to make this easier for her."

"In fact," he added, looking at Emily, "I've agreed with Emily that I would actually be willing to meet with Jimmy at some stage. Just to meet him, not to be a best friend," he smiled. "Probably just once. But I have an idea that it would help Lily, and would smooth things over a bit more, for Daisy's grandfathers to have a kind of peace-inducing powwow."

Archie looked quizzical at the archaic, maybe even politically dangerous language, but heard what Luke was saying. "Brilliant suggestion," he said. "And I've said the same to her. Just when she's ready, I would have a one-off meeting with Jimmy."

Emily listened, and didn't comment. There was still some residual pain. All of this was because of her history, her actions years ago. But which had produced the most beautiful daughter, and it was the role of all of them, her, Luke, Archie, Jimmy, to ensure happiness and peace for Lily. And for Daisy.

The main course arrived, vegetables served in individual portions, and appropriate sauces brought as requested. Wine and soft drinks were poured, and the water jug topped up.

They talked about other sundry matters. Archie had a good team in his department, and was enjoying training up some excellent new doctors. Luke was thriving with his art gallery involvement, non-executive roles pending, and opportunities to speak both French and Italian on the horizon. Emily was thrilled that Maddy and Tom's extension work was under way, and looking fairly close to schedule. She had a new client, an artist looking to add a studio to her Highgate home, which would double up as an exhibition space. As they continued their meal, she enthused about her profession with that dedicated commitment she'd often shared with Luke. "The bottom line is that I'm an architect because buildings really affect people, hopefully and more often than not, for the better," she said. She hesitated a moment as they tucked into their food. "In fact it's even more powerful than that. What we architects do is actually quite thrilling; our work can change people's lives, not simply slightly affect them and, after a commission is finished, what we've enabled will, we hope, have an ongoing daily impact." They were all silent for a moment, acknowledging Emily's words.

Main course was followed by dessert. Dessert was followed by coffee. Coffee was accompanied by *petits fours*. Before they realised, it was nearly three o'clock. "Shall we go for that celebratory drink at Deacon Brodies?" suggested Archie. "I don't have to set off for the airport until five-thirty. I can leave my bike here, and collect it later."

"I'm afraid I'm really tired, and we have that wonderful concert at seven-thirty," said Emily. "Do you mind if I cry off?"

"I'll join you," volunteered Luke. "Did you say 'celebratory drink'? Is that a politically celebratory drink, Archie?"

"Freudian slip," replied Archie, winking at Emily.

"Let's get a taxi there," suggested Luke.

***

After their sumptuous lunch, Emily was glad to wend her way back to the Balmoral, and luxuriate in its attentive environment. Their room was in pristine condition, bed made and dressed with multiple cushions, toiletries replenished, surfaces all cleaned and dusted. She collapsed into a welcoming armchair by the window, and picked up a magazine. Sun flooded into the room, and she relaxed, retrospectively enjoying the meal all over again.

The phone rang; it was Lily. "Hi darling," said Emily, "Is everything OK?"

"Almost," said what sounded like a tearful Lily. "Have you got a moment? I know you're away with Dad."

"Of course, I have a moment. What's wrong?"

"It's just..." Lily was silent for a moment. "It's just that when I met Jimmy, I asked if he had a picture of you both, from when you met." Emily's heart sank. This sounded potentially like emotional blackmail, and from the sounds of it, was upsetting her daughter.

"Well, this morning he sent me just what I'd asked for. He managed to find an old photo of you and him together, which he's taken a picture of on his phone."

"I'm sure it's a horrendous photo." Emily was doing her best to dilute the emotion of the situation.

"It's actually quite a nice one, although a bit faded. It seems to be on a walk, in the countryside. You are wearing flared jeans, and a kaftan-style top, and he's wearing jeans and a checked shirt. Your hair is really long. He has way more hair than when I met him the other day. He.... he has his arm round you, Mum."

"Yes, I think I remember. We'd gone on a walk in the Pentlands with another friend, who I guess took the photo."

"Well, what I wanted to say, Mum, amidst my tears, was that you both look really nice, and in fact in a way it feels good for me actually to see how I started. In what looks like a loving relationship, even though it petered out quite soon afterwards. So, although I sound upset, I'm really sort of happy to have the picture. Shall I forward it to you?"

In her heart of hearts, the last thing Emily wanted was to see this picture. A picture of the relationship which ended so dramatically, and so long ago. But she rallied.

"Yes, do send it. I'll be intrigued to see it."

"I'll WhatsApp it now. Sorry, I've got to go. Daisy has just woken up. Let me know what you think!"

Two minutes later, the picture came through onto Emily's phone. Her 2014 face gazed at her 1970s countenance, and at the image of a young girl arm-in-arm with her boyfriend. *Love's Young Dream,* she thought, *for a measly two months.* It was a stark cameo of her stupid fling with Jimmy, whom she'd met at that crazy student party.

Emily suddenly felt deeply sad. She certainly didn't wish that she and Jimmy had ended up together; what she had with Luke was significantly deeper, more solid, and lifelong. In fact, what she really wanted was something totally impossible. She desperately wanted Luke to be Lily's father and indeed, for Jimmy simply to disappear again. Emily sighed, a deep long sigh. She didn't look at the picture again. In a few days she would quietly delete it.

Then uncharacteristically yet for once decisively, Emily took herself in hand, and mentally gave herself a shake. This was Lily's story now, this business with Jimmy, she told herself firmly, rising from the chair to gaze out on Edinburgh. Not her story, but her daughter's. Enough of all the worry; she recalled Luke's advice. With insight borne of too much mental travail Emily resolved no longer—borrowing vocabulary from Victorian romantic fiction—to think of Jimmy as a "bounder", nor as the "usurper" which was how she suspected Luke had viewed him, nor as the selfish twenty-year old who had walked off and left her with a lifelong responsibility. He simply had to be a new Jimmy. She must, and she would, consign her own part in the opening chapter of that story to history, and mentally hand him over to his daughter. It was a moment of pure clarity, and of relief; it felt cathartic, a time to move on, and a decision made in the city where it had all begun.

She sank back into the armchair, and enjoyed its comfort for a few minutes before she heard a text pinging into her phone. By now the meal was definitely having its full effect, and Emily was starting to feel drowsy, a sensation compounded by the few tears she had silently shed while Lily was recounting the photo tale, and by her mental resolution of the Jimmy conundrum.

Should she look at the message, or simply drift off to sleep? It was ever so; yet again, her curiosity got the better of her. The text was from Tina. "Hello Emily," it began. "How is it all going? What's happening with Lily and Jimmy? Some better news from me. I'm now living with Friedrich full-time!"

It sounds like a job, not a marriage, thought Emily.

"Yes, there was another woman hovering around Friedrich, but he's assured me that it never really took off and that nothing happened between them. I believe him."

I would believe Friedrich too, Emily's mental commentary continued. *He has integrity and wisdom.*

"So when we visit you next week we'll be completely back together. Great news. I've been so stupid not seeing what a great man I married."

"Hi Tina!" Emily hit the minute keys with vigour. "I'm delighted to read this news. Well done to both of you. Luke will be thrilled too."

As she was tapping, another text from Tina appeared on the screen. "And we've even – wait for it – talked about renewing our wedding vows."

This calls for caution, thought her friend. *Extreme caution. Give it time, Tina*! But after a sharp intake of breath Emily continued composing her warm reply, simultaneously wondering why she was so addicted to looking at her phone while on holiday.

"It will be great to see you both soon. Come and stay if you have time. We can celebrate with you!"

She sat back in the armchair and pondered the message from her friend. Tina and Friedrich were very different. Yet if they were both committed to rebuilding the marriage, those contrasting personalities could be complementary, and even a source of strength. Edinburgh had been a key feature of the whole relationship, from Friedrich's visit over thirty years ago when he'd succeeded in bringing Tina back to Germany, to the hovering presence of Ricky over the years as he'd fathered Fergus from Scotland, to Tina's city-break in March this year and her emotion-filled stay with Ricky and Jane, and on to today with this unexpected text winging its way into Emily's Edinburgh hotel room.

She was deeply glad to hear the news. Emily had always admired Friedrich for the gracious way in which he'd accepted Fergus and had forgiven Tina for having a baby with someone else in the early years of their marriage. It must have been very hard for him. And it wasn't a one-off action, to forgive Tina. It had had to be a conscious ongoing decision, day after day, week after week, year after year. Forgiveness was on Emily's mind a lot at the moment; thoughts of Luke, Lily, and even Jessie and Xander, inevitably involved as well in the Jimmy situation, all jostled for attention.

She was very tired, and really wanted to luxuriate in that delayed nap. But first she texted Tina again. Emily wasn't usually blunt or forthright. But occasionally, and for the sake of the person she was addressing, she did speak her mind. So she didn't need to double-check this particular message. "Tina, you married a good man. Don't let him go. This may be your last chance. Just enjoy him. See you very soon!"

Emily switched off her phone. She walked to the other side of the room and put it on charge. Then at last, feeling peaceful and vaguely hopeful about everything, she lowered herself into the corner chair with its comfortable headrest and footstool and feeling the sun on her face, relaxed, and was soon asleep.

***

Luke and Archie got a taxi in no time, and were soon strolling towards Deacon Brodies. As they approached the tavern Archie said, "It looks extremely closed. Maybe terminally closed? There's a notice on the door." They read it.

We are sorry that Deacon Brodies Tavern will be closed

until November 1ˢᵗ

This is due to a family bereavement.

We apologise to all our faithful customers.

"Well, let's go for a walk instead. How about Arthur's Seat?" said Luke. "We could do with walking off that lunch, and it's only ten minutes from here. After all, today, thirty-six years on, I don't have an essay on Pascal to write. I finished it!"

"And I have no Physiology to study. Definitively all done," added Archie.

"This is beautiful, breathtaking", said Luke, as they walked through Holyrood Park, Arthur's Seat ahead of them. "Did we come up here much for walks?"

"I don't think so," replied Archie. "I was either working, or partying, or loafing around at the Union."

"And I was working, maybe just a little, partying like mad, and playing cricket."

"Look at that view," said Archie. Can you think of another city with a comparable one?"

"London, from Primrose Hill; Rome from one of its seven hills; Florence from Piazzale Michelangelo; Paris from La Défense; Canberra from one of three mounts," said his friend, listing options from travels over the years.

"But nothing like this one, Luke. This is our view, this is our city. We own it. Even though bits have changed dramatically since we were students," he said looking at the Parliament Building and Dynamic Earth.

"Do you know, looking at this landscape, and taking in the view over Edinburgh reminds me of two films."

"Oh yes?" said Archie, not as familiar with films as his friend, who was a bit of an expert.

"Yes, *Mary Queen of Scots*, that ancient one."

"Ancient?" responded Archie, thinking back to silent movies.

"Well, 1970s. Not so ancient maybe. Mary, played by Vanessa Redgrave, was walking imperiously in these green areas with her entourage, all dressed up to the nines as they were in Tudor times. And suddenly they came upon a wild-looking man, really long hair, beard down to his knees, ranting loudly; he looked like an absolute nonentity, and not particularly clean. So she asks in disgust, "Who is that man?" And they reply with conviction, "That's John Knox, Your Majesty." He was actually big news at that time in Scotland. He had lots of followers, as well as lots of opponents of course. Neither a nonentity nor a wild vagabond.'

"Yes, I've definitely heard of him," responded Archie.

"So in response to the Queen's disgust on screen, cue lots of laughter from the cinema audience, doubtless because I saw the film in Edinburgh and also I guess there were a fair number of Presbyterians amongst them. And then," warming to his theme, "there's *Chariots of Fire.*"

"Oh yes, I saw that film," responded Archie, gazing at the view.

"So do you remember when Eric Liddell and his sister were walking right here, overlooking Edinburgh, and she was nagging him to go to China as a missionary and not continue with his running? And he said, "God made me fast, Jennie. And when I run, I feel his pleasure." They were right here when he said that."

"And this is our film, Archie," continued Luke, with a dramatic smile. "Look at our plot. Met in Edinburgh, found our wives because of this city, sort of and then, we have an errant father surfacing after thirty-five years, a murderer unmasked after ten years, a client of mine who is miraculously resurrected, justice done in an old folks' home, and here we are back in Edinburgh for our closing scene."

"Our film, eh?" was Archie's dreamy comment. He was studying the landscape, his gaze darting from one area to another.

"And in the end, I think our film is all about justice. I don't know who made me so fervent about fairness, Archie. Was it actually God, or some other force? But when I see justice done, like Liddell yes, I feel someone's pleasure, but also certainly, my own."

"I'm sure you have a point."

"It just feels right when justice is done, whether for Giovanni, the old folks in that Home, Xander's pupils who've unfairly been given detention, poor Timmy Johnson and his family, and all the other plotlines I've just listed. It goes with the territory of being a lawyer, I guess. We've seen some wrongs righted recently, and others, well others are a work in progress. And then there are scenarios like the Jimmy one, which were always threatening to happen, and we just have to make the best of those."

"Indeed we do," commented Archie soberly. He was listening more intently now.

"Let me quote Aristotle," said Luke, "and then I promise to end my personal rant. Maybe this green area is where people rant, both John Knox and I." He paused. "Are you ready for this, Archie?"

Archie turned. "Yes, what's the quotation, Luke?"

Facing his friend, Luke adopted a dramatic pose, hand on right hip, the other one flung out pointing into the far distance for emphasis. "This is what Aristotle said, "At his best, man is the noblest of all animals; separated from law and justice he is the worst."

"And I think we should give him the last word," concurred Archie.

Together, they had come to a place of justice. Just for a moment all conversation ceased, and they were both silent as they gazed upon this city, this centre of study, this place in their hearts where they'd first met, wordlessly musing on the dramatic recent events enumerated by Luke.

ABOUT THE AUTHOR

Elisabeth Ludlow is a linguist and development professional with a doctorate in history. Married with two children and two grandchildren, she lives in a small English village where sweeping views of the countryside inspire. With a background in academic writing, forays into journalism, and a local history book, A Place of Justice is her first work of fiction.